Beyond the Horizon
By
Kristen Kehoe

To my sisters, for never leaving me behind.

Chapter One
Mia

My brother Joe left the day of his high school graduation.

I wasn't particularly surprised, though a part of me had hoped long and hard that he would change his mind, that he would go back to being the Joe he had been before he met Morgan, and before he decided our family wasn't enough.

He had done the cap and gown thing just this morning. He had walked across the stage and smiled for the cameras as they announced that he would be attending Stanford; he had grasped his diploma and held it up to the crowd, his perfect smile in place. But I knew it was a lie; the smile, the gesture, everything. And so did my parents.

They were silent throughout the entire ceremony. Once, my mother shed a few quiet tears, which she diligently wiped away until her face was clear and dry. My father sat like stone; not once did he laugh, cry, smile, or shout. Their faces were blank slates, their emotions carefully hidden as they sat perfectly still and watched my brother slip out of their lives.

It hadn't always been quiet, though. For the last ten months, they had been fighting about everything from his choice in music to his clothes, his hair that he had let go shaggy. My mother, a born micromanager, made it her goal to get Joseph back on track, to make him see what she and my father were offering him. But he'd never given in. Instead, he had ignored her for the first time in seventeen years and done what he pleased, which was everything she asked him not to do. My father never said anything to him—he simply shook his head, looked at my mother and told her that Joe was ruining his future and their name.

Joe never altered his course toward independence, but in the end he bent a little and did what they asked of him during those final events leading up to this day; he stayed to finish high school, he applied and was accepted to Stanford, and he walked across the stage at his graduation ceremony, allowing all of his peers and their parents to believe that he would be off to begin the prestigious life that they expected from our family come August. He was an Evans, and so he had done his duty and worn the proper hat in public. But my parents knew it was a façade, and no matter how well he played it, they couldn't smile. Their eldest son had veered off of the path they had groomed him for, he had taken a step back from the tradition that had been set in place long before he was born, and they didn't know how to bring him back.

When the ceremony ended, the twins, almost four years my junior, went with our parents, and Joe and I went with Lily, who was in between us in the birth order. Lily drove us home in silence, though I could see the words ready to leap off of her tongue at any minute. Lily was Mary Poppins, perfect in every way. She was the perfect student, earning straight As in all of the hardest courses offered, while still being the captain of the academic team, and an all-state tennis player. She would be a senior next year, and she already had her sights set on college. Stanford was her future, where she would obtain her degree before going on to law school afterward and then joining the family business of buying land, renovating it, and developing hotels.

Our father was a fourth generation hotelier. Eleven months ago, he moved us from our home in Portland, Oregon to here, the small community of Verrado in Buckeye, Arizona, where he began a new project. In Phoenix, which was twenty-five miles away, he would build another hotel, and then Verrado, would be home to our very first

Inn, a small, intimate place that would be just as chic as the Evans' Hotels, only smaller in size.

It was always expected that Joe would continue the tradition of buying and developing when he graduated from Stanford. Then Joe met Morgan, and my parents watched their first-born son reject not only their way of life, but their name and what it stood for.

No one said anything when we got home. Lily slammed out and into the house before Joe and I unbuckled. Shaking his head, Joe quietly stepped out of the car and went in through the garage door that led straight up to his room.

Instead of going in, I stepped out and walked to the front porch, where I sat on the bottom step and curled my arms around my legs. The sun was hot but that didn't bother me; it was a welcome relief from the chilly silence I had been surrounded by all day. Sitting there in my new white sundress chosen by my mother specifically for this day, I rested my chin on my knees and wondered who was to blame for my family falling apart.

I was fifteen and just finished with my freshman year in high school, but I knew that my life was changing. Even as I thought it I heard a car starting up and watched as my parents drove around the circular drive and out into the cul de sac. I didn't know where they were going but I knew why. Earlier in the week they had been fighting with Joe again, trying to change his mind about his future, as they had been trying to do for the last two years.

They had taken first step when he met Morgan. Everyone saw the changes in him instantly—his interests changed, his attitude toward his future and his family changed. No longer was he the golden boy who went to basketball or baseball practice and then went to do a separate workout before coming home and studying for two hours each night. No longer was he the president of National Honors Society or the Environmental chairman. All of his extracurricular activities stopped, and Joe became a boy with one focus: Morgan Andrews.

She was a petite girl, with strawberry blonde hair that she kept in a short bob. Her fingernails were always painted in a wacky color and most of her clothes were made out of some sort of recycled or eco-friendly material. She wore sandals in both the winter and summer, and she dedicated her life to serving others. We were developers; we tore homes down and did our best to invade sacred wetlands in order to put up giant hotels. She was the Save-the-Whales girl, the person who chained herself to trees to keep them from being cut down, the first in every picket line for any cause.

When Joe first mentioned putting his future at Stanford on hold to roam around the United States helping the poor with Morgan, my parents solved the issue by packing us up and moving us almost 1200 miles away to Arizona. They said it was for the hotel, that this project needed special attention, but we all knew why. Even the twins knew the hotel was only part of the reason.

Rather than bringing Joe back to his original focus, moving held adverse effects. He got worse. His first two months in Arizona he hardly spoke. He didn't go out for basketball workouts, didn't try out for the team in the winter. He never even mentioned baseball. He dropped all AP classes and received barely passing grades. Our parents had removed Morgan with her free spirit and odd nail polish, but they couldn't remove the desire for freedom that she had implanted in Joe, and in the end, he not only rejected them and their way of life, he rejected everything they had ever given him.

Now, as he stepped out onto the front porch with a duffel bag in one hand and his motorcycle helmet in the other, I knew he had left us long before this moment.

I stayed where I was as he walked down the driveway to where his motorcycle was parked and began loading the bags in the small compartments. Before he got even the backpack secure, Lily came slamming out of the house.

Her pale hair flowed behind her and was whipped at impatiently by her fingers. I couldn't see them, but I knew her light blue eyes would be blazing with anger, as they invariably were when she was upset. She stopped an inch from Joe's bike and planted her hands on her hips. She was wand slim and pale, a direct replica of our mother physically; emotionally, she was completely Thomas Evans. Our mother's entire life centered on doing what was right, doing what was proper in the eyes of her husband and parents, making certain that her children's lives were perfect and that those on the outside looking in would see exactly what she wanted.

That was me, not Lil.

Lily was proper in every way, but it wasn't because she wanted acceptance from others. Lily didn't care what others thought, she only cared about being the best; in life, in school, in everything.

A person who just glanced at her wouldn't know that beneath the lean and narrow figure was a spine of steel, that beneath the pale blonde hair and light blue eyes was a lethal mind that remembered everything and always had a response. And right now, her response to Joe's decision was pure disgust.

"What about Stanford? Dad spoke to the admissions director. You've seen the acceptance letter. You're in, Joe. You could go to Stanford next year despite your grades this year."

"Stanford's not my dream, Lil, and I never asked him to do that."

"It's not just about you," she shot back. "It's about tradition and our family. You've been given the tools to succeed, Joseph. You can't ignore that. You can't just walk away from everything, from your education and a chance at a real life, from us. It's not right."

He didn't say anything, just continued to secure his bag down. I wanted him to stop what he was doing and rant and scream. I wanted him to tell Lily that he didn't know what was going on, that he just needed something else, some time to see some other places. I wanted him to do anything that would show me he was confused, that he was thinking of staying. Anything that might show me he still wanted to be a part of our family, and that we hadn't lost him yet.

Tears filled my eyes as he did none of those things, as his face stayed blank and he continued to systematically secure down the few items he was taking with him.

"Mom and Dad are going to be crushed, Joseph," Lily said for the third time, her tone taking on that of a scolding school teacher. "Do you think this won't affect them? You're their oldest son, the first of the Evans' children to graduate and start their life. You're the heir to their namesake, the next in line to continue the business. How do you think they're going to feel if you just leave, if you don't even try?"

"Probably the same way I would if I stayed. I can't be what they want, Lily, and I can't continue to ignore what I want."

"Oh, how do you know what you want? You've been moping since we moved here. You haven't even tried to look around and make a life for yourself."

While Lily continued to try and convince Joe to stay, I sat very still and wondered what was going to happen. For my entire life, we had been a close family. There were expectations from our parents, but they had never seemed unreasonable. We never had to ask or want for anything. We travelled all over the globe, to Europe and Asia, down to South America. Never before was there been something that separated us. Until now. Until Morgan.

I wanted to blame her, to hate her as my parents did. To make all of this her fault. But I had watched Joe in the last year, and somehow, I saw more than just Morgan. Joe wanted freedom, and that was the only thing our family name couldn't buy. We could go on trips around the world; we could stay in the best and most expensive hotels around the United States on a day's notice. We could get into the best colleges after receiving the worst grades. But we couldn't be free, not in the sense that most people could. As an Evans, there were expectations, and one of those expectations was that you worked toward the future and its opportunities. Joe was done working, and I knew it.

Yes, I wanted to blame Morgan, but watching Joe with his bronze colored hair that was shades darker than my own, lightened and highlighted by the sun, his eyes that were more gray than blue, so focused and drawn, I knew it wasn't Morgan. It was our family.

"Couldn't you try?"

Both Lily and Joe stopped their argument and turned to stare at me. Clearing my throat of tears so my voice was stronger, I asked again. "Couldn't you go to Stanford and try? Maybe you'll like it."

Joe sighed, his shoulders falling a little with the motion, and then he walked toward me, his long legs eating up the ground at a steady pace until he was sitting next to me. I turned to him and tried pleading.

"We can talk to Mom and Dad, we can tell them that you'll try if they'll try. That if you go to Stanford, they have to be nicer, they have to listen. Maybe they'll agree...maybe they'll even let you go see Morgan."

With another sigh, he put his arm around me and rested his chin on my head. Comforted despite the ache spreading through my stomach, I leaned into him. "It's not about Morgan, Mimi."

I heard Lily snort and then quiet when Joe speared her with a look. "Not just Morgan," he amended and I leaned back to look at him. "It's hard to explain, Mia, but this is something I *have* to do. I won't be happy if I stay, no matter what changes. Does that make sense?"

I nodded, but a part of me didn't understand. Would never understand. "Is it because you're always driving me and the twins around? I'll be sixteen in May, I can find a ride until then."

He shook his head and brought me close again. "No, Mimi, it's not because of that. I love you and Ethan and Joshua. I even love Lily," he said, and I looked over when I heard Lily choke out a laugh. Tears streamed down her face and her arms were wrapped protectively around herself.

"I have to go, Mia, and find what's going to make me happy. But I promise I'll find a way to stay in touch, okay?"

I nodded and held on when he hugged me. He was four years older than me, my big brother who had been more a father than my own. The one who had taught me to ride a bike, who had scared the crap out of the first boy to pick on me in elementary school, and who had chaperoned my first date in middle school. He was everything that made our family work and he was leaving us.

When he pulled away to stand, I wrapped my arms around my legs again and hugged them to my chest as I watched him walk toward Lily and his bike. I smiled a little when Lily launched herself into his arms and hugged him fiercely before turning and walking inside without a backward glance.

I stayed where I was as he put on his jacket and helmet, as he checked the security of his bags before straddling his bike and kicking it to life. I stayed even as the taillights disappeared around the corner and the sound of his engine became nothing more than a distant rumble. I stayed where I was as my tears began to fall with the sun, and I realized that my life had just changed forever.

Chapter Two
Ryan

3 years later

Two weeks after my eighteenth birthday, I was positive of only three things in the world: (1) baseball was the greatest game in the world, no matter what those soccer freaks said, (2) Super Mario Bros. was the best Nintendo game ever invented (the original, not this new shit), and (3) if I failed Senior English, my mother was going to kill me.

It was that fact that had reduced me to following Nina Torres around and begging until she agreed to tutor me.

Nina being Nina was opposed to the idea, and was making this much harder than it needed to be, forcing me to follow her through the hallway—walking upstream after school, like a goddamn freshman—dodging people. During this pathetic display of begging, I came to another realization: she might only be 5'1", but the girl could move.

"Nina, it's not like I'm asking you to do my homework here, or to work miracles. I'm not an idiot like Logan Walker is, and you helped him raise his grade in math two months ago so he could keep playing football." I hated that my voice had a whine to it, but seriously, didn't she hear me the first time when I said my mom would kill me?

"Why don't you ask Max? He's *your* best friend, and apparently he's going to be valedictorian, so I don't know why you'd want me, a lowly salutatorian, to tutor you." She swung open the door to the library quickly enough that I thanked God for my reflexes and slapped a hand on it, narrowly avoiding another broken nose. Refusing to be intimidated by a girl who was half my size, I pushed through the door and followed her in.

"I did ask him to tutor me, and you know what I got on Freidman's test?" Nina plunked her back-pack down and I winced at the resounding thud. How someone that small carried around a bag that big without falling over was beyond me.

"I'm riveted." Her sharp tone normally put people off, but I just grinned at her. She'd been like that since we'd known each other, and I wasn't afraid of her. Much.

"I still got a D, Nina. You know Max, he's on a different wavelength all of the time. I barely understand any of the words that come out of his mouth when we're talking about baseball, let alone some Greek freak that's poked his out eyes because he slept with his mom."

"Oedipus," she corrected and rolled her own eyes. But I saw her smile and I knew she was coming around.

"Please, Nina? I promise not to hit on you like Walker did, and I won't ask you to do my homework. Just help me study for the tests and write the occasional paper. Freidman is killing me, and if she keeps it up, you won't have to worry about tutoring me because my mom will kill me. Dead."

She raised one, thin black eyebrow above her thick black framed glasses that were as much a part of her face as her nose. "Afraid of your mommy, Ryan?"

"Hell yes," I told her, and grinned when she finally laughed. "She's a scary woman. Remember the time she caught us trying to make fire with a magnifying glass and the sun? She almost skinned us alive."

"You were a little smaller back then. And chubbier."

"Growing," I said with a wince. "I wasn't chubby, I was growing, so I carried some weight. And it doesn't matter—5'2" or 6'2", when Joanna Murphy wants you dead, you're dead." I picked up a book that she'd laid out and scowled at her when she yanked it out of my hands and set it back down in its proper order. "Please, Torres? I'm begging."

"I would, but I'm not an English tutor. Math," she said when I let out a stream of cuss words. "I tutor kids in math, Ryan, and I've seen you in Calc. You're not a genius, but you're not exactly an idiot."

"Thanks a heap."

She grinned then, her perfect white teeth glowing against her brown skin that was a testament to not just the Arizona sunshine, but her Mexican-Asian heritage as well. She'd looked the same since we were little—petite frame, small features, big dark eyes that made her oddly good looking if you got beyond the scowl. And the attitude.

"Can you at least tell me who tutors people in English? Mrs. Friedman told me you could help, and I assumed she meant you would be my tutor."

Nina shook her head and opened a textbook and a binder simultaneously. "National Honors Society tutors people. Each member picks a subject. I'm math, so is Max, though he rarely ever does." She scowled again and I interrupted before she could detour and start razzing me about my best friend for the hundredth time that week. Nina and Max had been battling for grades and top honors since middle school and I knew once she started complaining about Max, she would never stop. It was the same with Max. I didn't even let him mention Nina's name anymore.

"Do you have a name, Nina? I'm going to be late to practice as it is."

"Sorry to keep you waiting," she said dryly. She motioned behind me. "Mia's an English tutor. You can ask her. Or Sarah Long, but I realize that might be a little more awkward for you, considering your history."

"Thoughtful of you," I muttered before taking a deep breath and turning.

It was always like this—a fist to the solar plexus each time I saw her. It didn't matter that we had lived across the street from each other for the last four years, or that I saw her every day at school and when she was leaving her house to run at night. It didn't matter that her face was burned into my mind, never to be erased. The sight of her still never failed to take my breath away, to impair my senses so that everything around me dimmed except for her.

Golden hair poured over one sun-kissed shoulder and rained down to her elbow. She was petite, only 5'4" or so, but her legs were long and showcased in the white shorts she was wearing. Her blue tank top was loose and flowed around her, accenting her delicate frame. I knew her eyes were almost the same color.

I watched as she strode toward me—what was it with small girls and their fast pace?—her face trained on the paper in front of her, and I felt my heart beat a little out of rhythm. There she was, the girl I'd been waiting for, for forever, really.

Chapter Three
Mia

I heard my name and looked up from the paper I was reviewing over Bradbury's *Fahrenheit 451*. I knew that if I was going to tutor Chris Stewart over the book and its characters, I would need to be prepared, because Chris wouldn't be. He never had been in two years.

I looked at Nina first, who jerked her head to Ryan, who stood next to my best friend with a look of shock on his face. He replaced it with a stupid smile as I stepped closer.

"Hello," I said and he nodded.

"Hey."

He didn't say anything else, just stood there with that stupid grin, and after a few seconds I raised my eyebrow. I didn't have time for both Chris and Ryan Murphy today. One was bad enough, but two clueless, slow witted boys? It was too much.

"Did you need something?"

As if someone had shocked him back to life, he jerked a little and then laughed, running a hand through his hair to smooth over the awkwardness. God save me from jocks who thought they were charming—like the fact that they're beautiful and can throw a ball makes up for the fact that they're socially inept. I purposefully looked at my watch.

Nina rolled her eyes behind him. "Smooth, Murphy."

"Shut it, Torres," he said without looking at her. "Yeah, sorry,

I was thinking of something else."

Thinking, sure—what party he was going to, what girl he was going to meet, when he was going to life weights next. But I smiled and nodded, hoping to push him along a little faster so I could finish my review.

"I need a tutor for English. I begged Nina, but she said you were the one to go to. Which is good, because Nina's not very friendly."

I didn't glance at Nina and glare at her, but I wanted to as I looked at the self-involved, thought-he-was-charming jock in front of me and wondered if I could actually say no as I mentally went through my schedule. I already saw Chris two days a week for an hour after school, and Elisa Lemus, a junior girl with concentration issues who claimed ADHD, directly after Chris. If I took on Ryan, too, that meant six hours a week that I was dedicating to other people and their work, while still having all of my own homework and work at the Inn all day on Saturdays. I was a reporter for the newspaper, a member the yearbook staff, social chairman for student council, a runner...

"Please?"

I looked at him, trying to ignore the grin that spread across his incredibly gorgeous face, and let out a quiet breath that was more resigned than distressed. What was one more thing on my plate? At least it would keep me away from home longer, and I wouldn't be subject to the long conversations about my future with my mother that she had taken to having every time we were alone at home together. They were really more like monologues than conversations. She would talk, telling me exactly how my future would be, where I would go to school and what I would study, who I would marry and when, what I would do, when I would have kids, where and when I would travel. Then she would pat my knee, tell me to study, and leave for one of her socialite meetings with the girls where they all tried to make their children sound more impressive than their friends' child. Sure, Ryan would be yet another person who got a tutor because they were too lazy to do their own work, but by adding him to my caseload, I could all but eliminate my time at home.

Everybody wins.

I nodded. "I have time on Wednesdays and Fridays from three to four."

He winced. "I have baseball practice every day after school."

"It's November. Baseball season is in the spring."

"That doesn't stop Coach from making us practice every day, or from running a player into the ground if he misses."

"Please tell me when he does that to Max," Nina interrupted. "I would sell my GPA for a chance to see him throw up."

I grimaced and shook my head at her. Ryan rolled his eyes, the only sign that he actually heard her. "Could we possibly do this around six on those nights? My house? Or yours?"

"You're telling me you want to be tutored at six o'clock on a Friday night?" I shook my head. "You really are desperate."

He grinned and I did my best to ignore the sheer beauty of his face, but it was next to impossible. The light green eyes that turned almost gray in the light, framed by lashes so long they were almost feminine, were set off against the dark blonde hair that was starting to curl at the ends because it was just a little too long. His face would have been almost pretty with the way his lashes curled against his lids, but the square jaw and slashing cheekbones covered in taught skin evened it out to one gorgeous package. Even in my constant state of irritation with underachievers like this one, I had to admit that if I was the looking kind, I would have to look no further than Ryan Murphy.

"You have no idea. I would settle for Saturday night at nine."

His voice snapped me out of my reverie, bringing me back from my perusal with a snap. Straightening my shoulders, I shook my head. "Well, I won't. Your house, six to seven, Wednesdays and Fridays. Not a second later or I'll leave. Your schedule might be flexible, but mine isn't." My voice was frigid and unbending, as was my attitude, but something about the way my body wanted to react to him had me on edge.

"Deal," he said. "How much does it cost? Walker said it was

forty a week."

I quirked my brow and behind Ryan, Nina winced. When I speared her with a glance, she shrugged her shoulders.

"Mia, listen to me, he was an idiot," she explained. "He tried to hit on me twice, and then told me that if I did his homework for him, he'd take me to homecoming. As if he's irresistible and I, being such a nerd, should be grateful for the opportunity."

"We do this as volunteers, Nina. Your IQ is large enough to know the meaning of that word, isn't it?"

"I do, I swear, Mia, but you should have seen this kid." She looked to Ryan for help, pointing her finger at him. "You know, tell her. Explain how awful Logan Walker is."

Ryan shrugged. "He *is* an idiot."

"See, and Ryan's not even that smart."

"Jesus, Nina."

"Well, you're not, and even you know he's an idiot. I should be given an award for helping him pass his trig midterm."

I shook my head and turned back to Ryan. "We'll start tomorrow. Be prepared. Don't think I'll come in there and tell you what the books are about so you don't have to read."

He nodded soberly and straightened into a salute. I felt my lips twitch but refused to smile. I knew his type and far too many people smiled at them for having a pretty face. "Go away, I have an appointment."

"Thanks, Mia," he said as he started toward the door. "Oh, and Nina, Max said to tell you he got a ninety-nine on his AP Calc test. He said you'd know what that meant."

Nina's eyes narrowed to lethal slits and her jaw clamped together so tightly I worried the enamel on her teeth cracked. Ryan laughed the rest of the way out of the library.

"Bastard," she muttered and went back to the physics book she was reading. I said nothing, knowing a diatribe on Max Canfield and his annoying habits would ensue if I did. Instead, I wandered over to my preferred table by the window and set up to wait for Chris.

Our appointment was at three every Tuesday and Thursday, as it had been for the last three years. And as per usual in the last three years, Chris was late, dawdling in at three fifteen, headphones on, pants below his butt so his striped boxers hung out—a look I thought had gone out in the late nineties along with adult overalls and hair scrunchies. My sneaking suspicion was that his mom threatened his life if he didn't meet me, but I didn't know if even that would hold as a threat much longer. He, quite simply, didn't care if he graduated from high school, let alone got a passing grade in English.

"Music and boarding," he told me the first day I tutored him two years ago. He'd been a freshman, I a sophomore, and he'd sat there ignoring my questions and knowledge about *Of Mice and Men*, until I set the book down and asked him what caught his attention outside of school.

"What kind of boarding?" I asked and he shrugged, his eyes never leaving the table where he traced his finger in the same pattern over and over. "Long, short, skate, wake, snow...doesn't matter. I do it all."

"Where do you go for the snow?"

He shrugged again, a movement that I would soon learn meant he was thinking. "Flagstaff, and when it's vacation time or I get good grades, my parents send me to Utah or Colorado."

And there it was. The reason that two years later, Chris and I were still working together. He wanted to snowboard in more places, I wanted the boost in my resume` and to fulfill my NHS obligations. It worked for both of us. He had been reading the same book for a few weeks now, and was doing fairly well. Because of this, I hadn't expected a ton of work and was half hoping that today would be more of a review than an intense one-on-one. My own homework was waiting for me, and I had a charity event to plan for the weekend.

My hope immediately deflated when Chris finally sat down and placed a paper on the table between us. I looked down at the red number over fifty and winced. Fifteen. Resignation settled over me as I looked up at him.

"What's this from?"

"Reading quiz. Mr. Gregg graded mine early so I could show it to you, get help, and retake it from a B starting point."

Perfect. I looked over the quiz and resisted scrubbing at my eyes, barely. There were questions over chapters that he was supposed to have read last night, I guessed, but there were also questions over the chapters we'd discussed together in depth last week. Obviously, something between us wasn't working since he only got eight of those right.

"Okay, why don't we start with you giving me a summary of what you remember from the chapters that we talked about last week and then we can go from there."

"Some freak works as a fireman burning books. The people let him because they'd rather watch television and drive nice cars. Sounds like a good deal to me."

I waited a beat, refusing to be irritated. That was his game. Irritate someone so much that they tell him he's trying to fail and leave. He goes home and continues failing. It was a classic cycle I had seen too many times to give in.

"Anything else?"

He shrugged. "Sparks notes didn't really have anything much else to say."

I sighed. "Chris, this is your junior year. You're lucky that Mr. Gregg will let you retake it all instead of giving you the F you earned."

His shrug was more of a jerk of his shoulders this time and I stopped. He was usually a little disinterested, maybe a little angry or annoyed, but never mad. Today, he looked mad. His gaze was riveted on the table where he traced a pattern with his finger, and while I watched him, noticed that his shoulders were slumped and his expression dour.

Knowing we wouldn't get anywhere if he was this angry, I set the test down on the table and folded my hands on top of it. "Want to tell me about it?" I asked.

He jerked one thin shoulder again while his eyes remained fixed on the table and his invisible pattern. "There's not really anything to talk about. My parents decided last weekend that they want me to get into ASU or U of A." He scoffed and his fingers stopped so he could throw his hands in the air. "A couple of decent test scores, an average PSAT score, and they think I'm good enough for Universities now. Are they nuts? I have a 2.6 cumulative. They were originally cool with the community college in Phoenix, but now, no no, they want something more." He leaned back in his chair and crossed his arms over his chest. "I'm not smart enough."

I stopped him there. "If you don't do your work, you're never going to know if you're smart enough."

"It's not just that," he said after a minute. "I don't want to go to one of those schools. I don't really want to go to school, but we made a deal, so here I am working toward graduating and thinking about community college. That was the deal. They can't just change the deal."

Hearing Chris's words made me think of my own family. Parents, even with the best of intentions, could manage to hurt us in the most basic way. My parents hadn't been able to accept Joseph and his needs. They could only see what they were offering him, but it never occurred to them that his needs were different, simpler in a way. Just like Chris's needs were simpler. He didn't want a master's in business or a degree in literature. He wanted some freedom, some time to bum around and figure out who he was. It wasn't ideal for most people, but it was him, and by changing the rules, they were rejecting who he was and trying to make him different.

And he was rebelling against them, as Joe had rebelled against our parents. Only Chris's parents were still trying, I thought with an inward sigh. My parents had simply cut Joe out, ignoring him as if he didn't exist. Lily became the favored eldest child, and Joe obtained freedom. All he had to do to get out from underneath the microscope our parents had put him under was sacrifice his existence. And he had. He didn't exist to them, they didn't exist to him. And we all lived happily ever after.

A glance at Chris had me frowning. I knew there was nothing to say that would make him feel better, so instead, I reached over and opened the book he had plopped onto the table with his test.

"Let's start by rereading certain parts, making a character outline, a plot outline of setting, symbols, themes, etc. Even the community college won't take you if you fail high school, Chris," I said when he stared at me. "Where you go is your choice, but you're limiting it if you fail."

After a moment he shrugged. I wanted to tell him I understood, but I had learned a while ago that words weren't useful, actions were, so I began to explain the points we had been over last week instead, noting that as the minutes ticked away, Chris got a little less angry and a little more involved in the story. Sometimes, happiness was too much to ask for, but every now and then we could accomplish something and that felt almost as good.

We took a little over an hour to go through the characters and the plot line. On Thursday, we would meet again and review the rest before he made up his test on Friday.

I glanced at my phone when he left. There were two text messages from my mom, and although Elisa was already setting her things down in Chris's vacated spot, I answered them quickly before closing the phone to begin again. I had another hour here and then I would pick the twins up at basketball practice before going home, running, and then starting my own homework. I needed to revise the essay I was sending out to Stanford for my application, which was due in less than a month. I had other essays and responses for schools, too, all due by December first. But Stanford was the most important, I thought, hearing my parents' voices in my head. Stanford had not been forgotten when Joe had rejected his acceptance there and broken a longstanding tradition amongst Evans males. If anything, it had become more important. It had become the proof that we were the family we showed to the world. Stanford was our tradition, and if I was who my parents wanted me to be, cardinal red was my future.

Without warning, the image of Joe as he rode away that last day came flashing to the front of my mind. I saw him then as I had seen him a hundred times since that day: free, and I wondered how it felt.

Because I didn't want to think about why that was, I pushed it back before looking at Elisa. Her red hair was cut to her chin and curled wildly. She had on leg warmers with ballet slippers, a miniskirt with so many rips in it I didn't know why she bothered wearing it, and tights of bright fuchsia.

Though I wasn't surprised with her choice in color, I took a moment to wonder whether or not she was hot with all of those separate articles of clothing on. It was November, but November in Arizona was like summer everywhere else—seventies and sunshine.

"Can we cut it short today? My band is practicing at five and I can't be late." She wiggled her small butt onto the chair and leaned back. "I'm the lead."

"A band? I thought you were painting."

She shrugged. "I was, now I'm not. Painting's so solitary, you know? Like, I was always alone and it made me dark. But then last week I was in the music store with my boyfriend and I was totally inspired. So we decided to start a band and our first practice is tonight."

"Good for you," I managed and tried to sound believable.

When we met at the beginning of the year, she'd been a dancer, wearing nothing but leggings and sweaters, walking on her tiptoes with a forced turnout. Recently, she replaced dance with painting, channeling her inner person, she called it. That had lasted a month, three weeks less than dancing. Her short-lived interest in hobbies was a direct mirror of her short memory. Her parents called it ADHD. I called it lack of focus.

Knowing well that she would have forgotten everything we talked about without them, I set the notes from our session last week on the table and looked at her.

"Where are we in our book?"

At the end of the hour, we had spoken about the chapters, along with her musical inspiration—her boyfriend, of course—and poetry, because she was really getting into song writing. I placed the notes I had written carefully next to hers and made sure she took them both. When she came back Thursday, we would go over them and add the next chapters on before her big exam.

She took off in a hurry, her red hair bouncing behind her, her long earrings with multi- hued stars clinking. I watched her leave and rolled my eyes before I sat back and checked my watch.

I had twenty minutes until the twins were done with basketball practice, so I pulled out my phone and began checking my email and my text messages for confirmations for the Fun Run Challenge I was organizing for this upcoming Sunday. It was a morning 10K run that would help raise money for Healthy Arizona, a foundation that worked toward bringing physical education and athletic teams back to underprivileged and low income schools in the state of Arizona. Originally, I signed up to help, until my mother pointed out that it would be a better investment to put on my college applications if I was in charge of the whole thing. At which point I gave in and did as she said, as I did with all things, because that's how our relationship worked.

After Joe disappeared and I saw how much it hurt my parents, I began working even harder, hoping that my accomplishments would show them they still had a daughter left who loved them and wanted to make them happy—or at least give them a sense of pride to cover the hurt. But, as of late, my mother's quest to make me the perfect individual had become more of an obsession, and while I wanted to say it was because she cared so much about me, I was starting to feel that it was because she didn't believe in me at all. Every piece of praise had a reminder with it, a small statement designed to put me neatly in my place and show me that life wasn't easy, nor was it meant for dreamers.

Like she thought I was going to leave her, too, I thought, so she disappointed me to keep me from disappointing her. Joe had once been a boy who dreamed of playing college basketball, who dreamed of going to Stanford like our dad had, as his dad had before him, and adding to the Evans name. Then he met Morgan and she changed him—or more accurately, she showed him a different way of living. I had a feeling my mother was afraid that this would happen to all of her children and she would then be the person to blame instead of Morgan.

I didn't really blame Morgan, not anymore. Joe had made his decision. She had been herself and Joe had allowed that to change him. And in the end, he was the one to walk away from our family. For that I would never been able to forgive him. He changed all of us because he changed—because he had chosen a new path—and now we were all left wondering why. It was the hardest on my parents' relationship, and I was aware enough to understand that was part of the reason I wanted to please them so much. I loved my family, deep down, despite the times I felt as though they based their affection for me off of my accomplishments, and if receiving an A on a math test or organizing a charity event made them happy with me, it was my hope that it would make them happy with each other as well. So far, my results weren't as successful as I would like.

Joe still wrote to me every month like clockwork. His emails were long and involved, telling me of all of the places he'd traveled, of all of the odd jobs he'd worked. Last week his email was full of the sunshine—he was in Costa Rica, tending bar and surfing, and having what sounded like a great time as he waited out the winter storms in most other places.

I never wrote back; there didn't really seem to be a point. At first because I was so hurt, so angry that he had just left us, that he hadn't tried to stay and be a part of our family. And then, as time passed and life moved on, I realized that he was happy, and that hurt more.

He wasn't living as a nomad, migrating place to place and job to job on the back of his motorcycle to make my parents angry, he was doing it because it made him happy. I didn't understand that, didn't want to, so I hadn't responded. But I read his news every month, no matter how long and involved or short and quick it was. I had read one email a month for the last three years and tried not to resent the fact that he could hurt me just by being happy. His departure from our family had led to many more—Lily, skating off to college and rarely coming home. My dad, jumping from one project to another, flying all over the world to "review" our hotels and others, to make plans. Anything that kept him from being with the rest of us. Anything to keep him from remembering that he still had a family who needed him so he could forget about the son who hadn't wanted him.

So, I read Joe's email with an ache deep inside, and I tried not to dwell on the fact that lately a part of me wondered what it felt like to be that free, that unencumbered with responsibilities and expectations, what it felt like to be a person instead of an accomplishment.

Chapter Four
Ryan

My little sister, Caitlin, and I stared at Max as he got into the car, his mouth already running a mile a minute. Bits of his Danish flew as he rambled on and on, stuffing his bag at his feet at the same time that he stuffed more pastry into his mouth. Grimacing, I lifted the paper towels from beneath the seat and handed one to Max.

As usual, he held onto it and never used it.

"Max," I interrupted when he finally took a breath. "What the hell are you wearing?"

Max paused in the act of shoving the rest of his breakfast into his mouth and grinned sheepishly before brushing his fingers down the front of his bedazzled t-shirt. They smeared pastry icing, but he didn't notice.

"I'm going for a new style. What do you think?"

"Teenage girl?" Caitlin asked sweetly from the backseat and I took a moment to give her knuckles.

Max scowled and looked down at his gold lettered, rhinestone bedecked t-shirt. "No, GQ. This shirt cost me almost a hundred dollars."

"Jesus," I said as I backed out of Max's driveway and back onto the main road. "And what prompted you to buy something with glitter on it and deck your hair out like..?" I trailed off and looked in the rearview to Caitlin for help.

"Cristiano Ronaldo?" she supplied.

"Yeah. Why do you want to look like this Ronaldo character? Doesn't he play soccer?" I winced. "Means he's gay, Bro. You don't want to look gay, do you?"

Max brought a hand to his gelled hair and patted it gently. "Dude, girls dig him, but that's not the point."

"There was a point to this outfit?"

"Murph, it's our senior year. Haven't you had that t-shirt since you were a freshman?"

I glanced down at my beloved Cardinals shirt. I *had* owned it since I was a freshman, but I'd also grown eight inches and put on thirty pounds. It might be the same shirt, but it didn't bag at the shoulders and hang to my knees anymore. Thank God for that.

"So?" I asked.

"So," Max said turning to me. "It's your senior year; no, it's almost halfway through your senior year. Don't you want to change your style up a little, have people look at you differently?"

Caitlin giggled from the backseat. "What's your look supposed to say, Loverboy?"

Max laughed at that and shrugged his shoulders, unbothered. We had been friends for so long that Caitlin was like his little sister, too. She ragged on him as much as he ragged on her.

"Hey, Caitlin, what's this I hear about you hanging out with Josh Evans?"

She blushed a little, her skin going pink at the cheeks until she had to look down. "We just study together at school sometimes," she mumbled.

Max smiled and looked at me while I tried to process what I had just heard. "Man, your little sister's making better time with the Evans than you are."

"Shut up, Max," I said without heat. Josh Evans? They just studied together? Christ, was Caitlin going to start dating now? Was she already dating? Was I supposed to do something about it if she was?

An image of me from freshman and sophomore—okay, and

junior—year flashed through my brain, a quick slide of every asshole thing I had done to girls, girls who had let me, and I looked in the rearview at Caitlin. Oh, *hell* no.

"When Mia came over to help him study a couple of nights ago, he showered and made sure he was ready before she got there. He didn't wear sweats or anything, but jeans," Caitlin put in so cheerfully that I wanted to strangle her—almost as much as I wanted to lock her in a room and make sure no boy ever looked at her again. I remembered holding her as a baby and now she was dating?

To show her what I thought of her big mouth and her social life, I scowled at her in the rearview, but she ignored me and continued, scooting forward in her seat a little. "He even cleaned his room, changing his sheets and throwing all of his dirty laundry down the chute, as though she'd being going in there and sitting on his bed." She shook her head at that, the look on her face clearly stating *boys*.

"You can shut up, too, Caitlin. And you can also tell Josh Evans that if he wants to keep his legs in working order, he'd better keep his hands to himself."

"You wouldn't dare, Ryan."

"Push me and find out, *Caitlin*."

Satisfied that my point was made, I pulled into the parking lot. Caitlin had her door open before I'd finished parking, and was already halfway across the parking lot by the time I got out. I narrowed my eyes and watched her cross paths—on purpose, goddammit—with Josh Evans. He must have said her name because she stopped and turned, a smile blooming on her face as she waited for him.

I watched them walk away together and wondered for the second time this morning when the hell Caitlin had gotten old enough to date. And what the fuck I was going to do about it.

"She's good," Max said.

"Who?" I asked as I spotted Mia across the lot. Today she was wearing a sundress with skinny blue straps that showed off her bare shoulders. God she had nice shoulders. And legs, I thought, watching the skirt swirl around her thighs, keeping her in focus until she and

Nina disappeared inside.

"Your sister. I wouldn't have even known what she was doing when she walked over there. It's almost like a coincidence that she and Josh are walking into school together right now. *Almost.*"

That had me snapping back and glaring at Max, but with a second glance at him I had to laugh. He was struggling to walk in the stiff new blue jeans he was wearing, and what appeared to be the world's heaviest leather sandals.

"Dude, your outfit is killing me."

He just smiled and swung on his backpack before sliding on gold rimmed aviators.

"Those make you look like a drug dealer," I said as I grabbed my bag and locked the doors.

"Murph, I get it; you're nervous that I look so good and I have a lot of classes with Mia. But don't worry, Bro, I don't poach. Besides, I've got my eye on someone else."

I walked with him toward the entrance, waving to people who said hi and shaking my head as people stared at Max and he preened.

"Who have you got your eye on?"

"Can't tell you yet, it would ruin the surprise. When she comes around, though, I'll let you know."

I opened the door to the senior locker area and walked through. "Okay. That's weird, but okay."

"Not any weirder than you having a thing for one girl and dating another one instead."

"Max, I'm not dating anyone."

"Anymore," he said and stopped at his locker to retrieve books. "And I don't know if what you and Sarah had could be considered dating, or just friends with benefits, but either way, you were with her and not Mia."

Sarah Long was just that—long and lean and not afraid to let a person know it. Even now I found her easily enough in the sea of people, her bleach blonde hair just a little lighter than all of the other blondes, her skin a little tanner. She was wearing a skirt that was short enough to show over three quarters of her leg, and a shirt that emphasized just how developed she was. And since she'd looked like that when she was fifteen, I cut myself some slack. What teenage boy would deny a girl who looked like *that* and had set her sights on him? Far be it from me.

For the last year and a half we hadn't really been in a normal relationship, but we had spent time together—in my bed or hers, in her car or mine. A handy closet, the gym bathroom. It hadn't really mattered at the time. She opened doors for me that most other boys only dreamed about—and had been a willing participant in her quest to explore new avenues of herself as well. But now, well, now it was easy to see where I'd gone wrong. She was hot, no doubt, but that's all I could say. I knew she was smart only because she was in some classes with Max, and he didn't take anything under genius level, but in our on again, off again time together, I hadn't really bothered to ask many questions about her brain, or anything else. Sarah and I had done one thing, and we'd done it well, but even with all of the time I'd spent with Sarah, caught up in what she was offering, I had known all along that it wasn't the real thing. She hadn't ever been fully mine, not the way a real girlfriend was, and when I realized that last year, I'd made the break from her, from us and who we were together, for good.

Sarah looked up from her conversation with one of her many followers and met my stare. I inclined my head and she smiled, the same inviting look she used on all guys worthy of her attention, but instead of driving me crazy as it used to, making me want to drag her off into the nearest corner and find that physical release that came so easily, this time I felt nothing. Without responding, I looked away and tuned back into Max, who was now talking about baseball.

"I'm telling you, if Sanchez grounds another ball during practice today, I'm tagging him with it. He did three yesterday, and we all had to run because he sucks. Put in Wilson, put in Richardson, put in any pitcher who can actually throw to me and get it all the way over the plate."

I nodded my agreement and was about to reply when someone

behind me called out my name. Turning, I felt the familiar stutter in my chest again, followed by the squeezing that made it hard to breathe.

Mia walked toward me, Nina beside her already shooting darts out of her eyes as she looked at Max. I heard Max say something under his breath, but I didn't know what it was and I didn't care, especially when Mia stopped in front of me in that sundress that matched her eyes—dark and deep as the ocean. When she looked up and smiled, the world around me went blank, and her face was the only thing that kept me anchored.

Chapter Five
Mia

Nina was beside me grumbling, but I ignored her easily enough as I approached Max and Ryan. I needed to reschedule our tutoring session for later tonight because my parents were having a small function at the hotel and it was "imperative" that I be there. When Margaret and Thomas Evans thought something was imperative, the entire world around them better, too.

In my renewed promise to not be annoyed with my mother and everything she did, I was working hard to take this in stride, but her pleas from this morning were making it difficult.

"Mia, I need you to be there. Everyone we know will be there and they're dying to see you. It's your senior year."

Like that said it all. Hey, it's my senior year, of course people want to see me. Except, they don't want to see me, they want to grill me to see if I'm really as amazing as my mother says I am. Honestly, I've thought about saving myself the time and sending a mass email explaining that I am, in fact, too close to average for my mother, and really, they have nothing to be impressed with and, therefore, no need to see me tonight. But again, the renewed promise to be a better person to my mother has me refraining.

That and the fact that my father already called this morning to set his non-arrival in play. He used the same tired lines he has for the past two years, phrases like "We'll see what my timeframe is," or "I don't get to choose when an investor sets up a meeting." My mother was near tears when I walked into the kitchen this morning, and because of that and the fact that she hadn't seen him in almost a month, I was going to the dinner and I wasn't complaining.

To her, at least.

"Hey, Max," I said and felt the daggers from Nina's eyes shoot straight into my back. Without acknowledging her, I turned and smiled at Ryan. His eyes were a little glazed over and his face carried the same blank, mesmerized stare that it had the other day. No wonder he needed tutoring, I thought. If the kid could space out in mid-morning hallway chaos, imagine how far he could go when he was sitting in an all-but-silent classroom.

"Ryan, can we talk a minute?" I asked.

He nodded but didn't answer. Nina solved it by punching him in the shoulder and snapping him back to reality. Max grinned, she glared, and I sighed. Ryan jumped back and started to babble, but I cut him off before he could get very far. I didn't have time to linger in the hallways this morning, waiting for some dim witted athlete to come to his senses. I still needed to go and see Mr. Black about the English paper that was due at the beginning of next week. *The Death of Ivan Illyich* was giving me more problems than I cared to admit.

"I have to change our tutoring session tonight."

He nodded his head slowly, as if this bit of information took time to process. "Okay," he finally settled on and I shook my head side to side to see if there was more.

Nope, nothing.

"Right. Well, I have to be at The Authentic around five for the meet and greet cocktail hour. Then there's dinner at six-thirty. I know its Friday night, so if you're busy and seven-thirty or eight is too late, we can reschedule for another day. Sunday I'm busy all day with the Fun Run, but I could do it Sunday night if that works for you."

He shook his head. "I don't have plans tonight."

Max shook his head behind Ryan, rolling his eyes, patting his chest, but I assumed it had something to do with Nina's presence and ignored him. "Good. I'll call if I'm going to be any later than eight."

"No worries."

"Be happy," I heard Nina say and for the first time, Ryan's expression changed from shocked to alert, and a smile broke out on his face.

"And he's back," I said and he looked at me. "I'll see you around eight."

I turned without waiting for a response—it would probably take him the better part of a year to form one anyway—and started toward the English wing, leaving Nina as she and Max were now in a heated debate about something on their physics homework. My day was full, as was my night and my weekend. I worked a full day at the Inn tomorrow, after which I would race to the starting line and make sure everything was in order for the run on Sunday.

My mother's description of me as dependable wasn't flattering, but it was accurate. Reckless just wasn't in my nature, no matter how much I wanted it to be. I tried to rebel, but French toast for dinner when my parents weren't home was about as crazy as my conscience would allow me to go.

I shook my head. Lord, I really was boring. Again, Joe flashed into my mind as he drove away, only this time, it wasn't pain I felt as I watched him leave, it was envy.

Walking into Mr. Black's class, I put that aside and focused on my immediate dilemma. I was an English tutor because I could read a book quickly and break down the plot line and characters. I knew the correct format for writing a paper, and I understood how to use the correct quotes and transitions in order to persuade the reader to see my point of view. I could teach someone to draw diagrams and charts, how to organize characters and their actions so they could choose which were the most significant. I could help someone search out and discover the symbols the author had left them with, and I could help them analyze these symbols. Like with all things in my life, it was easy when I was telling someone else what to do, but when I read a story and sat down to write my own paper, I was at a loss. None of the techniques that I used for others helped me in my own English courses. None of my charts or diagrams could help me answer the one question that I had to answer as I dove inside of a character and their actions; none of them could aptly answer the question *why*, and I found I needed that answer before I was able to understand the rest of the character.

What motivated Antigone to defy her family and defend her brother? What prompted the people of the *Brave New World* to question their happy existence and allow the drama of true life to break their euphoric feelings? What caused people of all places and times, of all worlds, to want something else? Something that was different than what they had, someone who was different than those around them?

Romeo and Juliet took their own lives, and for what? A moment's connection? Love? No way. MacBeth died and so did his wife, because they were so sure that their lives were destined for more, for what they considered better. Rarely in literature did characters who defied their place or their family survive. Wasn't there a reason for that?

I set my bag down on my desk and slipped out the neatly typed and stapled papers. For this paper, my job was to explain how Ivan Illyich had grown or transcended from his suffering. His emotions had changed, as had his actions. That I understood. When one suffers great physical pain, it was obvious that those things that once mattered—status, pomp, money—would no longer be in a place of utmost importance in a person's life. What I didn't know was if he had transcended from a person of pomp and greed who had only been concerned with his social appearance and status, to a person who loved his family above all else.

Was it enough that at the end of his life, Illyich realized that the love of and for his son and wife was more important than his social status? Why was it in death that people always realized the true purpose of life and what it meant to fulfill it?

"Perhaps it has something to do with the idea that nothing matters after we leave this life," Mr. Black responded when I asked him just that. "That in this moment we are able to see more clearly because life is no longer an issue." The look on my face made him smile. "You don't agree?"

"I don't disagree," I countered. "I just don't think that death can be used as a clarifying event. How does the looming darkness, so to speak, clarify anything for anyone? How can someone be sure this is a true change and not just something that comes because people think that those they're leaving behind need it? Illyich's entire life was made up of pomp and status until his final days. And even then it was prompted by the fact that no one wanted to be with him while he was on his death bed."

Students started to file in, but I stayed where I was, a frown on my face as I thought through my dilemma.

"You don't believe that a person can change through suffering?" he asked after a moment.

"I believe suffering can cause us to change. I don't believe change brought about by death is transcendental or valid—I believe it's trite. Shouldn't a person's character be judged on how they lived their life when it wasn't in jeopardy? When death wasn't the only thing left ahead?" I lifted my shoulders when he raised his brow at me. "It's great that he realized his wife and son were the most important part of his entire life, it's great that he finally accepted that relationships fulfill a person's life and not money, but isn't it a little late if they're dying when they come to this realization? Is a deathbed realization all it should take in order for someone to forgive a man who never thought of them on any other occasion?"

Mr. Black appeared to think about it while students continued to file in. I saw Nina and Max come in, still arguing. They sat down and Nina rolled her eyes before turning away from him and effectively ignoring him. Max just grinned.

"You're thinking about his life, Mia," Mr. Black said as he rose and brought me back to attention. "And you're thinking about his son and his wife and how they feel, though we know his wife was not compassionate by any means." I nodded. "The question is, do you really think they should ignore the change in Ivan Illyich and demand more before 'forgiving' him? Forgiveness by its very definition means compassion, acceptance, understanding—should a person have to earn those or is it the job of the person who is forgiving to give them without expectation?"

"What kind of question is that?" I demanded for the tenth time since English class that morning. It was time for the last period of the day and Nina and I were walking toward the newspaper room together.

"Forgiveness is given because people mess up—and this guy did. Why is it always that the people around those who make mistakes are charged with the task of forgiving and forgetting? Why can't people earn it? Ivan's a selfish man who doesn't realize that his life's a scam or that he's hurting those around him until the hour of his death. That's not an apology and it's not him changing. His wife and kid shouldn't have to accept it as such and forgive him."

"Why don't you just write what you know Mr. Black wants you to write and stop worrying about it? It's just a story written by a dead guy who nobody but high school English teachers remember."

I scowled because that was Nina's general feeling about all literature. "It's too subjective," she always said. "Math is easy—there's always an answer that can be found through various methods. And all people can find it if they know the correct formula. English is all about interpretation and making crap up. Who cares why some fictional character did something? It's not going to change the world we live in today."

I knew that I should just take Nina's approach and use the answer I knew Mr. Black was expecting. I could write it in my head right now—*Ivan Illyich lived an artificial life until his death, which was the moment of transformation for him. His life began even as it ended.* The issue wasn't in the writing itself, it was the fact that I didn't believe it. I didn't believe that this story was about change; I believed it was about heartache and too little, too late. No one should be able to apologize on their death bed and make it sufficient for a lifetime of pain, I thought as we walked into the newspaper room. No one should get to hurt people for years on end and ask for forgiveness when they had run out of options.

Joe and my father flashed in my mind and I gritted my teeth. No, forgiveness shouldn't be expected. A person had to earn it, otherwise, the rest of us were just walking doormats, waiting for the next person to decide when they were going to wipe crap all over us and move on.

My phone beeped and I took it out, trying not to grind my teeth when the message icon showed that it was my mother.

Your dress is on your bed, shoes next to it. Don't be late tonight.

I thought about not texting back, but I knew that would only elicit more messages until she knew I had received and comprehended hers. I shot off a message that simply read "Thanks," before sending. And then I reopened the message and sent an "I love you," before closing it again. Patience, I thought as I walked into the small, windowless room that was already filled with bodies. She didn't mean to irritate me, it was just who she was. It was just too bad that who she was, was currently driving me crazy.

I was eighteen—well, getting to be eighteen—and still, she had gone out and bought me a new outfit and laid it on my bed with the appropriate shoes. Which would have been a nice gesture, if it hadn't been the third of its kind this month. Or if I was ten.

My mother loved to manage and instruct, my father loved to oversee. Our family was like a well-run business, with only one failure in its twenty-two years of existence. A lot of that was due to the time and effort put in by my mother organizing the day to day operations. When Joe had left, she had been the most devastated because she was the one who had worked so hard to make him into the person he had been. Until Morgan.

It seemed this would always be a tag line when I thought of my brother Joe—one that had become ingrained in the last few years.

Joe had been a 4.0 student-athlete. Until Morgan.

Joe had been Stanford-bound. Until Morgan.

Joe had been the pride and joy of my parents' lives. Until

Morgan.

Joe had loved us. Until Morgan.

Our family had loved each other. Until Morgan.

Watching my mother cry over the disappearance of my older brother had been a motivating factor in my life, and since that day, I had worked hard to make certain that I didn't do the same. However demanding my mother could be, however upsetting at times because of her absolute refusal to see or accept anything that didn't mesh with her ideal, she was my mother—she was loving and caring and as steady a foundation as any child could ask for in their life. Joe had rocked her foundation, and I wanted badly to put it back on level ground.

More than I wanted anything in the world, I wanted to make her happy, and hopefully in time, that would erase some of the pain that still remained because of Joe's absence, maybe even bring my father back. In time, I prayed that my existence, my accomplishments, would be enough to fill the void that Joe had created inside of both of them.

My phone beeped again. *Don't forget about your math test next week. Every little point helps your GPA.*

But Christ Jesus I wished that time was sooner rather than later.

Chapter Six
Ryan

After two and a half sweaty hours of running, crunching, running, lifting, and more running, I eased my sore body onto the front porch swing and propped my feet on the rail, gently absorbing the slight rocking motion. With a sigh, I shoveled in a bite of rocky road from my bowl and hoped it would do its job. I'd lost five pounds since training started, and I was afraid I may lose five more if we didn't start to actually *hit* the ball.

I scooped up another bite and prayed to Christ that the sugar would make its way to my brain quickly. I was already mute when Mia was around me and I didn't need exhaustion slowing my brain down any more when she was around. I was seriously going to have to work on the whole talking thing with her, otherwise she was going to think I had a disability and that was really going to ruin my chances. It was bad enough that she thought I was an idiot because she had to tutor me in a class she made it clear she could ace in her sleep, but add that to the fact that I was unable to do much more than stare at her when she was around, and it didn't make me all that appealing.

On Wednesday when she'd come over, she had already been on her nightly run (I watched her leave and return, like the semi-stalker I feel like) and was freshly showered. Her hair had been long and damp and hanging over her shoulders and when she'd bent her head over my paper to read it, I'd lost myself for a minute and I actually lifted my fingers to run them through her hair. The look she speared me with was on level with the kind of look a woman gives a piece of slime when it gets on her shoe. So, tonight I really had to step up my game if I ever hoped to have a chance in hell of her seeing me as normal.

When her car pulled up to the curb, I realized I wanted her to see more than normal when she looked at me. I wanted her to see everything, like I saw everything when I looked at her.

Don't even go there, I warned myself and scooped up more ice cream. It was thoughts like those that had me going tongue-tied and brain dead and it needed to stop. What I needed was a plan. No more being shell-shocked by her looks or her scent; no more creepy moments when I was mesmerized by her hair, even if it was damp and smelled like wildflowers and made me want to see it spread out over my pillow. No, what I needed was to focus on her instead of everything I felt. That way I could show her I was different than what she thought, smoother, nicer, smarter. Less creepy.

I could start all of this by calming the fuck down and relaxing.

Taking a deep breath, I stayed where I was and watched her as she walked toward the front porch in sexy black sandals and a skirt that stopped mid-thigh. Her hair was all scooped up and coiled at her neck, except for the few strands that had escaped to float around her face, tickling her neck every now and then as the light breeze rustled them.

Grateful I hadn't called out so that I could take another moment to steady myself, I just watched her. As she stomped up the walk, I heard the faint sound of whispering, and with narrowed eyes, I watched as perfect Mia grumbled to herself. On a closer look, it appeared she was having a small temper tantrum, not unlike the ones Caitlin often threw when something or someone had upset her—or just told her no. Women were such fickle creatures, I thought, and wondered who had dared to upset my princess...and who had her talking to herself.

That one thing was like the antidote to my nerves, and all at once I found myself genuinely relaxed as I watched Miss Perfect walk up the drive, grumbling to herself the entire way. Enjoying the show, I stayed quiet as she got closer, making out phrases like "bamboo shoots" and "never again."

When she was almost to the steps, I called out to her and had the pleasure of seeing her head snap up as she realized someone was there. Mortification came and went on her face, followed quickly by annoyance, which was just as quickly replaced with a calm smile.

Impressed, I scooped up more ice cream and grinned at her. "Who were you talking to, Champ?"

Chapter Seven
Mia

I struggled with mortification as I realized that Ryan was sitting there watching me from his porch swing. The grin on his face was wide, showing off all of his straight teeth and making him even more attractive. Because that irritated me almost as much as the fact that I'd been caught talking to myself, I looked away and took a deep breath. Idiot, I thought as I walked the rest of the way up the stairs. But I didn't know if I was referring to him or myself.

I stopped a foot away from him and stood with my bag over my shoulder and my hands clasped firmly together. My feet were killing me and I had just spent the last three hours being toted around and showed off by my mother like some goddamn puppy (and I never cuss, not even in my head), all the while smiling like Miss America and pretending that I was oh-so-happy to be doing what I was, preening and answering questions, like a trained Labrador showing off her tricks.

I had actually been relieved to have the tutoring session with Ryan as an excuse to leave, knowing that otherwise I would have felt guilty for leaving her alone, and therefore compelled to stay and be with my mother, even though every other word out of her mouth had been like nails on a chalkboard.

My favorite part was when she told everyone I would be attending Stanford next year, and then added a sly "and hopefully she succeeds as Lily has done." Which really means, *Mia's an idiot and we hope she can make it at the smart kid school.* Nothing like a cleverly concealed insult to put me in my place and motivate me.

On the car ride from the Inn to Ryan's, I repeated every conversation, but this time I added in the things I really wanted to say and topped each statement with an eye roll, hoping that I would be rid of the sick weight in the pit of my stomach that seemed to appear more and more often these days after I spent any significant amount of time in the presence of my mother. And I hated that I felt this way, especially since I know she latched on so tightly tonight and other nights because my father—the infamous effing Thomas Evans—called with his excuses at just past five, when he knew my mother would already be too engrossed in her plans to complain. I saw it after the call came in, the hurt, the sadness, the loneliness, but before I could get to her and try to help, to offer comfort or someone to talk to, she was already setting that mask in place and moving forward. Her over bright smile and chirpy voice were a dead giveaway that she was upset, but as was expected of her, she went on.

Although I wanted to rage at her to stop pretending, to stop letting my dad walk all over her, to *stand up* for herself for godssake, I didn't. I took my cue from her and put on a pretty dress and a smile so I could pretend with her, because that's how our family operated. Show no weakness, no vulnerability; forge ahead and always come out on top.

"Fake it until you make it" should be written on our family crest.

All in all, my emotional wall was a success until I pulled up to Ryan's and he caught me talking to myself. If he had been inside like a normal person and I had just made it to the door without him seeing me upset, I would have been able to ignore the heaviness of the evening for the rest of the night. I was good at ignoring things.

"I didn't see you when I pulled up."

"Too engrossed in your conversation," he said and grinned.

Pretty face or not, the image of slapping him was becoming more appealing by the moment. I took another deep breath instead. It wasn't his fault that he thought he was funny, I reminded myself. Surely he had been told how adorable and amusing he was his entire life, how was he to know any better now?

Ignoring the headache that was beginning to brew behind my eyes, I made my lips curve. "Sorry, I was just reminding myself of some things. Should we begin?"

He nodded and scooted over, making room for me on the swing. I stayed where I was. "Out here? Isn't that going to be distracting to you?"

"Because it's such a rocking place?" he asked, and made a show of looking around at the quiet streets and glowing homes. Not one dog barked, no cars or music sounded, no one slammed a door or had a shouting match. It was more peaceful than most libraries.

"Right," I said and sat rigidly beside him, trying to find any excess patience that I had left. Though my feet were screaming, I refused to slip out of the sandals and become barefoot as he was. The sooner we began, the sooner I would be able to go across the street and inside and upstairs and go to sleep, where I didn't have to talk about college, or the future, or anything else that was unknown to me but already mapped out by my mother. That is, if I was smart enough to follow the map.

Irritated that I let my mind go there, I snapped back to focus.

"The last time we met, Macbeth and his wife had made a plot to kill Duncan and become the king and queen. Let's review everything up to this point, and then we'll move on with what has happened in the scenes since."

"Want some ice cream?"

I looked up as he shoved a dripping spoon toward my face, leaving me the choice to either open my mouth or be covered by creamed sugar and fat. I grimaced, swallowed, and held up a hand to stop him from getting a second spoonful and repeating the process.

"No, I don't want any ice cream, thank you." I bit the words off and began reviewing my notes. A moment later, he interrupted me again.

"Have you run yet today?"

I sighed hugely to make my annoyance known, and set my papers down so I could stare at him. He was sitting with his legs propped on the railing, gently rocking the swing back and forth. His now empty ice cream bowl was on the rail next to them, and his arm was slung out over the back of the chair. His beautiful hair was damp and curling slightly, his lids heavy over those glowing eyes that were alight with humor. He looked so relaxed that I was surprised the air around him wasn't glowing with it. Resentment welled up inside of me, and I once again worked to swallow it down before answering.

"No, I've been busy."

"Do you want to? Not run, it's too dark for you to go alone and I've had my quota of running for the day, but we could walk."

I would have to cut my feet off if I walked so much as a step more in these shoes.

"Ryan," I said, frustration coating my words. "We need to get this done. You have a test coming up and if you fail, your grade will drop and, as you say, your mom will kill you. You asked me to help you, but I can't if you won't focus."

He shrugged. "So we walk and talk about Macbeth and his crazy, power hungry wife at the same time. You look like you could use it," he said before I could protest again. "I'm betting that you put in a full day of school and committees and then you had this dinner thing with your parents and the bamboo princess, or whoever you were talking about, and you didn't get to run like you always do." My eyes must have narrowed in suspicion because he laughed. "We live in the same cul de sac, Evans. You leave every night about the time that I'm coming out here for ice cream and a place to hide from my mom."

"What I could use," I said through clenched teeth, "is to finish this so I can go inside and go to bed. And it's rude to listen to someone's private conversation."

Oblivious to my tone, he shook his head. "First, it's only a conversation if there's at least two people involved. And second, I don't think you could calmly go to sleep feeling the way you do. I know you're upset," he said. "Or as upset as you get. Why don't we just go for a walk and you can clear your head? You can't be any good at teaching when you feel like this."

It was the first time he had put together what appeared to be a coherent sentence in the last week, but instead of pride in my skills and ability as a tutor, I found my patience vanishing and my anger welling up too quickly to control.

An entire evening—hell, week of frustration boiled to the surface and bubbled over onto the overgrown jock next to me. I shut the book with a slap and shoved it into my bag before rising. My feet screamed at the pressure, but I refused to wince as I turned and looked down on him.

"What I need," I said, my words lashing out, "is for everyone to stop telling me *what* to do and *how* to do it. No, I didn't have time to run today. As much of a shock as this may be for you, some of us are too busy to fulfill our every whim and desire. Instead of running, I, like you said, did go to my meetings, I did fulfill my family obligations, in between which I took the time to prepare for this session because I thought when you said you needed someone to help you study, you meant it. Obviously, that was my mistake and I won't make it again. Especially for a dim witted, selfish jock who has the ability to get better grades, but simply lacks the desire to be a better person and work a little harder."

Satisfied that he was shocked speechless, I turned and marched down the stairs, each step I took causing my feet to weep in pain. I was burning these shoes first chance. Christ, was this my mother's idea of torture? Had she started finding ways to physically make me suffer as well, just to make sure I never disobeyed her? I could actually feel my skin going raw as the straps dug into my flesh.

I wasn't even halfway across the street when I heard him call my name, but I kept walking, trying to speed up without collapsing, or worse, giving in to the pain and pressure that had nothing to do with my stupid shoes and weeping.

"Evans, wait."

His fingers closed around my arm and I turned quickly enough that he took a step back and held up his hands.

"Hold on, Ace. I didn't mean to upset you."

"Well, side benefit, you did. And stop calling me Ace. Or Champ. I'm not some stupid baseball player."

"God, you're ornery tonight. I'm sorry, *Mia*," he said with great emphasis. "I didn't mean to tell you what to do or to upset you. I was just trying to help."

My energy was waning and with it, my anger, overridden by the pain shooting up out of my feet. Too tired now to care, I nodded. "Fine, let's forget it. We can sit down and go over the notes again." I winced as I headed back toward his porch, and then muffled a yelp as I felt myself being lifted off of the ground. "What the hell are you doing? Put me down. Jesus, what kind of person just picks someone up?"

"Calm down, Evans. I'm not going to take you upstairs and have my way with you. Yet," he added and roared with laughter when my eyes widened. But it wasn't just due to shock and embarrassment—for some reason, the picture his words painted in my head were scarily appealing, and I wondered what the hell had happened to me that an inappropriate innuendo from Ryan Murphy spiked my heart rate and made me think of things I never had before. Like how hot he was, and how good he smelled.

Ignore, ignore, ignore.

"You're limping and this will make it better."

Before I could come up with a response, I was being carried through his house and into his backyard. His sister looked up as we passed through the living room and out onto the patio and I closed my eyes against the mortification.

Just as quickly as he'd swooped me up, he plopped me down on a lounge chair and bent in front of me to unhook my sandals.

I slapped at his hands, my embarrassment growing with each second. And my fear. If he touched me now, I might just give in to my desire from ten seconds ago and jump him. Jesus, what was *wrong* with me? "I can take them off myself."

"Good. Come over here when you're done."

He went to the side of the in ground Jacuzzi and turned on the jets before sitting down on the ledge and sticking his feet inside. When I just stared at him, he grinned and patted the spot next to him. "Trust me, Evans."

Giving in, I undid the clasp to each of my shoes and felt my feet weep with relief as I removed them. Wincing only a little, I grabbed the notes from my bag and padded over, sitting down on the ledge with as much grace as possible in my skirt. The minute my feet hit the water, I felt instant pleasure.

"Better?" he asked,

I nodded. "Yes." And then I gave in and smiled. "Maybe you're not so dumb after all."

He clamped a hand on his heart and pretended to moon over the words. "Now you've done it, my heart goes pitty-pat."

"I take it back. You're an idiot."

"And she's back," he said, repeating my words from this morning and pulling another smile from me. "I really am sorry for upsetting you back there. I wasn't trying to tell you what to do. I just wanted to help."

Because I knew he was being sincere, and because I knew my frustration had little to do with him and everything to do with my family, guilt snuck in and I shook my head. "Don't worry about it. I was already on edge, so it wasn't really your fault. Of course, if you'd been inside like a normal person, I would have been able to compose myself before seeing you and none of this would have happened."

"But don't you feel better now that is has? You got your irritation out and now we can focus."

I nodded and moved my feet back and forth in the water, enjoying weightless feel. "I guess. We do have to go over these notes, though. You have a test coming up, and a paper to write, and you need to know what's going on."

He sighed and nodded. "Okay, Ace—Mia," he corrected when

I glared. "Hit me with it."

We spent the next hour going over the characters and their individual motives. He recited the events of the last few scenes to prove to me he had read, and I explained the purpose behind certain scenes and events to him. By the end, we had covered half of the play and I was feeling more relaxed than I had in a really long time.

"I'd better go," I said without moving.

"Okay." He shifted until our knees bumped and I looked over at him. His face was close and I could see the light from the house reflected in his eyes. For a minute I sat there, mesmerized by the contact. And then I heard the slam of the front door and I snapped back. For the third time that night, mortification swamped me. I turned away, hoping to find a graceful way to stand up in my already hiked up skirt. While I considered it, he stood and placed his hands at my waist, lifting me easily to my feet.

"Um, thanks," I said and didn't look at him as I walked over to get my things.

We walked around the side of the house this time, going through the side entrance to the yard. When we reached the driveway, I would have kept walking all the way to my car, but he said my name and stopped me.

"Hey, Evans."

I turned and bumped solidly into his chest before taking a huge step back. "Um, yeah?" Brilliant, Mia, way to act unaffected.

He smiled, obviously aware of the affect he had on me as he put his arms around my shoulders and brought me back, cradling me against his chest while I stood there, my arms filled with my shoes and my bag trapped between our bodies. I held myself rigidly, waiting for him to let go, praying that my body didn't give in to its own urges and do something embarrassing. Like kiss him.

When he continued to hold me, I gave him a small shove and hoped he'd release me and give me back my space. The need to drop my things and hold on was stronger than I had ever felt, and I was scared I would do that at any moment if I didn't distance myself.

Rather than let me go, though, Ryan came with me, and his head bent down until our faces were close, his lips at my ear. Goosebumps popped out on my skin as his breath whispered over my neck. Without thinking, I curled my fingers into his shirt and angled my head until my face was pressed into the curve of his shoulder and neck where I breathed in his scent.

I had never been held like this, was all I could think, and when his arms brought me to my toes and pressed me closer, I closed my eyes and drifted, not ready to think, not ready for anything but Ryan and what it felt like to just be with him.

My heart was beating loudly in my ears when his lips pressed to my temple. Unsure, I turned further into him, waiting, wanting, yearning for something that made me tremble in fear as much as desire. As if he sensed my hesitation, Ryan kept his hands light as they skimmed down my arms and back up to my neck, up further into my hair, where they loosened the bun and had it all spilling free. His lips were at my neck now, nuzzling, while his hands lost themselves fully in my hair, bringing me closer.

"Mia," he whispered, and like that his lips were on mine, covering them, devouring them, owning them in a devastatingly slow rhythm. Everything in my body tingled, and my hands that were trapped between us gripped my things so tightly I was sure my knuckles would break.

This was what it felt like to be reckless, I thought. This heated, spine tingling, heart thumping state was exactly what had been missing from my life. It wasn't safe here with his mouth on mine; I knew that even as I angled my head a little at the pressure of his hands and allowed him to sweep his tongue through my mouth and tangle with mine. But in this moment, I'd never wanted safe less. I wanted reckless, I wanted to go on feeling like this forever—tingling with need and desire, anticipation humming through my veins, blocking out all sensible thought.

As Ryan lifted his head and my eyes fluttered open to meet his, I wanted to drop everything and grab him, to yank him back to me and have his lips on mine, taking me to that place that we had just been. As I went to do just that, my phone buzzed in my bag, bring me back to reality with a thud. I blinked and looked around, as if just realizing where I was. I pushed away, but Ryan held on, forcing me to look at him. His eyes burned with need and I saw his intention as clearly as if he'd said it aloud.

"Don't." My voice was weak, as were my words, but he halted anyway. Panic was threatening again, and my breath was backing up in my lungs. "Please don't."

He stared at me and for one exciting heartbeat I thought he would do it anyway. The part of me that I didn't understand, that I didn't want to understand, ached, while the rest of me shook at the thought. He must have seen the fear, or something else, because a few seconds passed and he let me go. Scrapping my pride, I turned and fled.

Chapter Eight
Ryan

Although I've never been overly religious, I've always held strong to the fundamental Catholic—or maybe it was Jewish—teaching that Sundays were reserved for observing the Sabbath. Although my observance wasn't exactly in line with that of God's, or any other religious person's or figure's for that matter, I did believe fully in the idea of rest, relaxation, and celebration.

Especially when one was recovering from a minor hangover.

The hangover, combined with the early morning chattiness of the few hundred other community members standing next to me at just before seven-thirty in the a.m., and the already blazing sun beating down on me, were enough to make me want to kill someone. After I drank another gallon of water and got up the energy.

I'd thought about not going to Sarah's party last night—had even said no at first. But then some guys on the baseball team had reminded me that our free weekends were limited, and before I knew it I was being pulled into the frenzy of beer pong and flip cup. I'd stopped drinking at midnight since I had to be home at one, but the damage had been done—especially after almost three months of abstinence and sobriety—and now I was hung over.

My only relief came from the fact that I'd still had enough of my mind left to say no to Sarah when she'd cornered me. It had been close, and she'd been clinging to me like a barnacle to a rock, but after one sloppy kiss—or two, since I'm not a fucking saint and after three months of abstinence, sobriety, and celibacy, a willing female in a short skirt and tank top was a hard thing to resist—I'd come to my senses and managed to walk away from her, remembering why we had broken up in the first place.

She didn't care that it was me she was kissing, she just cared that she got what she wanted, and that was power. I'd said no before it had gone too far, and that was something to be grateful for. The only thing, I thought, and tried to find some shade and relief from the blazing sun. Still, it didn't erase the twenty minutes before I'd said no when we'd been making out like we had so many times before, but at least we hadn't gone all the way back to where we'd been. Making out was one thing—sex, well, that would have unleashed an entirely different kind of self-disgust, and in my already pathetic shape, I wasn't sure I could take anymore self-loathing right now.

I sipped from the bottle of water some chipper soul had given me that morning and swore for the hundredth time that I was going to kill Max at the next available opportunity. Not in front of all of these people, though. I took another sip to clear away the sand that seemed hell bent on building up in my mouth. Too many witnesses. No, I would wait, let the whole incident blow over and go cold, and then when Max was least expecting it, BAM! I would make my move.

Since the thought of punching Max made my head ache less, I entertained the fantasy until my brain grew tired and sluggish, at which point I switched to fantasies about my bed. I could just leave, just walk out without saying anything to anyone and go home and crawl back into bed, where the sheets would be nice and cool and the house silent.

When someone handed me a number with adhesive on the back, I gave a wistful sigh for what could have been before I took off my long sleeve and placed the number where they directed on the front of my t-shirt. For the last time, I wondered what the hell I was doing awake and getting ready to run at seven in the morning on a Sunday when I had only gone to bed six hours earlier. Coach didn't make us practice on Sunday, Mom and Dad had a landscaping job they were working on, so they weren't home to razz me about homework or chores. It would have been quiet bliss at the house where Caitlin and I could have shared some lunch, possibly played a few games of Wii tennis, and vegetated. Instead, I was getting ready to a run a 10K—a distance someone mentioned was equivalent to around six miles. Christ, I play baseball. The bases are ninety feet apart, and during some games no one hits for the first three innings and I stand in the shortstop position waiting for some action—why the fuck was I running six miles?

When Max walked up to me, grinning like an idiot, I thought fleetingly about murdering him again, but the thought passed when I realized how much energy that would take. Right now, it took energy just to stand and I couldn't spare any, not even for the pleasure of cold cocking my best friend. Especially since I knew Max could be scrappy when he wanted, and between the heat and the hangover, I was in no shape to start something. Instead, I focused fully on him for the first time all morning. He looked pretty normal today, which was a plus. I didn't know what had gotten into Max lately, but his outfits were getting crazier—along with his attitude. Why was Max smiling at seven in the morning when a six mile run loomed ahead? Max was the catcher, he hated running almost more than anyone else on the team. Sure, he had declined the party the night before and was, therefore, in much better shape than I was, but it was still seven o'clock in the morning. What the fuck?

"Murph, looking good. Athletic, ready to run."

"More like hungover. Is this why you didn't go to Sarah's last night, Max? You knew you were running at seven in the fucking morning?"

"Dude, I didn't go to Sarah's because she's your ex and I have loyalty. And because I knew I would be running," he said with a laugh that pierced through my already aching skull and threatened to split it in half. Christ, what I wouldn't give for some Advil. Or a hammer to just finish the job.

"What the hell's going on, Max?"

Max just grinned and took the water from my hand to sip from it nervously. His eyes continued to dart from side to side, and his already nervous habits became more pronounced. He sipped from the water again and went to hand it back. I shook my head and Max shrugged, a jerky motion that reminded me of when we'd been twelve. His movements had been spastic then, too, and he had ended up walking off of curbs or into walls and people for almost two years because he couldn't control his nervous energy.

"Max, you're about to jump out of your skin. It's Sunday morning, we don't have practice, you hate running for the sake of running, but you still woke me up before the fucking sun, and now we're standing around with real runners who do this every Sunday, charity event or not." I ground my teeth and glared at him as a group of women who were already chattering walked by, their spandex outfits spookily alike, making them into a clan. One of them was pushing a stroller that had multiple babies in it, who were also garbling about something. "For the love of God, Max, why?"

He just shook his head and looked around again, sipping from the water every few seconds. "You know, my mom's running, she told me about it and I thought it would be a good thing to do. Besides," he said, looking over my shoulder. "I thought you would want to be here, considering."

I followed Max's gaze and looked over my shoulder at Mia. Her hair was pulled off of her face, and she wore a white t-shirt with the race's information emblazoned on the front in bright pink and turquoise. Her shorts were the same turquoise, and she carried a clipboard as she talked to people.

Jesus, she looked beautiful for seven in the morning—and efficient. As always, I thought testily as my head continued to ache.

It was her fault I felt this way, really. The only reason I'd even gone to the party was because I'd had a harsh realization the night before when she'd run away from me like a scared rabbit runs away from a fox. Or like a smart person runs away from a leper. We were no good together, and she'd made that dead clear.

She was prim and proper and a rule follower. I was a delinquent who couldn't pass remedial English without a tutor. She organized Sunday morning charity events, I participated in Saturday night debauchery. We just didn't fit, and that had been hell to realize; just as it had been hell to realize that no matter how much she didn't want me, I may never stop wanting her. That, more than anything, had pushed me to Sarah's, to fun and forgetting the girl next door, just for a few hours. Too bad those few hours couldn't help a guy the next morning, I thought sourly and turned back to Max.

"How did you know she would be here?"

He shrugged, and this time it came out more like an intended action and less like a spasm. "My mom told me she was in charge of it, said it was pretty impressive. I figured you wouldn't mind the extra time spent impressing her."

If by impress you mean beg and plead, then sure, bring it on. I was pathetic. "I think it's better that I don't let her know I'm here."

"Trouble in imaginary paradise?"

"No trouble, just realizing how different we are. She's not what I expected, you know, and I'm not someone she can take seriously."

Max put his hand on my shoulder in a rare gesture of support. "Want to talk about it?"

"Nothing to talk about. I was wrong to think we could ever be something—she thinks I'm an idiot jock who's only after a good time and another party. After last night, I don't really know if she's wrong."

The hangover that had been raging was nothing compared to the disgust that swamped me now. One wrong turn with Mia and I'd gone straight back to the easy way—beer pong and Sarah and watching Mia Evans from afar, wishing that she would just look over and see me like I saw her. Fuck pathetic. I was a disgrace to men everywhere.

"First, I can't talk when I'm around her, so she thinks I'm some kind of retard. Then, I finally talk to her and start to show her that I do in fact have a brain, and I ruin it by making a move so obvious my grandma would have seen it coming. She all but flew she ran away from so fast." Disgust coated my voice as I remembered how small her voice had been, how shaky when she'd said no on Friday. "And if that's not bad enough, here I am, hung over at a charity event she organized, only proving to her that she was right to run away from me. What the hell's wrong with me?"

"Murph, cut yourself a break. She was probably just as nervous as you and that's why she left like she did. She's not the kind of girl you're used to."

"Exactly," I yelled. "She's nothing like Sarah, or anyone else, and I treated her exactly the same."

"So, fix it," Max said, still looking around. "Go up and tell her you're sorry."

I just shook my head and stepped up to the starting line. I was an idiot. One bad night and I returned to the person I'd been eight months ago, the person who was content to float through life without actually caring or trying. Not the kind of person Mia Evans wanted. Even as that thought crossed my mind, another followed directly behind that it wasn't really the person I wanted to be, either.

Mia or no Mia, I had known last year during baseball season that if I wanted to accomplish anything, I was going to have to make a serious change. And I did, for a while, until the one thing I wanted got a little difficult, and then I backed off and took the easy route. Tool.

I shook my legs out and stood next to Max as the starter explained the rules and the markers for the route. The people around us chattered on and on about the race, but I tuned them out and searched through the throng of bodies before finding Mia again, clipboard in hand still, eyes on the crowd. It would probably be better for both of us if I just backed off and let her go. We were opposites, and it was times like last night and this morning that reminded me why I hadn't made a move in four years of wanting her. She was event chairman, I was a lone runner who had only come because my best friend had gotten a wild hair and dragged me.

Even as I convinced myself that it was better for everyone that she'd run the other night, she looked my way and I knew that talking myself out of being with her wasn't an option anymore. Even before I'd had a taste of her, my body craved her like it had never craved anything or anyone else. Now, after remembering how well she'd fit against me on Friday, after remembering what her lips had felt like against mine, the small sound she'd made when my tongue had touched hers, I knew for a fact that my feelings weren't going away, no matter how hard I might try.

The starter went off and I surged forward to break away from the crowd. And because they weren't going away, I knew I needed to backtrack and fix my mistake so we could move forward, no matter how long it took her to become comfortable around me.

No more drunken Saturdays and painful Sundays. No more easy girls and frivolous times. I wanted someone who mattered—and I wanted to be someone who mattered. It was about time to show her and everyone else just who the new Ryan Murphy was.

Chapter Nine
Mia

"Great work, Sis."

I smiled at Ethan and Joshua when they plopped down next to me in the grass. It was just past three and all of the racers were gone and the tents taken down. Nina was busy making sure the last of the entry money got counted and sent to the correct people, and I was currently enjoying the sunshine and quiet. It was the first time since five-thirty this morning that I'd taken a moment to sit and now that I had, I wasn't sure I was going to be able to get up.

"Thanks. And thanks for all of your help with the heavy lifting. You two were amazing."

"You're telling me things I already know," Ethan said.

"Him and no one else," Joshua replied, and Ethan reached over and punched him.

"That's what you think. I saw Caitlin checking me out when I was lifting those tables today. Sorry, Bro, I probably should have worn a shirt with sleeves. I didn't mean to embarrass you in front of your girl."

"You're mistaken. She was in awe that twins could be so different—she's used to me and my arms and she felt sorry for you."

I sat beside them as they traded insults, smiling as I enjoyed just being there. In a moment I would have to get up and check how much we made, call the program director and let them know the final amount, find out where to deposit it, inform them of the contributors and such. There was a laundry list of things I still had to do in order to bring the event to a close, not to mention my homework that I had to review and complete, the English paper that I needed to go over one more time, and the rest of my college applications. But for now, with everyone else gone or occupied with something else, I took the chance to just sit and enjoy the sunshine.

"Hey, speaking of Caitlin," Joshua said and looked at me. "She said Ryan carried you through their house the other night and you guys went swimming." He wiggled his eyebrows and Ethan made ohhhing noises.

I reached out to hit both of them, embarrassed all over again at the memory. "We did *not* go swimming," I said and leaned back again. "And he was just joking around carrying me that way."

"That's not what she said," Joshua continued, and I wondered exactly what else Ryan's little sister had seen.

"Well, she's wrong," I replied.

"Why don't we ask her?"

I looked to where Ethan was pointing and saw Caitlin, adorable and petite in her running gear, her ponytail bouncing as she and another girl, who was a few inches shorter but just as adorable, walked arm and arm toward us. Trailing behind them was Ryan. The look on his face was anything but perky.

Irritated because just the sight of him had me flushing and remembering Friday night, I stayed where I was while the twins greeted the girls.

Apparently, this was Macy, Caitlin's best friend. They were going to Grazie's for a slice and wanted the boys to come.

They looked at me. "Ask mom. She's over by the sign-up tent."

They all trooped off, the girls already giggling, Ethan and Joshua razzing each other to show off. I watched them until they reached the tent, bracing myself when Ryan sat down next to me.

Can't put it off any longer, I thought, and turned toward him.

He was eating a Popsicle and without saying anything, he broke it down the middle and offered me one half. I shook my head no, but he just continued to hold it out to me.

"Don't worry, I didn't lick that side yet. At least not too much. It's hot out here, and you've been standing in the heat all day. Go ahead."

I was about to refuse again and then I looked at him. His eyebrow was raised slightly, his eyes steady on mine as he challenged me. I felt my back go straight and I held out my hand.

"Thanks," I said and took it from him.

Together, we nibbled our frozen sugar and sat on the grass in silence. I wanted to act casually, to say nothing of the other night and pretend as though this was a normal neighborly visit, but I was having a hard time. So, rather than relax as he was, I twisted the now bare Popsicle stick in my fingers and wondered what I was supposed to do.

"Why did the tomato blush?" he asked.

My head popped up and he raised his eyebrow again. "Come on, smart girl. Answer the question. Why did the tomato blush?"

"Because he saw the salad dressing."

"So she does read more than textbooks."

"No, my brother Ethan asks me that joke at least once a month after he eats a Popsicle. It's been there forever."

"Ahhh. That's too bad, for a minute I was thinking we were made for each other."

"Unlikely."

He laughed and stretched out his legs. "So, I should apologize for the other night then."

I looked at the ground and plucked at a piece of grass. "Don't worry about it."

"That's the thing," he said. "I wasn't going to. Last night I went out, got drunk—being the mature and emotionally stable young man that I am—and decided that I wouldn't worry about you. A failed attempt is what I was going to leave it at. No harm, no foul."

For reasons I couldn't quite figure, my mood plummeted with

his words. I plucked a larger clump of grass. "Well, great. Now that we've got that covered, I have to go to see Nina and find out how much money we made."

"It didn't work, though," he continued, as if I hadn't spoken. When I went to stand, he stood with me and put his hands on my shoulders. I took a step back and shielded my eyes as I looked up at him.

"How devastating for you. Not to worry, though, I'm sure there'll be another party soon and you can make another attempt."

"Funny. But that's just it, Evans, I don't want to forget it. Or you," he said and reached for my hand, linking our fingers together while I stared at him. "I'm sorry I was so abrupt the other night. I've just has this thing for you for a while now, and I kind of got ahead of myself. So to make it up to you, and to show you that I'm not really an awful guy—or an idiot—I figure we should hang out." He smiled at me and brushed his thumb over my knuckles. "What do you say, Evans? Want to hang out right now?"

More than anything, was the first response that popped into my head and it startled me enough that I had to blink. I stood there, staring at our joined hands, wondering why I didn't do the smart thing and just take mine back and walk away.

I had no reasonable answer for that, but I did know that hearing him say he didn't want to get over me made me feel like I never had before, and it was a feeling I wouldn't mind holding onto.

"I...I don't know. I have to go see Nina about how much money we made. And check out with Mrs. Blain before I can go anywhere."

"Okay, I'll come with you and then we can go from there."

Again, I wanted to tell him no, that it was better for him to get drunk again and work on forgetting it, but he was already walking, keeping my hand in his so I had to lengthen my stride to keep up.

Nina was hunched over a calculator when we reached her, with several other people around her who spoke to each other in between calling out numbers to her. Her fingers flew over the keyboard of the machine, and when I said her name, she held up a finger and indicated for me to wait.

Ryan and I stood there for three minutes before she finally looked up and smiled. Her hair was pulled off of her face, her glasses on. She wore roughly the same thing I did, except her shorts were narrow like her frame and reached almost to her knees. And rather than festive teal, she went for straight black.

There were no detours for Nina, not even in wardrobe.

"Hey, Captain. Murph. Eighteen thousand is your number, Mia, and that includes entry fees and extra donations made by runners and non-participants."

I raised my eyebrows. "Is that including the money we have to deduct and use to pay the vendors who didn't donate?"

She nodded and worked her head around, placing her pencil behind her ear in an old habit that always made me smile. It made her look like a thirty-year-old CPA instead of a high school student.

"Yep. You can call the higher powers or whoever it is that gets this check and tell them the good news." Then she grinned. "Holy shit, that's a lot of money. Way more than I thought some silly run would generate."

The people around her stopped mid conversation, startled by her revelation, and I shook my head. The soul of discretion she was not.

"Thanks for your help, Nina. I couldn't have done this without you."

"You're welcome, and you owe me. I'm not likely to forget that you promised me dinner next week."

"Next week's Thanksgiving," Ryan said.

"Ah yes, the day we stole our homeland from the unprepared, defenseless Native Americans. It's surely a time for celebration."

Ryan laughed and I rolled my eyes. Nina had something to say about every holiday, be it religious, national, or other. She never just enjoyed the break from school like the rest of us.

"Yeah, that one. The week after we'll celebrate with dinner and a movie. That way I can be finished with my college applications and have something to celebrate, too."

"I already got mine in."

Of course she had. Her future was in sight, and much like her wardrobe, there was no hesitation or detour there, either. She was moving forward, and happy to do it.

"What are you doing here, Murph? I thought you left with Canfield."

"Evans and I are going to hang out."

"Well, well," she said and wiggled her brows at me. "You two have fun."

"We will," Ryan answered before I could say anything.

When Mrs. Blaine came over to hug all of us, we were sidetracked for another fifteen minutes as she raved on and on about the revenue and generosity of which she'd never seen the likes.

"You girls simply did a marvelous job advertising. I'm so impressed. I can't wait to do it again next year."

Nina's face gave away exactly what she thought of that, but I smiled and nodded. "We're looking forward to it. Thank you for everything, Mrs. Blaine. We wouldn't have been able to raise half as much without your generosity and help with the sponsors and donations."

She waved her hand. "It was my pleasure darling. If there's one thing I'm good at, it's getting people to hand out money. Ask my ex-husband."

She barked out a surprisingly deep laugh and I felt one of my own bubble out in unison with Ryan's. Something about this woman who wore too much make up and not enough clothing had me actually considering working the same event next year. It wasn't about appearances for Mrs. Blain. She was a middle-aged divorcee` with no children, who owned and ran one of the boutiques off of Main, and who, despite what people said about her when she wasn't looking, was seemingly content with her life. Maybe there was something to be said for ignoring expectations, I thought as Ryan walked toward my car with me.

"So, what do you want to do?"

Of course, ignoring expectations didn't mean ignoring responsibilities, I thought. "I really do have a lot of homework," I told him.

"Evans, I'd put money on it that you've already finished your homework for the week."

"Not all of it," I said grudgingly. "I still have some math to do."

"And one hour won't kill you. Besides, I've spent the better part of my morning supporting your cause. Do you know how long it's been since I ran 6.2 miles, Evans? Never," he said before I could guess. "And I gotta say, it wasn't very much fun. In fact, I consider that false advertisement. That's liability for a lawsuit."

I smiled as I settled in and put my seatbelt on. "Did your sister drag you?"

"Nope, I dragged her, but the way she was acting with your brother today explains why she didn't complain very much. Max forced us both," he said at length, and adjusted his seat to accommodate his long legs. "He screamed into my house like a tornado on steroids this morning and woke me up. Since I was awake, I didn't want to let Caitlin sleep in and enjoy her Sunday, either."

"Sounds reasonable."

"Not at all, but it was that small pleasure which kept me from the larger pleasure of killing my best friend. I still have no idea why he even wanted to run in that stupid race—no offense."

"None taken," I said and turned onto Main Street. "We don't care if you liked the run, but we appreciate your money. As do the children of the greater Phoenix area, who will now be afforded physical education and sports teams."

"They should. I hate to run, that's why I play baseball. There are games that I don't touch the ball more than twice in an inning, and that's because the pitcher throws it to me when he strikes someone out."

"Sounds boring," I said. "No offense."

"None taken," he replied, and I could hear the amusement in his voice. "It is boring, that's what makes it exciting—you never know when someone's going to crack one and stir up the monotony. Keeps you on your toes."

"And Max ruined your monotony this morning, in a manner of speaking."

"Yeah, he infringed on my Sunday ritual of sleeping in, Wii tennis, and SportsCenter."

"Don't forget nursing your hangover."

"That, too," he said without the hint of embarrassment that had been there earlier when he'd mentioned it. "The weirdest part about the whole thing is I still don't know why Max wanted to run."

"Maybe he felt like contributing to a good cause," I said, and Ryan snorted.

"Max's brain doesn't work that way, trust me. It works in angles and equations, calculations and such. Emotions like generosity don't add up for him."

"Maybe that's what it was—a calculated move. He gained something from being there, but he wasn't ready to go alone, so he dragged you with him since you're his best friend."

"Yeah, but what? Max hates to exercise, so it had to be something big to get him to run—especially at seven in the morning. Do you guys have something against the afternoon, by the way? Why seven?"

"It's the time that's cooler—and more people are available if it's in the morning." I thought of Nina and how Max had been looking at her lately, but I didn't say anything to Ryan. It wasn't my place to gossip about Max—even if it was with his best friend.

"Whatever you say. What are you doing?" he asked as I pulled up to the curb outside of his house.

"Dropping you off."

"Turn off the engine. You promised we could hang out for an hour."

"No, I didn't. You asked, and I told you I didn't have time."

He reached over and turned the key himself, taking it out of the ignition and putting it in his pocket. "And you know your homework won't suffer if you take an hour."

"Ryan," I said as he got out of the car and started up the walk toward his house. "Fine, I'll just leave them with you. I have a spare." At least I thought I did.

"Okay," he called over his shoulder and kept walking.

Irritated, I stalked after him. "You can't just assume I have the same kind of time that you do," I said as I rounded the corner of the house and went through the side gate we had used the other night. I was brought up short when he pulled off his shirt. Momentarily stunned by the sight of his bare chest and rippling abs—and holy God, who knew that someone actually looked like that in real life and not just the movies—it took me a second to realize his socks and shoes were already gone. Shocked into reality, I averted my eyes, afraid that he would be in his full birthday suit soon.

"What the hell are you doing? Put your clothes on."

"No, we're going swimming," he said, and I looked over as he began to walk toward me. The bared skin was smooth and tan and made me want to reach out and touch. Irritated with myself, and with him, I scowled.

"Just give me my keys."

"Evans, I want to spend time with you. Just an hour," he said before I could interrupt him. "And then you can go and do your math homework and your college applications and write up your report on curing world hunger, or whatever else it is you need to do." He stopped in front of me and placed his hands on my hips. I detested the shiver of excitement that worked through me, and I forced my body to stay rigid. "All I'm asking for is an hour."

No. Absolutely not. Hadn't I just had this conversation with myself the other night and again twenty minutes ago? I didn't have time for this, I didn't need this, I didn't *want* this. And I was a liar. A big, fat, interested-in-Ryan-Murphy liar.

"Just one," I heard myself say as he swooped me off of my feet and had my arms circling his neck in terror. "You've got to stop doing that."

"Why? You weigh next to nothing."

"Because it's embarrassing."

"Relax, no one's watching."

"On the contrary," I said as he began walking. "Your sister told my brothers you carried me through the house the other night. They asked me about it."

"So?"

"So, if she keeps seeing you manhandle me this way, she's going to keep telling them and they're all going to think there's something else going on."

"There is something else going on," he said and jumped.

I barely got a scream out as we hit the water.

I heard him laughing as I came up sputtering and reached for the side, my shoes—which were still attached to my feet—obstructing my ability to stay afloat.

"Idiot," I spat as I hauled myself up until I was sitting on the side. He grinned and swam over, grabbing the side of the pool next to me where he rested his chin on his arms.

"Cooled off now?"

I ripped my shoes off and dump the water out of them before setting them next to me, face down.

"No, I'm soaked and my shorts are see-through."

"I know," he said and his grin widened. "Don't worry, I won't tell anyone."

A thought hit me and I groaned as I reached into my left pocket and took out my phone. "If this is broken, you're going inside and ordering me another one right now. And you're upgrading it as an apology."

Instead of looking remorseful, he took it from me, hauling himself out the pool and walking toward the slider doors. Even through my irritation, I couldn't help but notice the back view was as nice as the front. Who knew he had shoulders like that? And arms. Good God, he had muscles *everywhere*. My eyes wandered down despite my resolve to be aloof, and I couldn't help the small intake of breath. As if he knew what I was doing, he looked over his shoulder and grinned, slow and mischievous, and I snapped back, turning toward the pool.

His laughter disappeared inside with him and I closed my eyes, scolding myself to get a grip.

A moment later he came back out carrying a bowl filled with rice with my phone submerged inside of it.

"It'll be good as new in a minute."

"If it's not—"

"I'll get you a new one," he finished and sat down next to me. "Admit it, you're not that mad."

Since I wanted to laugh, I reached my left hand into the water and scooped some up into his face. "Not anymore."

He retaliated by grabbing my hand and dragging me back in with him. Without my shoes, I could tread as easily as he, and for a moment we studied each other, our heads above water and our bodies submerged.

"I'm glad you're here, Evans. Even if I did have to drag you again."

I gave in and smiled. "I guess it's not so bad. Even though you did ruin my outfit. And my phone."

"I guarantee the phone is fine. It's a fourth generation and you've got a case on it. Besides, it does my ego some good to see you a little messed up right now. Just like it did it some good to see you having your temper tantrum the other night."

"Excuse me? That was not a temper tantrum."

"Sure it was," he said easily, and continued on as I glared at him. "Don't be embarrassed. Like I said, it did me some good to see it."

"Why's that?"

"Shows me you're normal."

"Temper tantrums and soggy clothing are what you judge normalcy on?"

"They sure help."

"You're an odd one, Ryan."

Instead of commenting on that, he flipped around and swam to the side. "Come on, let's race." Twenty minutes later, after he beat me for a third time racing from one side of the pool to the other, I gave in and swam to the side, hauling myself up and out of the water until my feet dangled over the edge where I squeezed as much water as possible out of my shirt and hair. Ryan pulled himself up next to me and patted my leg.

"Don't be too hard on yourself for losing three in a row. I've got a good foot on you in height."

"Don't be too cocky about winning. I'm going home to practice and we'll rematch later in the month."

"Does that mean we're hanging out later in the month?"

I shrugged. "We won't be done with *MacBeth* for at least another two weeks, then there's your test we'll have to prepare for."

He just shook his head side to side. "Admit it, Evans, you had fun today."

I brushed at my sopping clothing and pretended mild interest. "It was a nice day to swim. Would have been nicer if I had an actual swimsuit on."

"Next time."

I looked over at him, his lazy grin in place, his eyes on me, and I knew that he was telling me, not asking me. Just as I knew he was right. I nodded. "Next time."

It surprised me how much I wanted to stay there with him, not worrying about school or my family, about college and the future. I wanted to laugh again, to make him laugh again, but I was already pushing the envelope. I hadn't even told my mom where I was and I was sure to have several texts and voicemails from her by now.

"I really do have to go. My mom's probably wondering where I am and why I haven't called."

He leaned back and grabbed the bowl of rice, holding it in front of me while I reached in and grabbed my phone. With one eye on him, I hit and held the power button, amazed and irritated when the screen flashed on. I ran through some apps at random, waiting for a line to appear on the screen or an error report to show. When nothing did, I sighed and held it out to show him.

"Like I said, good as new."

"Luck," I replied and took it back. When I saw the conversation bubbles from my mother, my mood lowered a few degrees. "I kind of wish it was broken," I mumbled and he raised his eyebrows at me.

"I didn't take you for the kind of girl who ran away from things."

"Not things, my mother."

"Ah, now that I understand. Mine terrifies me on a regular basis."

"Mine doesn't terrify so much as drive a person to the edge before slowly bringing them back, only to drive them to the edge again. It just so happens that I'm her focus right now, so I'm spending a lot more time considering whether or not I should just jump and get it over with, or continue living with her."

"That's quite a decision."

"You have no idea."

He shook his head at me. "She can't be any scarier than Joanna Murphy."

"Wanna bet?"

"Try me."

I raised my eyebrow. "When I was a sophomore, I got a B on an essay because the teacher thought that my voice was too apparent throughout the paper. He said it needed more research, basically. My mom went in at seven in the morning and slapped the paper on his desk while I cowered behind her. By the time she was done telling him what was right with my writing and what was wrong with his observations of it, he was babbling out an apology while reassuring her

83

he would be re-reading it shortly. Two days later, I got the paper back with a bright red A on the top."

He raised his brow back at me, unimpressed. "A changed grade, that's what you're going with?"

"You have better?"

"Please, Evans, my mother would have just been happy that I actually wrote the paper."

"Let's hear it then."

"Last year my mom caught me in, well, we'll say in a compromising position with a certain female. She and my dad came home earlier than they were supposed to and saw two cars in the drive. When I wasn't downstairs, they were concerned and she barged into my room while my dad stood outside, politely averting his eyes."

"Are you bragging or telling a story?" I asked and he grinned.

"I can do both. The door to my bedroom is still missing. I have no idea what she did with it."

"You lie."

"Swear on my Ted Williams baseball card."

I had zero idea who that was, but it seemed like a pretty solid oath. I sat there, my eyes wide as I stared at him, waiting for any flicker that would show me he was lying.

"We can go up and I can show you right now if you really don't believe me."

I shook my head and then just laughed. "How can you live without a bedroom door? Don't you need privacy to get dressed?"

"My room is at one end of the hall, Caitlin's is at the other, with the bathroom in the middle. My parents' is downstairs. I don't really have anyone who walks near or by my room. And in Joanna's world, my privacy went out the window the day I tried to abuse it."

I continued to stare, appalled at the idea that he didn't have a bedroom door.

"I can't imagine not having a bedroom door. My mother keeps all doors to all bedrooms closed at all times. She doesn't want people to look at anything that might show them people live in our house."

He nodded his head. "Like I said, my mom's a lot scarier than yours."

"We'll call it a draw. If my mother had caught me with a boy in my room, I'd probably be at boarding school. Or kicked out of the family, like my older brother."

Chapter Ten
Ryan

I watched shock register on her face right before it went carefully blank.

"What happened?" I asked.

She just shook her head and picked up her phone when it beeped. "I have to go."

She went to stand but I beat her to it, holding out a hand to bring her to her feet, holding her there when she would have pulled away. "I'll get you a shirt and some shorts to wear home."

"Don't bother, it'll take me twenty seconds to get in the car and across the street."

"But who knows who's going to see you in those twenty seconds."

"Probably no one," she said through her teeth, and tugged on my hand until I stopped dragging her toward the door. The uptight, irritated Mia was back, and I could see it in her face that she was already regretting spending time with me, already regretting letting me in just that little bit. "Just give me back my keys so I can go. We've spent at least an hour if not longer together and I still need to run before it gets dark, do my homework and check the Stanford website because, according to the last three texts my mother has sent me, there's been an update about Early Action applicants."

"Stanford? Wow, you really are smart."

"Not really, just motivated." She held out her hand and stared at me with her eyes carefully blank. "Keys, Ryan."

I shrugged and let go of her hand so I could walk over to my shirt and shoes and grab them. Jingling them, I walked back to stand in front of her.

"What just happened here, Evans?"

"We went swimming."

"Funny. I meant, why are you upset all of a sudden? Is it your mom, or your brother? Or is it the fact that you had fun with me when you really didn't want to? You don't have to say anything," I continued as her face reddened. "I just want you to know I'm glad we spent time together. And if and when you do want to talk about it, I'm here. Even if you don't want to talk about it, I'll still be here. I figure you should understand that now."

While she stood there frozen, I dropped the keys into her outstretched hand. "I'll walk you out."

"You don't have to."

"Nope, but I will anyway. Besides, maybe your mom will like me if she thinks I'm a gentleman. And if she sees me walking you to your car, maybe she won't notice that your clothes are wet."

"Not likely," she said, but she didn't object when I took her hand and started out of the yard with her.

"How about next week?"

"We'll meet at the same times."

"Great, but I meant are you free next week? Maybe we can see a movie. Get something to eat."

"It's Thanksgiving."

"Yes, but that's only Thursday. See a movie with me, Evans, eat some pizza with me." We stopped at her car and I turned her so that we were facing. "You and me, Mia. Let's hang out without the tutor pretense."

"It's only a pretense if it's unnecessary, and seeing your English grade, I can assure you it's necessary."

"Ah, there she is," I said and she let herself smile this time. For some reason, watching the hesitant curve of lips, I was certain that she didn't let herself smile nearly often enough. Not really. "Come on, Evans, it will be like today."

I saw her look up to the house before turning to face me fully. "Ryan, I don't know if this is such a good idea."

"The movie or the pizza?"

"All of the above," she answered. "I'm focused on Stanford right now, and so's my mom. It's not a good time to start something like this."

"Like what?"

"This," she snapped and gestured to me and then herself. "You don't know everything about me but if you did, you'd understand why we should leave our relationship as it is."

I put that comment on the back burner, because despite what she may think, I planned on getting to know everything about her. Instead, I focused on the next most important thing. "Evans, did you have fun today?"

She paused and I knew she was gauging how much she should say and whether or not she should lie. "Yes," she finally answered.

"Okay. Want to have fun again next week sometime?"

More thinking, I noted, but her shoulders had relaxed and she wasn't glancing up at her front door anymore. "Yes," she answered on an explosion of breath and I smiled.

"Great. I'll pick you up at seven next Saturday."

Then, before she could turn away to get into her car, I set my hands on her shoulders and eased her gently forward until her head was tucked neatly under my chin. I waited one beat and then another before I felt her arms circle my waist. Stepping a little closer, I leaned down and buried my face in her throat, breathing her in while keeping the pressure light so I didn't crush her. Or scare her off. She needed time, I reminded myself, and was rewarded when I felt her tilt her face into my shoulder and wrap her arms a little tighter. We were close enough that I knew it would only take turning my head a fraction and my lips would be on hers. I knew how it would be, how she would taste. But I also knew it would ruin whatever we had just started, and for the first time in my life, I realized that what might be was more important than what was right now.

With more regret than I ever remembered feeling, I breathed her in one last time before stepping back. Too soon. What I wanted from her was scary to me—if I gave in and took her mouth with mine, it might not stop there, and then she'd run like hell and never come back and I wouldn't be able to blame her.

Instead, I ran my hands through her damp hair, from her crown to her shoulders and watched her eyes flutter open when I settled them at her ribcage.

"I'll see you at school tomorrow."

She nodded and stepped back, jerking nervously when I leaned close enough to reach around her and open the door. I grinned and she cleared her throat, turning to get in and neatly clicking her seatbelt into place.

"Good thing you did that. You know how many crazy drivers there are in this area."

Her lips twitched with a small smile and I brushed my fingers through her damp hair one more before stepping back. "Bye, Evans. Thanks for the swim."

Chapter Eleven
Mia

Holidays were meant to be fun, and when Joe had still lived with us, for the most part they had been. But like everything else about our family since he left, holidays had changed. We were together because we had to be, not because we wanted to be, and rather than thankful for the time with my family, I was wondering when the best time to make my escape and go for a run would be.

The only saving grace was the fact that my aunt and uncle still flew in from Portland with their daughter, Cora, and their family drama always seemed to trump ours, if only because they were so vocal about it.

Aunt Suzie was my mom's older sister and uptight about life. How she had managed to marry a sweet man like Uncle James was one of life's great mysteries. Uncle James was laid back, happy, and absolutely content with his life. He was an architect and his firm did the drawings on Dad's hotels. Uncle James worked hard, but in all of my life, I had never seen him yell at anyone or treat someone with disrespect. Even when his wife was demanding and his daughter rebellious, he plodded along, listening to everyone around him, asking questions instead of making statements. Where my own father questioned ruthlessly and then gave his judgments and opinions, Uncle James nodded his head and encouraged, if only by showing interest. He was the light in this dark hour of family togetherness, and sadly, even he couldn't save his daughter from her mother.

Aunt Suzie was the polar opposite of her husband. She was uptight, controlling, and, in a much heavier way than my own mother, a micromanager. Both had learned from their own mother, and the apple had not fallen far, but where I knew deep down that my mother genuinely wanted the best for all of us, even if she thought she knew what it was and refused to acknowledge something different from her own plans, Aunt Suzie was dramatic and selfish. Everything was about her—what she wanted, what she had, what she didn't have, what she gave to everyone else, what no one gave back to her—which was probably why my cousin Cora enjoyed upsetting her so much.

Cora was a few months older than me, and her one desire in life was to shock and upset her parents—specifically her mother, who had taken to being disappointed in everything Cora had done since the day of her birth. From the text Cora had sent me last week, I was pretty sure Aunt Suzie's latest contention with Cora was her choice not to attend college, but go to fashion school, which was absolutely unacceptable to Aunt Suzie and she had been telling Cora that since her daughter had broken the news.

Which was probably why Cora showed up to Thanksgiving dinner in a black tank top with a plunging neckline, and a skirt so short she had a hard time sitting down. Her heels were spiked and black, and her fingernails were painted the same color. Her long blonde hair was pulled off of her face, and every now and then she would look at me and smile before making some obscene gesture.

We were an unlikely pair, but somehow our differences, which were legion, made us closer. Maybe what they say about inmates is true, and Cora and I simply bonded because we both felt we were being held hostage by the ever-growing expectations of our perpetually dissatisfied mothers.

Lily and Cora, however, lead a love/hate relationship that was borderline volatile most days. Both viewed the other critically and verbalized their criticism nine times out of ten. For Lily, who had appeared home from school late last night looking too thin and more worn down than I'd ever seen, Cora and people like her were the root of the problem for women in our society. Women's suffrage happened to free women from the charges of men, to allow them to make up their own minds. In Lily's world, any girl, woman, or grandmother who spent her day trying to look nice and attract men had missed the point of history, and were consequently responsible for any sufferings—political or otherwise—that women had endured since 1788.

Currently, the twins were in the game room alternating between watching football and having the ultimate PS3 football tournament. My dad and Uncle James were golfing and would be all day—a fact that seemed to quietly relieve my mother. She'd been on edge since he'd been home, most likely due to the hushed arguments they'd been having. This morning, when I'd walked out of my bedroom and headed downstairs, I was stopped by the sound of their voices, my father's so controlled and deep, my mother's so quiet and a little shaky, arguing but not. No one in my family really had arguments anymore, and I don't know if that fact pleased or frightened me, like somehow we had lost the passion to say what we really felt and instead, our house was haunted with the words that forever lie on our tongues never to be said.

While all of the men were enjoying what Aunt Suzie termed their "manly ritual," a phrase which made Lily's teeth grind together every time it was said, Mom and Aunt Suzie were in the kitchen, fretting over the turkey and the stuffing, the dressing, the vegetables—which meant my mother was cooking and Aunt Suzie was knocking back gin and tonics while she carried on about the hardships in her life and my mother reassured her that none of her problems were her own fault. It amazed me that my mother, a woman who simply did not accept less than perfection from anyone, was such an enabler when it came to her own sister.

Cora, Lily, and I had been in the kitchen attempting to help, but Cora had been dropping small comments meant to irritate her mother. Since Aunt Suzie had taken the bait each time, she was on the verge of a total meltdown when my mother demanded we leave the kitchen and have girl talk in the living area.

Lily had flopped down on the couch and picked up the first magazine at hand, her sneer as she read its cover a clear indication of what she thought about *Cosmopolitan* and its sacred word. She knew it was Cora's magazine, which was half the reason she had picked it up.

Cora flopped down on the couch, some miracle keeping her skirt below her butt. I curled my legs under me in the chair next to her.

"So, fashion school," I said and smiled. "Aunt Suzie sounds thrilled."

"You would have thought I told her I was moving to Russia and becoming a call girl instead of Los Angeles. I mean, it's still school, right?"

"If you're a Barbie," Lily said from behind her magazine.

Cora just smiled. "Lily, don't be jealous of my bust line. I told you, there are surgeries that can help you with your inadequacies. You should get your nose taken care of while you're at it."

I shook my head as they picked at each other and attempted to change the subject. "Have you applied?"

Cora nodded. "Yeah, but I won't hear back until April, just like other schools." When her phone buzzed, she slid her thumb across the screen and began typing.

"Another one night stand on the rise?" Lily asked.

"Jealous?" she asked without looking up.

"So jealous. I can't wait to go the health center at school for an antibiotic that'll cure the clap." Lily mocked a smile and held up crossed fingers. "I hear accidental pregnancies are rampant right now, too. Maybe I'll get lucky."

"No worries on that front, Lil. Your chastity belt seems tight enough that you'll escape college before you even need to get on the pill."

"It says here that the average teenager will have sex with at least one person before they turn eighteen." She raised her eyebrow at Cora. "Well, it's the first time you've been ahead of the curve, isn't it?"

I tried to think of something to say that would interrupt their conversation, or at least redirect Lily's attention, but I was too slow. Cora stayed sprawled where she was, pretending indifference. But I knew that she cared, and watching Lily, I also knew that she was out for   blood.

"It also says that there are over eighteen thousand sexually transmitted infections each year, and half of those occur in people your age or younger." She glanced at Cora over the magazine. "When's the last time you went to the doctor, Barbie?"

"Not everyone who has sex gets a disease, Lily. Rule number one, use a condom." She smiled, but it came out more defensive than anything. "Trust me, you should try it, it might loosen that stick that's crammed up your ass."

"I thought it was rule number one, learn his name, rule number two, use a condom."

Cora shrugged, reading her screen as it lighted up again. Lily wasn't ready to let it go, though. "Not all condoms are one hundred percent accurate."

"Not one hundred percent is accurate enough for me."

"Maybe it's not for him," she pushed on and pointed to the phone. "You can't be careless with everyone else, too, Cora, even if you don't care what happens to yourself. Maybe they don't want your STDs. Or your babies. Ever thought of that? They might—"

"Shut up, Lily," Cora said. Her voice wasn't bored or amused now, and her body trembled when she pushed off of the couch.

Lily was standing, too, but she wasn't seeing the look on Cora's face that I was seeing. "Does the guy your texting know you haven't been a virgin since you were fourteen? Or that your one skill in life is sleeping around?"

Cora winced as though she'd been slapped and Lily stopped where she was, the full impact of her words hitting her. There was a moment that all of us stayed where we were, silent, unable to talk or move.

It was Cora who broke the silence first, her face pale, her words radiating anger and hurt when she looked at Lily and spoke. "Just because I'm not some shriveled up, know-it-all prude like our mothers have made you doesn't mean I'm a diseased slut." She turned and took a step away before turning back. "And that person on the phone? It was a boy. And he does know. And you know what else? He doesn't care about that, he only cares about me. See if you ever have someone who feels that way about you."

When Cora left, Lily and I stayed where we were, quiet, watching her go. The silence was heavy, and when I finally looked over, Lily shook her head, but her normally confident posture was hunched with embarrassment.

"You know her, Lily," I said. "You know who she is, what she goes through every day. Why would you say those things to her?"

"Why is it my fault?" she asked, tears welling in her eyes. "Why isn't it her fault, too?"

"I'm not saying it's someone's fault, I'm asking why you were purposely mean. Don't you think she's been through enough? Don't you think having your mother tell you what a failure at life you are is enough?"

She shook her head and wiped at the tears that trailed down her cheeks. "You don't see what I do every day, Mia. You don't know what it's like. At school," she clarified, when I furrowed my brow. "On the streets when I'm walking around. Everywhere there are people who are sick from a disease or who have been abused in a relationship. Around campus there are girls who drop out because they're traumatized by an incident at a party, or because someone did something to them they can't remember." She looked at me, her eyes dark and clouded, before shaking her head and speaking again. "I don't want that to be her, and if she moves to Los Angeles, trust me, she could hurt herself if she's acting like this. Portland is bad enough, but she knows people there for the most part. What's going to happen when she doesn't know people, doesn't know where to go when something happens?"

Lily wasn't soft, but she did feel. And she was feeling scared for Cora. As they had the day Joe had left, her emotions had heightened and come out in a torrent of anger and fear.

"I can't watch her ruin her life and not say anything." She shrugged her shoulders in a gesture of utter defeat. "I just can't." She looked at me then, and her face was just as pale as Cora's had been, and for a moment, I wondered if there was something wrong with Lily. I'd always thought of her as indestructible, but watching her now, I wondered if she was more like me than I really knew.

I stepped forward to put my arm around her shoulders, trying to offer comfort even when I knew it wouldn't be welcome. She remained stiff and unmoving, but I held onto her for a moment anyway.

"You can't save her, Lil, just like you couldn't save Joe. People have to live on their own."

She nodded and tears continued to stream down her face. "I don't want her to get hurt, Mia. I shouldn't have yelled at her," she said and I felt her shoulders relax a little. "But I just can't seem to get over the thought of losing someone else, you know?"

In that moment, I did know. Lily was working with the same fear that I was—the fear that our family was breaking, and if we didn't fix the crack soon, we never would.

"It's like everything around us is changing, and every time I come home its worse. I barely recognize Mom, the way she flutters around hovering over everyone and everything, trying to smile as though she isn't nervous when really, it looks like one good gust of air will knock her over. And the way Dad barely looks at anyone, how he only asks one question and then disappears. I mean, he didn't even talk to the boys today. When he asked Joshua a question, he was already thinking of something else before Josh finished answering. It's like we don't know how to be a family anymore."

Lily's words instilled a kind of fear in me that had a sick weight sitting in the pit of my stomach. It stayed even when we went to look for Cora and found her sitting on a bench in Poets Park, amongst all of the quotes and plaques, smoking a cigarette.

She was lonelier in that moment than anyone I had ever seen, and it took me back to the afternoon Joe left and I had been on the porch staring after him, as if that would change what had happened. Cora sat with her shoulders hunched, her eyes on the ground, and her legs tightly crossed while she puffed smoke. I knew that Lily thought the same thing, because it was she who reached out first, saying Cora's name as we neared her, sitting next to her and surprising all of us when tears shone in her eyes as she apologized.

"I didn't mean to hurt you, Cora. I'm just in a mood right now."

"Chronic PMS?" I said as I sat on the other side of Cora and both of them smiled.

"Maybe. Might be chronic fear," she mumbled and both Cora and I looked at her.

"What the hell are you scared of?" Cora asked.

"Everything," Lily mumbled and had Cora and me gasping. "I was so sure when I was leaving for school that everything would stay as clear as it was that day. I would get my degree, get into law school, pass the bar, become a lawyer, come back and work with Dad. Make him proud."

Cora held out her cigarette and after a minute, Lily took it, puffing quickly before handing it back. "And now?"

Lily shook her head. "I don't know. Nothing is like I thought it would be, nothing really makes sense. I don't know what I want anymore, or who I am, and it scares me."

Cora watched her, and then she stamped out the rest of her cigarette before linking one hand with Lily and the other with me.

"I know what I want," she said. "But it doesn't make getting it any easier. Especially when everyone who's supposed to love you tells you that what you want is wrong."

"Or that you're not smart enough to have it," I muttered.

Lily's eyes met mine and held for a minute. Then she nodded in understanding and we all sat there, linked together as we wondered what we were supposed to do.

Chapter Twelve
Ryan

My Saturday night date with Mia didn't go exactly as planned, and it all began when Joshua Evans asked my little sister to the movies. At first, I was shocked by the fact that Caitlin was even old enough to go on dates, and then immediately irritated when I said as much to my mom and instead of agreeing, she asked me to play chaperon and to drive Caitlin there and back. Even when I explained that I already had plans to take Mia to the movies, her only response was to pat my cheek and say how nice it was that we would all be in the same place.

When I called Mia to confirm our plans, I learned that Nina had told Mia she was desperate for a distraction from her aunt who was visiting "indefinitely" and Mia had generously offered to take her to the movies with us, an offer that Nina snatched up. And Mia's cousin was still in town, so she was coming, too. Since all of my plans for romance and getting to know Mia on a more intimate level were now trashed, I called Max to go with us and at least distract Nina.

Caitlin was no happier with my role as chaperon than I was, which, perversely enough, made the entire situation more bearable. As long as she understood I was a chaperone, then maybe she'd behave. I said as much while we drove out of the cul de sac and she responded by crossing her arms over her chest and staring out the window without saying anything. She stayed that way until we pulled up to Max's house, where she heaved a sigh before climbing into the backseat and resuming her position of crossed arms and a solemn look. She wasn't happy that her big brother had interfered, and she was less than happy that I was bringing along an entourage of people.

"You couldn't have asked Mia to go to get something to eat?"

"Get over it, Caitlin. We already had plans, and if you think Joshua Evans is going to get the time and chance to make the moves on you, you have another thing coming."

She rolled her eyes at that. "Please, Ryan, Josh wouldn't do something like that. I would," she said and had me grinding my teeth together. "Besides, how pathetic is it that you're using my date to make one of your own?"

Breathe, I reminded myself and counted to five before responding. "Just to clarify, Mia and I already had a date planned. It's you who's tagging along."

"I wouldn't have to if you hadn't said something to Mom and made her think I needed a chaperone." She leaned forward far enough to punch me in the arm as Max came out the front door. "Don't be a jerk to Josh, okay? He's really nice."

"Don't let him touch you and I won't have to be a jerk."

"Oh, please, Ryan, it's not like we're going to jump each other in the movie theater. I'm not like you," she said with a grim smile that had my eyes widening.

Max climbed in before I came up with a response and I heard her laugh. Hoping that was a good sign, I glanced in the rearview to see her grin and roll her eyes at Max—our version of a truce—before turning back to the Enrique look alike who was currently stinking up the truck.

"You've got to be kidding. Max, do you ever want to get laid? By a woman?"

Max just smiled and patted his perfectly shaped hair. "Like the do, Murph? I thought I'd change it up from the everyday messy muss."

"To what? Gangsta's paradise?"

"Latin Lover," Caitlin said from the backseat and I burst out laughing, as grateful for her sense of humor as I was for the fact that

Max created a diversion so I was no longer dwelling on Caitlin's comments. It's not like I'd ever had sex in a movie theater. Exactly.

"Max, you look ridiculous."

"Dude, the white v neck is simple and sexy, GQ said so."

"Did it also say that too much cologne can kill? I'm dying here." I rolled down my window and let in the cooling desert air, taking in the rest of Max's appearance as I did. He was decked out top to bottom in a white v neck and jeans that were torn in strategic places, but still managed to look brand new. He wore the same thick leather sandals he had the other day, and a belt that was more of a prop than a tool, as his jeans appeared tight enough to keep themselves up.

"Max, what's with the clothes lately? You looked normal the other day, why did you revert back?"

"It's not about the clothes, Murph, I already told you that. It's about what the clothes say—to me and you and everyone else. I'm different. I, Max Canfield, am a different person than I was last year. I have different interests, I like different people. I *am* a different person."

I rolled my eyes. "Settle down, Gandhi, I get it. You're enlightened, you've changed. But *why?* What was wrong with how you were before? When you looked normal. And straight."

"I get it, Max." I glanced in the rearview at Caitlin and she shrugged. "I do. He's letting people know that he's expanded himself, that he isn't just the person they think he is, or that he should be. Like when your older brother thinks you should be a little kid forever," she finished off and glared at me.

"Exactly, Caitlin," Max said before I could let off the biting remark on my tongue. "You're exactly right. Which is why Ryan here is going to the movies with me, and you—the grown up you—are going to the movies with Josh Evans. You're changed, multifaceted, and open. Ryan, however, is not. He's the same, and because of that, he's scared to ask Mia out and settles for me instead."

"Try again, Enrique. Mia's meeting us there. And has everyone forgotten last Sunday? Mia and I hung out, I told her I liked her? We had a civilized hour together and made plans to hang out again? Oh, and would you look at that, we're hanging out tonight, and she's bringing her cousin and Nina, so behave, Max. I don't want you pissing Torres off and making them leave."

He patted his hair again. "Trust me, Murph, Torres won't see me coming."

"That's because she'll smell you first," I muttered and pulled into the parking lot. Caitlin was already jumping out and heading toward Joshua, who had magically appeared the moment the truck stopped.

"Caitlin," I called out before they could walk away. She froze, turned, and slit her eyes.

"Yes, Ryan?"

"Be out in front of the theater around ten-thirty so I can take you home."

"Fine," she said and started walking again. I frowned at their backs and wondered what the hell I was supposed to do now. We were seeing a different movie—what if Joshua tried to make a move on her in the theater, where it was dark, and secluded? Before I could take a step after her, Max's stepped up beside me.

"Wow, Caitlin's dating. Caitlin's going to the movies with a boy, where it's dark." Max shook his head and patted me on the shoulder. "You know what they say, man. With boys, parents only worry about one penis, but with girls, they worry about them all."

My lungs backed up and for a minute, my vision got hazy. Giving in, I bent at the waist and breathed air in nice and slow. *Jesus Christ.* "Thanks, Max, that's really helpful."

He grinned. "Anytime. Hey there, ladies. How's it going?"

I didn't rise right away, but shifted so that I could watch as Mia walked toward us with Nina on her left, and who I assumed was her cousin on her right. Before I could stand all of the way and introduce myself, Nina let out a whooping laugh. "Who's your date, Murphy? She's pretty."

I shook my head as Max's face fell. "Take it easy on him,

Torres, he's remaking himself."

Mia stepped in and made the introductions to the tall blonde standing next to her. "Ryan and Max, my cousin, Cora."

Max gallantly offered his hand and started babbling so that Cora laughed. Nina narrowed her eyes and muttered something, but I ignored them all and focused on Mia. As always, she was put together in a way that made me just want to look at her for a while. Her hair was pulled off of her face, spilling down her back loose and free and making my fingers itch to dive into it.

Tucking them safely into my pockets, I took in the rest of her. Her outfit should have appeared plain, almost nun-like next to Nina's stark black and Cora's bright red jumpsuit that clung to every curve, but instead, it made her look sweet, almost vulnerable. Her sweater was beige and long and fell over leggings. She wore boots in the same color that ended just below her knee. The hint of nerves in her face didn't bother me, or not nearly as much as the desire coursing through me did. In order to ignore it, and to keep her from bolting, I held out a hand and smiled.

"Let's go see if we can spend more than an hour together, Evans."

Chapter Thirteen
Mia

When Nina called earlier, she'd been desperate for me to hang out with her and save her from her aunt.

"My parents are gone for the night and she's been making noises all day about margaritas and pedicures," she said, panic streaking her every word. "The fact that I'm not twenty-one or the least bit interested in touching her feet hasn't even registered with her. You have to save me, Mia."

For her sake—and the sake of her aunt, who was basically a thirty-something-year old woman with the interests of a college student—as well as mine, I told her to come over and we would hang out with Cora. I had planned on calling Ryan and telling him tonight wasn't going to work—and pretending I wasn't disappointed about it—but then Josh called Caitlin and made plans, so we all piled in the car to go.

"There are a lot of us," I told Ryan as we walked up to buy tickets. "We probably won't all be able to sit in the same row." It was silly that I was nervous now, when I had been so relieved to not have to cancel. If I was honest, I would admit to him that I'd been looking forward to this all week, but because I wasn't honest, not about those kind of things, I tried to keep my distance.

"Don't worry, we'll find a way," he replied and put money on the small space. "Two."

"Paying for Max?" I asked and smiled.

"You, Evans. We had plans, remember?"

I stood there frowning as Cora cooed over Ryan and told him how sweet he was. When he handed me my ticket and held out his hand again, I hesitated, unsure of my moves and his.

He raised his brow as he left his hand out, standing there smiling at me. "Did you want me to pick you up again? I'm trying my hardest here, Evans, but if it's what you want..." he trailed off when I slapped my palm into his and ignored Cora's laugh.

I knew it was stupid, but being here, in public, wasn't the same as it was at his house. When it was just us, it was easier to relax, to believe that he was sincere. But, here...here we were surrounded by people we knew. Holding hands was bound to cause people to talk, and really, for what? We weren't together, not the way I was sure the girls who were behind us from the sophomore class were gossiping about right now. We were barely even friends...I didn't even know his middle name. Surely I should know that before I held his hand in public. Or made out with him in his driveway while he was half dressed. My bad.

Nina was already seated when the rest of us walked into the theater, and she grabbed Cora's arm and pulled her down in the aisle seat next to her, forcing Max to sit next to me.

"Torres, I didn't think you went for things like this."

"I'm surprised you *can* think at all with that cologne clouding your brain. Less is more, Maxine. Remember that the next time you think about poisoning the rest of us with that crap you've sprayed yourself with."

"You sure know how to sink a guy's sails, Nina. Here I was trying to look nice for you, and all you can do is insult me."

"If I'm nice to you will you go away?"

"Probably not," he said with a good natured shrug. "Besides, I kinda like it when you snap at me."

Nina turned her head and scowled at me before rising. "I'm getting a soda."

"Great, I need some sourpatch kids, I'll come with you."

Before Nina could object, Max was already up and leading the way out. I saw her hesitate, as if wondering how badly she really wanted a drink, until she finally stomped out after him. I shook my head, wondering about Max's strategy. Sure, she was talking to him, but if looks could kill, *Maxine* would no longer be with us.

"I don't know why he actively goes out of his way to irritate her," Ryan said as we all watched them go.

"I have a few guesses," Cora said and I smiled. "And personally, I think it's good for the scientist. I mean, he's definitely going to have to step up his game if he wants to melt her icy exterior anytime soon, but I think he's already made progress."

Ryan furrowed his brow as he picked up my hand and began to fiddle with my fingers. When I tried to take them back, he only tightened his hold. "What is she talking about?"

"Max and Nina," I said as they came back in.

"Cora, would you like to sit next to Mia? The aisle seat can be so daunting."

"What's he doing?" Ryan asked. "And since when does he care who sits where?"

When Cora rose, Nina clamped a hand on her arm and I grinned. "It looks like he's irritating Nina until she goes out with him."

"Cora, you can't be serious," Nina said. "You're fine on the aisle. Hey, here, take my seat, I'll take the aisle."

Cora shook her head at Nina and then patted the other girl's cheek. "Nina, this hot boy wants to sit next to you, and I think you should let him. It might do you some good," she said before walking up to squeeze in next to Ryan and me.

"You know she wants to kill you now, right?"

She fluffed her hair and then slicked her hands down her sides, adjusting everything so that her cleavage was at its best. "Oh, but she'll want to thank me later. I'd put money on it."

Ryan was still gaping at me and I took pity on him and squeezed our linked fingers. "Get over it, Murphy," I murmured as the lights lowered and the previews rolled onto the screen. "Your best friend likes a girl and he's working to get her."

He just sat there silently for a moment before standing and walking out.

"Freaky Abercrombie Genius boy down there isn't the only one working some game," Cora muttered, and I shook my head.

"Trust me, Ryan's just showing off. He expects girls to fall all over him. Besides, you're more his type," I whispered. "He likes luscious and obvious. No offense."

"Cousin, I'm everyone's type," she purred, while settling back. "But I don't think he's expecting so much as hoping this time."

I didn't say anything, wondering if she could tell that I was secretly hoping as well.

When Ryan came back five minutes later, his arms were loaded down with candy of all different varieties and one large bucket of popcorn. Sitting, he looked over and grinned at me.

"Hungry?" I asked and snagged the chocolate covered raisins.

"Nope, just taking a page from Max's book and working to get the girl."

~

We all went to eat after the movie, Joshua and Caitlin climbing into the back of Ryan's truck, and Cora telling Ryan we would love to meet him. As Nina, Cora, and I then piled into my car and followed them out of the parking lot, Nina's fist bopped Cora—who had claimed the front   seat—on   the   shoulder.

"What is *wrong* with you?"

Cora glared and rubbed her arm. "What the hell are you talking about? And don't punch me again, I can't wear my new jumper if I have bruises."

"This is so typical. You like male attention so you make the rest of us suffer with you. Why did you have to accept their offer for pizza? Why did you move and make me sit next to Max all night?"

"Why are you still pretending to be mad?" I asked and earned a gaping stare from Nina. I just shrugged. "You could have asked to switch seats with me, you could have just left or refused to get a soda when he went. But you didn't, which tells me you're not really as annoyed by him as you say."

"Agreed," Cora said. "You're not annoyed by him, Bill Nye. In fact, you're slightly flattered."

"I am not," Nina shot back. "I just didn't think about moving. I didn't want to be rude."

I didn't say anything because I could see that Nina was on the verge of going hysterical, but Cora waved away Nina's statement and continued to tease her the entire three minute drive.

When we pulled into the parking lot of the pizza place, I let Cora get out first to catch up with the crowd. When Nina got out, I patted her arm. "Are you okay?"

"I. Do. Not. Like. Max. Canfield," she said between her teeth. "And I am not flattered by him. Ever."

I nodded. "Okay. But what we were trying to point out is that Max appears to like you."

"I can't, Mia," she said quietly and stopped. Her eyes traveled to the window where Max was already seated with everyone else, his hands gesturing as he engaged them in yet another story. "I get what he's doing, and maybe I am a little flattered. But I just can't. I'm not like that."

I nodded again and rubbed her shoulder for support. I understood what she was talking about and I understood what she meant. Some of us knew our roles in life, and we knew that venturing out of them could be dangerous and painful. Wasn't that why I was who I was? Because it was expected of me and doing the expected was easier than dealing with the consequences of the unexpected. Easier, I thought with a glance through the window at Ryan, but I was starting to wonder if I was ready for complicated.

"It's okay, Nina, you don't have to like him back," I said and she breathed a quiet sigh of relief. "But I think you should know he does like you, I mean, really like you, everyone sees it, and I don't think he's going to back off." With that, I walked inside, hoping the seed I had planted would bloom a little thought.

If I thought it was sweet what Max was doing for Nina, I was unsure if I thought what Ryan was doing was sweet or terrifying. Or both.

There was already a bottle of water at the seat right next to him, and when he saw me he raised his own before taking a sip and keeping a steady gaze on me. I thought about taking my own advice and going to the chair at the opposite end of the table next to Max, and then I thought better of it. It would've been nasty after all he'd done tonight, and worse, it would've been a lie. I did want to sit next to him, because whether or not I understood why, and no matter how hard I tried not to, I was beginning to like Ryan Murphy. More, I was beginning to like who I was when I was with him.

A little shaken at the thought, I sat and took a small drink, avoiding his eyes as I watched Cora already flirting with the boys in the booth against the wall. When I told her they were freshmen, she just smiled.

"No male attention is wasted, Cousin, remember that."

Nina walked in and plopped down on the chair between Max and me. Taking his glass of soda, she gulped from it and then sputtered before slapping it back on the table. "What the hell is that?"

"Mine," he answered and slid it back in front of him before sipping for himself. "And it's swamp water. All of the sodas mixed together," he told her when she stared at him with a puzzled expression.

"Max, are you five?"

"Nope, I just like sugar. Must be why I'm drawn to you," he said and I saw Nina's eyes narrow.

"Stop, that's it," she said and held up her hands. "I know what you're doing and you haven't got a chance. So stop being nice to me. Go back to being rude. At least I can stand being around you that way."

Max never missed a beat. "Fine, I thought your newspaper column from last month that stated seniors who apply to more than three schools are flaky and irresponsible was awful. Maybe they can't decide, or maybe they want to see what their options are. Who are you to judge? And you misused the word 'vocation' in the second paragraph."

Nothing could have been better designed to engage Nina, and as the pizzas arrived and we ate, she did exactly as Max had hoped: she spent her entire hour yelling only at him. While they argued, I ate one slice and tried to settle my stomach. Ryan was talking and laughing, between which he consumed at least an entire pie by himself, causing me to raise my eyebrows at him when he finally sat back.

"Finished?"

He grinned. "I'm a growing boy, Evans, ask anyone. Besides, when I'm not at home, I eat big. It makes up for the meals we miss or have to struggle through valiantly after my mom burns something or forgets to cook it all the way."

That had Caitlin launching into a story about their mother's turkey dinner a few days ago. I was still laughing as we walked out and began our goodbyes.

"Hey, Evans?" Ryan said and I turned to look at him, aware that Cora was watching us. "Why don't we let your cousin take everyone home? Come somewhere with me for a while." He reached out and ran his hand down my arm before he linked his fingers with mine. Even through the fabric of my sweater I felt the heat of his skin burn into mine, causing a shiver to run through me.

"Um, I have to drive Lily to the airport tomorrow and her flight is early."

I heard Cora groan, but before I could look at her and glare, Ryan stepped up so that our bodies brushed, sliding his other hand down my arm until both of his hands were linked with both of mine. I caught my breath and tried to appear casual as I looked up and met his eyes. "Come on, Evans. I'll have you home in a couple of hours. I want some time with just you, Mia," he said more quietly, and I felt goose bumps pop up on my skin.

"Oh, Jesus, Mia, just go with him so the rest of us can go

home," Nina yelled.

"Better yet, go with him so you can make out," Cora said just as loudly.

Heat seeped into my cheeks when Ryan grinned. "I like your cousin, Evans. Has a real smart head on her shoulders."

"Yeah, that's what most guys notice about her. Her brains." I gave in and tossed my keys to Cora. "Don't drive fast. My mom's not supposed to be home, but if for some reason she is and asks where I am…"

"Cousin, I have it covered. Turn your phone off, and think about what I said," she said with a wiggle of her eyebrows as she walked around the car and got into the driver's seat.

I watched as they all piled in, laughing when I heard Nina lecture Max not to let his greasy head touch the leather seats. When they were gone, I turned to Ryan, who was began pulling me toward his truck.

With one last thought that this was a very bad idea, I ignored my own instincts and allowed myself to be pulled along. For once, I was going to do the unexpected and damn the consequences.

Chapter Fourteen
Ryan

I took her to The Authentic and laughed when I saw her face. "Relax, Evans. I brought you here to swim, not to get a room and have my way with you."

Relief washed visibly over her before she shook her head. "We can't. The pool's closed."

Was it any wonder I adored her?

"To guests," I said and waited for it to sink in. The horror on her face made me want to rethink my earlier statement and throw her over my shoulder before finding a dark place where I could make her mine in every way possible. I shifted in my seat and tried to block out that image.

"It's not really breaking and entering, Evans. You own the place."

"My family," she corrected. "My family owns it. Ryan, I don't even have a key."

I smiled. "But I'm betting you could find one, if you really wanted to."

"That's not the point. I don't have a swimsuit and I refuse to go in the water fully dressed. *Again.* This sweater is cashmere."

I turned off the engine, angling my body toward hers so I could look at her while I waited. I knew her sense of propriety was warring with her sense of adventure—just as it had the last two times we'd hung out. I was starting to understand her and I was realizing that Mia Evans wasn't immune to me, but she wanted to be. That little fact made being with her twice as fun.

Her face went from scared, to annoyed, and, finally, to thoughtful. The moment she decided to get the key I knew, but I waited for her to tell me to wait, and I did, watching while she dashed inside of the main entrance and came out a moment later, motioning for me to get out of the truck and follow her.

"Shane's on until midnight. The pool technically closed at ten, so you have to keep your voice down. I don't want him to get into trouble."

I grinned and saluted before stepping through the gate ahead of her. It was a small rectangular pool, but in the darkness the water sparkled and the twinkle lights that were wrapped around the base of the trees glowed, offering us our only light. This was no backyard swimming pool and an impromptu dip, not like the first time. This was a date, and whether or not she wanted to, I was determined that Mia was going to see that.

"Here," she said, handing me a plain black pair of board shorts. "You're not swimming in your clothes, and neither am I."

"No clothes? Even better."

"Put on the trunks," she said on an exasperated laugh. "I'll be right back."

Chuckling to myself, I found a small room to change in and swapped my clothes for the shorts. Leaving my clothes in the corner of the room, I went back to the edge of the pool and leapt into the water, pushing my way from one side to the other before coming up for air. When I raised up out of the water, a movement had me looking over my shoulder just as Mia executed a clean dive into the water. She came up laughing and my heart rate, which had spiked considerably with that small vision of her in a skimpy bikini, tripled at the sound.

"Maybe this was a good idea."

"You should know by now that most of my ideas are good

ones."

We swam toward the middle, both treading water as we looked around. "You know, this is the first time I've been in this pool since we opened the Inn."

"You're joking."

She shook her head and I stared at her as she took in the details, the lights, the quiet, the moon on the horizon, before her gaze shifted back to me. "No, I'm not. This pool is for hotel guests. If we want to swim, we need to wait until we get home to our own pool."

"You're a real rule follower, aren't you, Evans."

Her face changed immediately, and all of her earlier pleasure was gone when she looked away. "Unfortunately," she said and swam toward the stairs. Following, I shook my head.

"That wasn't meant to be an insult, Evans.

"Forget it."

I reached out and snagged her wrist before she could rise out of the water, panic causing me to grab with more strength than necessary. "Mia, I'm sorry. Don't leave."

She looked over her shoulder at me and for a moment I thought she was going to shrug me off and go. We were both standing now, the upper half of our bodies out of the water. Her face glowed in the half-lit pool and for the second time that evening, I was reduced to just looking at her. Even with her mask of composure back in place she was striking; strong cheekbones, a pointed nose, full lips. She'd taken her hair down so it streamed down her back in a waterfall of liquid gold. I wanted to bring her close and hold her, to tell her I was an asshole and that if she left it would kill me. Instead I waited, knowing that she needed to accept my apology first.

"Mia, I'm sorry. I was teasing, being an idiot."

She stared at me a second longer before she finally nodded. My breath eased out of my lungs and I took a chance and ran my fingers through the tips of her hair.

"Sorry," she said and turned fully until she was facing me, wiping her hands over her face. "I guess I'm a little sensitive."

I released my grip on her wrist, turning my palm over until our fingers were laced. "I really am sorry. I wasn't trying to insult you."

"No, I know that, and you're right, I am a rule follower. I always have been."

"That's not a bad thing, Evans."

"It didn't use to seem like it," she murmured, looking over at the mountains, illuminated by the sliver of moon. "I mean, rules are rules, right? You follow them, things go the way they're supposed to. If you break them, there are consequences. Isn't that the way it's supposed to work?"

Her voice was a little desperate now, her fingers white as they squeezed mine. I nodded and ran my thumb up and down the side of our joined hands, hoping it brought her comfort.

"The thing is," she said and looked down at our fingers that were twined together. "I've followed the rules my whole life, done everything that was ever asked of me and I've never questioned whether it was right or wrong, I've just done it because I had to."

"And now?" I kept my voice gentle because I could see how hard it was for her to share, and how much it cost her to admit that she may not want to be a perfect.

"And now," she said and looked up at me again. "Now, I don't know if I want to anymore." Her voice was almost a whisper, as if admitting what she wanted was a foreign and uncomfortable thing for her. I inched closer and wrapped my arms around her, bringing her gently against my chest as I tried to ease some of the tension out of her body. It took her a minute, but in less time than the last, her arms circled my waist and her face pressed into the curve of my shoulder.

I rested my cheek on the top of her head and gently ran my hands up and down her back, hoping to bring her as much comfort and contentment as she brought me.

"There's nothing wrong with following the rules, Mia," I said at length. "I think what you might not realize is that not all consequences are bad, and sometimes breaking the rules is necessary. Not just because it can be fun," I said with a grin, and pulled away to look at her. "But because you have to figure out who you are, and sometimes that means being someone different than who everyone else wants you to be."

"How do you know?"

I smiled. "I've broken a lot of rules, Evans, and disappointed a lot of people."

"And now?" she repeated my earlier words.

"And now," I said with a slow exhale. "Well, I still fuck up—like getting drunk a couple of weeks ago when I thought I'd blown my chances with you."

"A very sensible decision," she said with a small smile.

"As most of mine are," I teased and ran my hands over her back again. "But, other than a few slips, I'm in a good place right now. A place I've wanted to be for a long time. I just had to decide to make the move and get here."

Her eyes were steady on mine, her heartbeat fast enough that I could feel it. Hoping I was seeing what she was offering, I slid my hands down her arms to her wrists and gently slid them from their position around my waist, bringing them up and around my neck.

My eyes still on hers, I brought my hands to the sides of her ribcage, holding her gently even though every fiber of my being was urging me to pull her against me and take anything she was willing to give. "Where do you want to be, Mia?"

She shook her head back and forth, her eyes big and dark as she stared at me. "I don't know anymore." And then she gave me what I never thought I'd have. "But I'm glad I'm with you right now."

My breath caught and my body stilled as I stared at her, my eyes searching for the meaning behind her words. When I found it, the air rushed back into my lungs and I carefully slid my hands up her side, brushing against the side of her breasts, pausing only slightly at the sharp intake of her breath before I continued, out to her shoulders, along her neck and up so I could slide my hands through her hair, traveling down its length past her shoulders and the sides of her ribcage again, to her back, memorizing her shape as I brought her close.

I couldn't see anything but Mia as I lowered my head until our mouths were only inches apart—didn't want to see anything but her. My eyes never left hers as I closed the small distance between us.

I watched her lashes flutter until they rested on her cheeks, and felt her arms tighten around my neck as she rose a little higher with the help of the water, pressing her chest to mine so we made one long line until our mouths were lined up. I could see and feel and think of nothing but her as I took her mouth with my own, wrapping her closer until not even water came between us.

Here was everything I'd ever wanted. I might only be eighteen, but something inside of me told me I hadn't been wrong when I'd fallen in love with her all those years ago. Holding her, kissing her, I knew I'd never felt like this before and I knew I wouldn't ever again. This was Mia, and with one kiss, she'd given me everything.

It flitted through my mind that she also had the ability to take everything, but I pushed that terrifying thought aside and focused only on her and this moment. I swept my tongue across her bottom lip and was rewarded when she parted them slightly, allowing me to slip inside and taste all of her.

A small whimper sounded in her throat and she reached up to tangle her fingers in my hair. Taking a bit more, I changed the angle of the kiss, drawing her flavor deeper into my mouth as my hands explored her exposed flesh, memorizing the shape and texture of her, getting to know her with my fingertips only.

When her breath hitched, a small catch in the back of her throat, and her body arched into mine, my blood went from a slow simmer to boil and I knew I had to stop before I gave in and ripped all barriers aside to claim her where we stood.

I eased away gently, placing one last kiss on her lips. I didn't release her yet; instead, I held her close and watched her face as she realized what had just happened. I waited, my heart rate spiking. If she pulled away and left now, I might not recover from it. It wasn't my first kiss, not by a long shot, and still I knew what had just happened between us was as new for me as it was for her. I watched her, waiting for some sign, relief flooding through me when her lashes fluttered open and a smile curved at her lips. The breath I had been holding expelled in one loud whoosh and I dropped my forehead to rest on hers.

"Evans, you can't know how long I've wanted to do that."

Chapter Fifteen
Mia

Accepted.

The first Saturday in December, I stared at my computer screen and read the words that told me everything I'd worked toward had finally happened.

And I wondered why my stomach should hurt so much at the thought of it.

I hadn't expected anything different, not really. There had been a few moments in the past year when I worried over the idea that I wasn't good enough, that I would be seen as too normal and be rejected. And then my parents would have to do for me whatever they'd done for Joe to get him in.

But they didn't, because I'd gotten in all on my own and now I was following my dreams. Wasn't I?

I closed the lid to my computer and sat staring at the wall, ignoring my phone when it beeped, and again when it rang. It was my mom. I knew she would call, even though she was in Phoenix doing something at the bank for my dad. This was the day she'd been waiting for, and she hadn't been wrong last month when she told her friends that I was going to Stanford.

I was going to Stanford.

Tears pricked my eyes, and for reasons beyond me, I laid my head on my desk and wept.

~

My parents took me out to dinner to celebrate, but halfway through the evening the air was so thick with tension I could hardly breathe. I wished desperately that Joshua and Ethan hadn't had a birthday party to attend so that at least their chatter could serve as a distraction from the shouted silence of my parents' interaction.

They both spoke only to me, my father to ask the obligatory questions in between checking his phone and looking at his watch, my mother to prattle on and on about how she had never doubted me for a moment and how proud she was that another Evans would be following the tradition and becoming a Cardinal. I tried to smile, tried to act grateful for her enthusiasm, but all I could see were the nervous glances she sent my father's direction, or the small slices of hurt that flashed in her eyes each time he picked up his phone or made a noncommittal sound instead of really engaging with her.

He hadn't looked at her once, and she'd hardly looked anywhere else. It was in that moment that I realized just how broken we were, and how much I didn't want to be there. Really, how much none of us wanted to be there.

When my mother spoke about how much she missed her own days as a college girl, my father gave a small laugh and made a comment about Stanford being different than the state university my mother had attended before digging into his chicken.

My mother's face remained frozen in a smile, but the sheen of tears in her eyes was unmistakable, as was the quaver in her voice as she shrilled out a laugh and agreed with him, dismissing her own college education as "flighty fun." At that moment, I wished for some of Cora's brashness, or, in the very least a little courage to help the icy words in my throat rip free. I wanted to lash out at my father and force him to feel, to see what he was doing to my mother, to our family, but instead I let the moment pass, realizing I was no better than he as I gave only mumbled responses around my lobster bisque, wondering how much longer I had before I could escape.

The rest of the dinner passed in relative silence, my father's only comment to remind my mother that he would be driving to Phoenix to catch a plane early tomorrow morning. After that, she hardly spoke, and though I seethed that my father could be so cold, so careless with her feelings, I was grateful that she excused herself to her room with a headache when we got home.

My father had already changed his clothes to go workout and was texting on his phone as he came down the stairs. He paused a moment when he saw me.

"Good work, Mia, but I never expected anything less. Remember, don't stop working hard now that you've been accepted. More than thirty percent of college students drop out in their first year."

With that little morsel of wisdom, he nodded and strode out of the house and toward his car.

Watching him go, I wondered what it said about me that I was relieved he wasn't staying past morning.

As I walked up the stairs to my room, I realized I wanted to be anywhere but in this house, where the emotions ran as cold as the concrete floors, and the expectations that always loomed overhead were punctuated with icy tones and easy dismissals. Silence surrounded me as I walked down the hallway past all of the closed doors toward my room, and as my hand reached for the nob, I was frozen by the unmistakable sound of weeping. My body stilled, my breathing stopped, and I stood there in my party dress that I hadn't chosen with the matching shoes, listening to my mother sob. It was a sound I'd never heard, one that skittered across my skin with sharp little nails and pierced my heart, making the breath whoosh out of my lungs.

And because I was my father's daughter, I turned back the way I had come and walked down the stairs and out the front door.

I ignored the guilt that wanted to creep in as I started across the street, just as I ignored the sick weight in the pit of my stomach. I didn't want to feel hollow tonight—didn't want to feel sad or stressed or worried. I just wanted to feel. Stepping onto Ryan's front porch, I didn't give myself time to analyze what I was doing before I rang the bell.

A minute later, Caitlin answered the door and I smiled when she looked over my shoulder and asked if Joshua was with me. "No, sorry."

"Oh, well. Ryan, your girlfriend's here," she shouted as she walked away and had my face flushing with mortification as I stood there. A second later, I heard footsteps and then he came into view, his jeans loose and low on his hips, his dark t-shirt faded from so many washings and just snug enough that I could see the planes of his chest, the strong build of his shoulders. His feet were bare.

Suddenly, I felt like an idiot, standing there in my fussy dress and high heels, uninvited on the porch while I interrupted what sounded like a party.

"Evans? I thought you had dinner with your parents," he said reaching for my hand and bringing me inside the entryway.

"I did," I answered and looked down the hall as raised voices carried to us. "I'm sorry. I got done and wanted to see you...I should have called. I didn't think," I said, miserably awkward.

"Called? Mia, you live across the street. It's faster to walk over than to call, and this way, I get to see you."

"You're having a party."

He glanced over his shoulder at the voices and then back at me. "A party? No. My parents and I are just battling out some Wii with Caitlin. I was hoping I would get to see you tonight," he said and stepped closer.

"You were?"

He nodded and dipped his head down, pausing a breath from my lips. I stayed perfectly still, my eyes on his, my breath clogging in my lungs. An inch and our lips would touch, and then I would feel everything that had been missing inside of me before him, a thought that should terrify me but didn't. Instead of closing the gap, though, he remained an inch away, staring into my eyes.

"Yeah, I was. I miss you when I'm not with you, Mia." His lips brushed mine softly, once, twice, a third time and my eyes fluttered, my mind already going to that place where all I could think of was him.

And then he leaned back and smiled, taking my hand and tugging me down the hall after him.

I followed, slowing as we passed through the kitchen to the living room where his parents were sprawled with Caitlin. The scene was so polar opposite of the one I had just left in my own home that mortification swamped me once more as tears threatened to prick my eyes.

"Mia, are you okay?" Ryan asked as he turned to me. I nodded, but he continued to study me for another minute, as if he already knew how to look beneath my words to their real meaning. When I offered him a bolstered smile, he linked our fingers more securely before turning to his parents.

"Hey," he said to the room and heads turned. "Mia's here. We're going to go out for a bit."

"Afraid I'm going to beat you again?" his mom asked and did a short victory dance. When her laughter rolled out, it sounded so much like Ryan's, I felt my own lips twitch. Ryan just shook his head.

"One time," he said. "You beat me one time, and since then I've beaten you at least a dozen."

"Please, I'm on fire tonight. I'll wash the floors with you."

"Careful, Mia, they're in a never-ending competition." This time his father spoke, walking to stand next to his wife and hug her to his side.

"I'm sorry to intrude," I said and his parents both waved me off.

"Of course not. Go, be young. *Young*," his mother emphasized to Ryan. "Not a day over eighteen, you hear me? Alcoholic beverages are *not* something an eighteen-year-old consumes. Are we clear?"

"One time," he said again and tugged me out of the kitchen and into the garage.

He opened the door to his truck and I glanced at him. "Let's go for a drive, Evans."

~

He took me to Lost Creek Road and parked in the gravel lot that looked up at the mountains on one side, and over our small town on the other. He couldn't know that I ran here every day, or that by bringing me here, he was showing me one more reason that I wasn't satisfied with who I was anymore.

"The name of this road has always drawn me," I said, staring out at the mountains. "Since my first year in Verrado, this road has always called to me." I didn't want to look back toward the lights yet, the city where people and expectations waited. I wanted to look at the darkened horizon, illuminated only by the moon, and believe for a night that my life held possibilities that I didn't know about yet.

"I have a blanket in the back, and a sweatshirt you can wear."

I nodded and opened my door, stepping out onto the gravel and walking around to the back, where I met him before hoisting myself onto the tailgate. He stood in front of me and tugged his sweatshirt over my head, lifting my hair out and combing his fingers through it as it sifted down over my shoulders.

He didn't say anything, but I could see so much in his face, so many words, and after the evening I'd spent with my parents, I wanted nothing more than to feel with him. Taking a chance, I leaned forward and pressed my lips to his, savoring the small intake of breath and tensing of his body before his hands went to my hips and pulled me closer. His head angled and his tongue swept out and tasted my lower lip. I mimicked the motion with my own and heard the low rumble deep in his chest.

He didn't push, though, even as a part of me wished he would. It would be so easy to forget when he took me to the place that was only feeling and being, the place that I could only find when he was touching me. But he didn't. Just as he had stopped an inch in front of me at his parents', he stopped now, kissing me once more before pulling back and hopping onto the tailgate. Scooting back, he grabbed me around the waist and hauled me with him, snuggling me into the crook of his arm as he covered us both with a blanket.

For a while, we sat there, content with the silence, his fingers tracing the palm of my hand, his heart beating against my side.

"What happened, Evans?"

I didn't look at him, but snuggled deeper into his body, pulling at a thread on the blanket. "What do you mean?"

"You know what I mean," he said and put his finger under my chin until I had no choice to meet his eyes. "What happened to make you run, to make you look like you were on the verge of tears tonight? To make you afraid." The last part wasn't a question, but a statement, and that more than anything had my eyes filling again. Tilting my chin down, I started pulling at the thread again, taking small comfort in the feel of his heart beating, strong and steady, beneath my cheek.

"My brother Joe left," I explained after a moment. "He didn't see eye to eye with my parents—or they wouldn't let him see anything differently than they did, so he ran away. Got his high school diploma and loaded up the back of his motorcycle the same day. That was three years ago. I haven't talked to him or seen him since. I guess he's still running, like me," I murmured.

"Why do you run?"

I shook my head, wondering how to answer, whether or not I could find the words to explain. "I don't know. I was so upset, with him, with my parents, with everything. I wanted everyone to stop fighting and try to make it work, but they wouldn't. My parents drove away and Joe came down the stairs with his things already in a bag, like he'd known from the very beginning he would leave. I started running after he disappeared, pushing myself to get away from the house and everything that had happened there. I saw this road that day he left, Lost Creek Road, and I took it, thinking it was exactly like me."

The tears that had been backing up since I saw my mother shrink to a shell at dinner spilled over one by one, but I made no move to wipe them away. Oddly, after all of this time holding them in, afraid of what they would mean, it felt too good to let them roll, and to know that no matter what the consequences of my admission, I had finally trusted someone enough to be honest.

"I remember that day," he said.

Turning my head, I stared at him. "What?"

"I remember that day your brother left." His voice was low and when I just stared at him, he cleared his throat to continue. "I'd just gotten home from baseball practice and went to put my glove in my room before dinner. The air was on the fritz so the window was open. I heard you first," he said, and brushed his fingers through my hair at the temple. "When I went to the window, I saw you sitting on the front step, your arms wrapped around your legs while you sobbed into your knees. I sat with you," he admitted on a slow expulsion of breath. "I didn't know you very well, but I couldn't leave you even then. Something about the way you looked, the way you sounded, it hit me hard. I didn't understand why, not really, I just knew I couldn't leave you. That I didn't want to leave you."

I couldn't form words, couldn't seem to bring in enough air to say what I was feeling. My heart thrummed in my chest, and my hands trembled as I looked into Ryan's eyes. He'd sat with me while I cried. Without even knowing me, he'd cared enough to stay with me when I was in pain. Just like he was with me right now, because I'd needed him.

"Ryan." That was all I said, just his name, and as it breathed through my lips, I understood what it meant. I was lost to him. Him, this boy, who had sat with me while I cried, and now held me while I trembled, he had somehow become more to me than anyone else, and though it scared me, it also liberated me. Desperate to convey how I was feeling, I reached a hand out, placing it on his jaw. Unsure, hesitant, I traced the curve of his chin, the sharp line of his cheekbone, up into his hair before tracing the same steps back down, hoping that what I felt in my heart, he could feel through my fingers. I wanted him to know that he had touched me in a way that no one else had, that he meant more to me than I ever thought anyone could, but I didn't know how to say it. I stopped at his lips, unsure of my next move even while I knew what I wanted.

As if he knew, too, he rolled until we were face to face, each of us on our sides, the only light coming from the moon that filtered through the building clouds.

He was braced on his elbow, one arm supporting him as his other hand journeyed from my face to my hair, down my shoulder to my hip, lower until the fabric of my dress gave way to skin. My breath caught and I stared at him, my eyes never leaving his as his hand continued its journey, down my leg to the back of my knee and then my ankle, back up again, over my hip, my waist, under the sweatshirt to my ribcage, the side of my breast. His eyes never leaving mine, he continued to touch me, light caresses that left a stream of electricity in their wake, and when his lips finally found mine, I reached out to grip his waist and then we were rolling until he was braced above me, until our bodies were fitted together and I could feel all of him.

I ran my hands down his back and up again, under his t-shirt to the skin beneath, back down to his hips, resting them at the waistband of his jeans. With a small intake of breath, he grabbed my hands, linking his fingers with mine and dragging them above my head. His lips brushed mine, once, twice, coming back and staying longer the third time, his tongue tracing my bottom lip until I arched under him and silently begged for more. Emotions swamped me as his lips met mine again and again, their tender assault too much, and without warning, my whole body began to tremble.

"Shh, Mia, it's okay. I won't hurt you."

His words floated over me and when I felt him pull away, I was snapped back into reality as a blast of cold air replaced the warmth of his body. Before I could blink, he was pulling me close again, wrapping his arms around me so that my arm was wrapped around his middle and my head was resting on his shoulder. I could feel his heartbeat pounding out a rhythm that matched mine, but his hands were gentle as they stroked my back.

"I'm sorry," I whispered and squeezed my eyes tight, wondering if these damn tears would ever go away.

His body stiffened, and before I could blink he rolled over so he was braced above me again.

"Evans, look at me."

His voice was rough and when his fingers came to my chin, I looked up at him, my traitorous body melting at the mere sight of his face this close. Even in the shadows, I could see the intensity of his eyes, which were deep and serious and never left mine as he spoke.

"Don't ever apologize—not here with me, not like this."

His hands stroked my face, and that was all it took to have the tears that threatened spill one by one down my face.

"Oh, baby, did I scare you? I'm sorry, Mia. I won't ever hurt you, I promise. I won't push you or ask you for more than you can give," he murmured, kissing my cheeks as he wiped at the tear that continued to fall.

I shook my head, curling into him as he gathered me close again, grateful for his warmth and the feeling of his hand as it stroked my hair. "It's not that. I'm not scared of you, of this," I mumbled into his neck. "Not really."

"Of what, then?"

I sucked in a low breath and wondered if I could say it—could I tell him out loud what I'd never admitted to myself? Could I release the words that ran through me, set them free and hope that it changed nothing even when I knew it would change everything?

"I got in to Stanford," I said and I felt him shift so that he could look down at me, but I didn't look up. Instead, I watched my finger trace the ridges of his abdomen. "I've been working toward that for years, and finally, I got accepted."

"Jesus, Mia, that's amazing. You should have told me and I'd have taken you to celebrate."

I continued tracing the patterns, barely hearing him as the words inside of me boiled up and over. "My whole life, Ryan, I've worked my whole life for it. And now..." The words stuck in my throat so I had to stop and clear it. "And now," I continued, finally looking at him, "I'm afraid it doesn't matter, that it will never matter the way I thought it would."

"Why do you say that?"

"Because Stanford can't save my family." My voice sounded small, sad, even to my own ears, but I couldn't bring myself to make it stronger. "It can't bring my brother back, or make my father love my mother. I saw that at dinner with my parents tonight, and after watching them together, I had to face it: being accepted to Stanford doesn't mean I'm suddenly going to be enough for my parents, or that they're going to be enough for each other, or for me and my brothers. Stanford is an illusion, like everything else in our family, and tonight I realized that I don't want the illusion, I want something real. I want to feel something like this, like what I only feel when I'm with you." Finally, I tilted my head back and looked at him, reveling in the fact that he was here, that he was mine. "I don't want to keep living for someone else, Ryan. I'm just afraid it's too late to stop."

Chapter Sixteen
Ryan

Mia managed to avoid me for almost a week after that night.

Each time I texted her or tried to get her alone, she always had an excuse. Tutoring, work, winter workouts for track, prom meetings, newspaper editing, the list went on. Because I knew she was struggling with more than just a busy schedule, I eased back and let her get away with the excuses. She'd discovered something the other night, something I didn't even fully understand, but something I knew was important enough that she needed time to let it settle. But by Friday, a week after she had moaned my name right before she'd cried on my shoulder, I was done being patient.

She wasn't outright ignoring me, but I could sense that she was doing her level best to put some distance between us, to get back onto even ground as she saw it, and go back to the way things were. Since there was no way in *hell* I was letting that happen, I was searching the courtyard and the lunchroom like an idiot trying to spot her so I could convince her to hang out tonight. Convince her, sure—more like force her. I'd texted her earlier and she had replied with a maybe, but that wasn't enough. I needed face-to-face.

"Dude, relax, you look like a puppy trying to find his owner."

I scowled at Max as he shoveled in potato salad like it was his last meal, but since I was afraid he was right, I forced myself to stop scanning the throngs of people and picked up my lunch.

"So, you're just ignoring Nina now and acting like always? How's Torres responding to that?"

Max shrugged and shoveled in some carrots on top of the salad. I leaned back a little to avoid the debris that was sure to fly out when he spoke.

"The usual. When I got put into her study group in math, she gave me the cold shoulder for a while, but then I ignored her and she finally started talking, asking me what the hell I was doing there, wasn't there some willing freshman I could go prey on so she could actually work. You know, her way of whispering sweet nothings I guess." Max grinned and swallowed down the carrot-potato concoction in one gulp. "Then I threw her off and asked her what her plans were for the weekend. She bristled and said some scathing thing, so I shrugged like I couldn't care less and told her not to worry, I'd catch up with her some other time and I left."

"Sneaky."

"Wasn't it? I mean, it's not swimming in the moonlight or sitting in the back of a pickup looking out at the stars, but it worked for her. I think I'm going to try and catch her up at the base this weekend."

"Why the base?"

"She goes there to watch the planes. She's been into aviation since we were kids—she wants to build planes when she graduates from college."

"No shit? That's pretty awesome."

"And really hot," he said with a grin.

I shook my head and dug into my second sandwich. "Well, let me know if you need reinforcements. I can ask Mia to put in a good word for you."

"Speaking of Mia, what the hell's wrong with you?"

"What?" I asked and rose when the bell rang. "Nothing's wrong with me. What are you talking about?"

"What are you doing, Murph?"

I frowned. "What do you mean?"

"I mean, you've spent the better part of two months getting to know her, even though you've been in love with her for years—don't deny it," he said before I could speak. "Then, you finally work up the balls to make a move, and now you're just moping around waiting for her to come to you." Max shook his head and I narrowed my eyes at him, partly in annoyance, partly in reaction to the balls comment. "It just seems wrong. I've only had a thing for Nina for a few months and already we're at the same place as you and Mia."

"I hardly think that tricking a girl into hanging out with you and then ignoring her in some twisted mind game is at the same level as Mia and me. At least Mia knows I like her. You've got a strategic battle plan going to keep your relationship alive."

He grinned. "Yeah, but it's a brilliant plan." Then he pointed ahead. "Isn't that your girl there, talking to Sanchez?"

Jealousy had never been something I'd wasted any energy on, with girls or anything else. I figured I would get what I worked for, and I worked for stuff that mattered. With Sarah, I just hadn't cared enough to bother being jealous of anyone who was with her when I wasn't. And the other girls, well, they hadn't lasted long enough. But seeing Mia walk down the hallway and laugh while Sanchez settled his arm around her shoulders and continued talking, I was eaten alive with it.

Mine. I knew it was possessive and stupid and archaic, but that didn't change the fact that it was the truth. She was mine and it was about time everyone knew it. Herself, included.

I was three strides away from Max when I heard him yell, "I've got an extra set of battle plans if you need them." I held out my middle finger as an answer while I continued to push my way through the crowd, saying her name when I was only a few feet away. Her eyes met mine and I had a brief moment to see them light up before I swooped my hand around her waist and brought her to her toes so my lips could take hers.

At first, she was too stunned to do anything, but when I changed the angle of the kiss, her lips parted and I swept my tongue out to trace the line of them. Her breath caught, and soon she was kissing me back, her hesitant tongue mating with mine and causing my whole body to go on alert.

Suddenly, I was back in the bed of my truck with her underneath me, her hands streaking under my shirt as she begged me with her lips. I'd wanted her more in that moment than I wanted to breathe, and then she'd trembled, so hard, so quick that I knew she wasn't ready. Just like I wasn't ready, not until she knew how I felt. Not until she knew that this was *real*, and she couldn't just walk away when she got scared.

Even though every ounce of me begged to bring her closer, to continue devouring her until neither of us could think of anyone or anything else, I could hear people whistling at us and I knew I was already on thin ice, so I gently pulled away, keeping my hands at her waist as her eyes fluttered open. "A week's too long in between kisses."

When I bent my head to press my lips to hers once more, she slapped a hand on my chest and stepped back.

"Hey, Murph, good to see you," Sanchez said, grinning like the idiot he was. Because I was feeling pretty idiotic myself, I grinned back.

"You, too, Sanchez. Can I get a second with my girl?"

"Sure thing, Boss. See you at practice. Oh, and Mia, if you need any more material for your article, I'm your guy." With that he saluted and turned to jog away, yelling at someone to wait up for him.

Since she was looking at me like I'd grown three heads in the last ten seconds, and I knew if I tried to approach her now she may slap me, I refrained from reaching out for her and instead dipped my hands into my pockets, studying her as she glared at me.

She was wearing jeans tucked into boots and an oversized shirt that made her look even smaller than usual. The fact that I couldn't see her skin didn't keep me from remembering what it had felt like under my hands, just as the fact that her eyes were piercing me didn't erase the memory I had of them clouded with need.

"What was that?" she said after a moment. Her voice was low and harsh and I smiled, shrugging my shoulders as I nodded at the people who passed us.

"I wanted to talk to you."

"That's funny, I didn't hear you say anything but I sure as hell felt your tongue somewhere else."

I grinned, loving that even as she said it her cheeks went pink. "Well, I should say I wanted to talk to you, but once I saw you, I realized I wanted to kiss you more."

When she opened her mouth to yell again, I held out my hands to stop her. "I've missed you, Mia. I haven't seen you since last Saturday, and since you've been going out of your way to avoid me, I decided I should let you know that I'm not going to let you walk away. No matter how scared you are."

Her cheeks flushed again, but I couldn't tell if it was in embarrassment or anger. "I told you, I wasn't scared of this."

"And we both know that's bullshit. Otherwise, you wouldn't be avoiding me."

Because she knew I was right, she crossed her arms over her chest. "So you thought the best way to keep me from being scared was to accost me at school in front of everyone? People were staring, Ryan. They still are," she said and motioned to the people who walked by us grinning.

"So? Look, I'm sorry, I should have taken it slower, not grabbed you, but I'm not sorry people saw us. I want to be with you, Mia, all the way with you. If it takes kissing you in the hallway to let you and everyone else know that, too, well, that's what I'll do."

"Did," she corrected, but I could hear the anger fading. "That's what you did."

"Did," I said and reached a tentative hand out to her. When she didn't slap it away, I took that as a good sign and wrapped my other one around her waist, bringing her up against me again. "Didn't you miss me, too?"

She shook her head, but I saw her smile as her eyes fluttered closed.

"Don't be afraid of me, Evans," I whispered and bent my head and to brush my lips against hers. "Don't be afraid of this." I nipped at her bottom lip and then pressed my lips to it when she gasped, pleased when her arms wrapped around me and her body melted into mine. When she would have taken the kiss deeper, I drew away, teasing her with light kisses over her jawline.

"Ryan," she said and her voice was rough and throaty.

"Hmm?"

"Kiss me."

"I thought you didn't want me to." I pressed my lips to the pulse at her throat and heard her light groan.

"I lied." Then her lips were on mine while her fingers curled into my shirt at the waist and brought me closer. I could have devoured her, and she would have let me. It was as if time ceased to exist for us. I couldn't think of anything but her, and I knew she was only thinking of me. Somehow, everything I'd ever wanted was here, right now, and a little shot of panic whipped through me as I realized I didn't know how I was going to keep her.

When I finally pulled back, she buried her face in my neck for a second and I breathed in her scent, that light and floral scent that reminded me of a meadow in the spring. When the bell rang, she jumped and I smiled, running my free hand down the length of her hair.

"Can I walk you to class?"

She nodded, her cheeks a little pink from the kiss and the audience. "Sure."

"Can I see you tonight?"

Her smile was slow but beautiful and something tightened in my chest as she nodded. "Sure."

As I held her hand and walked with her through the now deserted hallways, I realized for the first time in my life that it might not matter how hard I worked for Mia. The choice was always going to be hers whether she stayed or left, and just like that, I could lose the one thing that was beginning to matter the most.

Chapter Seventeen
Mia

The weeks following my acceptance letter, I tried to go on as normally as possible, but there had been a definite change in me that was hard to ignore. Stanford and everything it had once stood for no longer shined bright and heavy at the forefront of my mind. Instead, Ryan did. Rather than feeling weighed down when I ran, I now felt as though I were running toward something, not away.

I tried to remind myself that it was dangerous to think that way, that in doing so I was making the same mistakes as Joe. And then I wondered if Joe had really made a mistake. Could I really blame him for my parents' relationship? Now, after I'd seen how callous and cruel my father could be, didn't it make more sense that it wasn't Joe who had made their lives miserable, but them? And a logical conclusion to this would be that even if Joe had done as they asked and gone to school, even if he had remained a puppet in this family play, just waiting for his strings to be pulled and point him in the right direction, their relationship would have eventually ended up here?

I didn't know whether I thought this because I was beginning to envy Joe his disappearance, or because every time I looked at my mother she seemed to get smaller and smaller, not just her physical size, but her personality, and it was a direct result of my father's actions, or lack thereof. My mother was a rock on the shore, trying to hold the shoreline and support the ecosystem that had built itself around her, but the constant pounding of the elements surrounding her was causing her to break apart and disappear, bit by bit so that by the time New Year's Eve rolled around, she was even more jumpy and frazzled than usual.

Preparations for the party had begun at promptly eight a.m. this morning, when the party company came to set up all of the different tables, and the caterers took over the kitchen to prepare all of the food. By ten thirty, our home had been transformed from desert modern to Monte Carlo, with its colored lights and craps tables, a roulette wheel and a blackjack table. Candles had been put into the pool, and there were several different stations for food. I did my best to stay out of the way, and when Cora arrived with her parents around noon, we offered to drive Ethan and Joshua to their friend's house, making a quick exit while Aunt Suzie and my mother gathered around the event staff and drilled out commands.

It was a toss-up who was most surprised when Lily went with us.

"I can't stay here," she said and walked out to get in the backseat next to the twins. "Seriously, if she suggests another article of clothing for me, I might freak out. Why does it matter so much?"

"The fact that you have to ask answers your question," Cora said and I winced, waiting for Lily's rebuttal.

When she smiled and mumbled, "Point taken," I glanced at Cora. Cora widened her eyes but made no comment as we started away from the house.

After releasing the twins to their freedom, we stopped for coffee at Mocharavia, where the coffee girl congratulated me.

"Stanford, wow, you must be really smart. Congrats!"

I mumbled my thanks and kept my head down, noting that Lily and Cora both watched me skeptically. Just then, we saw Nina at a table in the corner where we learned she was hiding out from her Aunt.

"She's going with my parents to your parents' tonight, so that's something, but the damn woman won't leave me alone," she complained as we sat down at her table with her.

"A pedicure is hardly Mexican torture, Nina," Cora said as she sipped from her latte and eyed the boys who were passing in front of the window. One of them held a Frisbee, and the rest walked next to him, their faces sweaty, their shirts showing signs of grass and dirt stains. Cora smiled coyly when they looked in the window, and the one holding the Frisbee paused for a minute, looking her up and down, his face full of appreciation. Then Nina turned and glared at them and had them moving again.

"Thank God," Lily said and sipped from her glass of water. As a rule, she didn't drink caffeine, which was probably for the best since she was already the highest strung person I knew, save our mother.

"It's not Mexican torture for people like you, Barbie," Nina said without sting. For whatever reason, she and Cora didn't have the volatile relationship that Lily and Cora had. Instead, they seemed to accept the other for who she was while remaining grateful for the fact that they weren't that person. "But for me, the idea of someone playing with my feet and asking me personal questions about my sex life is akin to having someone shove fire pokers in my eyes."

"We'll get you a sex life, Nina. I mean, we're getting Lily one, so it's no trouble." Cora smiled at them both, and again I waited for a snide and ripping remark from Lily, but none came. Her cheeks turned pink and she rolled her eyes, but nothing else. Encouraged, Cora set down her coffee and leaned forward. "I guarantee then that you'll enjoy someone playing with your feet...even if it's just a stop on their road to someplace further up."

"You're a real friend, Cora," Lily said and met Cora's eyes. Cora stared at her a moment, gauging her reaction, before she inclined her head and smiled.

"So I've been told. Speaking of sex lives," she said and turned to me. "Aunt Margaret said something before we left about someone named Jonathan. Like, 'Don't forget that Jonathan is coming over tonight.' Cousin, please tell me you're not letting your mother set you up on a date for New Year's Eve. That's more horrifying than the fact that this one over here is actually going to use her science book as a date, and the second one is actually jealous about that."

"I'm not jealous," Lily corrected, showing some of her old spark that had been missing since she arrived home for Christmas break. "I simply don't understand why it matters what color shoes I wear. Who cares what I stuff my feet into?"

"It's too easy to turn that into a crude comment, so I'll pass, but trust me when I say what you wear on your feet can oftentimes determine whether or not you get a date."

"Seriously?" both Lily and Nina asked at the same time and I laughed.

"Seriously," Cora said and shook her hair back. "Jesus, are you two from the dark ages? Let Aunt Cora help—heels lift your butt and lengthen your leg. And those two items are necessary in the battle between men and women."

"Christ, that's disgusting," Nina said and tossed back the rest of her coffee in one shot. "I'm a 4.3 student and my IQ ranks as one of the highest in the nation for my age. Why should what I wear be the deciding factor as to whether a guy's interested in me or not?"

Lily didn't say anything, she just watched as Cora laughed at Nina's rant. "Nina, if you're so smart, riddle me this: Does it make you less smart if you put on a nice outfit and a pretty pair of pumps? No," she continued, happy to score a point. "And before you say its objectifying women, may I remind you that it's no different than you checking out a guy for being hot."

"I don't check anyone out," she said.

"That's for another time," Cora said. "But let me give you one last morsel of wisdom. Do those ugly pants and sweaters you wear make you smart?"

"Of course not."

"Then why would high heels make you stupid?" Satisfied with Nina's silence, Cora turned back to me. "Spill it, cousin. Did your mother really set you up tonight?"

I shook my head and sipped from my small coffee. "No. Jonathan's parents had a dinner at the Inn before Thanksgiving and I set it up for them. Before I could leave, Mrs. Petersen cornered me and told me how her son Jonathan had been in Switzerland for the past two years and now he's finally coming home for Christmas. Then she asked if I would show him around, befriend him in a way, and since they're coming tonight, I guess she figured it would be a good setting for him to get reacquainted with people in."

"Is he cute? I can reacquaint him with certain things if that's the case."

"Always the giver," Lily said.

"Oh, I'm a taker, too," Cora replied.

"The last time I saw him he was wearing all black, including fingernail polish, and he was sulking in the back of English class. I don't gather a couple of years away have changed him that much."

"Oh, well, a girl has to ask. Maybe we can set him up with Lily and they can be tortured souls together."

"I better borrow a pair of shoes from you first, just to make sure he notices me," Lily said sweetly.

"It's going to take more than a pair of shoes, Lil, let's be honest." Then Cora pursed her mouth and looked at Nina. "Are you doing anything tonight, Bill Nye, or are you really using school as a lame excuse for not going out?"

"I don't need an excuse, lame or otherwise. I don't believe in these trite holiday rituals."

"I'll take that as a no. Why don't you come to the party, you can be my guest since aunt Margaret is such a stickler for that. We'll get you dressed up and wearing some makeup—who knows, you might even take off the frames and enjoy yourself. I believe I heard a certain someone is going to be there."

Nina purposefully adjusted her glasses and kept an amused smile on her face. "Again, to you that's a night worth remembering—to me, it translates into the tortures of Hell. Thanks, but my physics book and I have a date. It's getting serious."

"Lucky," Lily grumbled.

Nina left a few minutes later and Cora shook her head as we sat there, watching the people go by, prolonging the process of going back to the house where we were sure to be put to work, or worse, subjected to the fluttering of our mothers.

"It pains me to think that she's going to sit home all night and study. The girl's gorgeous and she doesn't even know it."

I nodded and a thought slipped into my head. "I think we can find a way to make sure she isn't alone tonight, even if she's set on staying home."

"Oh really?"

I nodded. "But you can't tell anyone I did this, okay? Because she would never forgive me." I looked at both of them to make certain they understood.

"Mia, I never spoke with anyone when I lived here, why would I tell someone something now? Especially when I could care less what it is you're going to do."

"Seriously, Mia, you're under the impression that I have friends here," Cora said. "I don't. I don't really have friends anywhere," she added quietly.

"Welcome to my world," Lily said and looked over at Cora.

They shared another moment of silence, another round of understanding, and then Cora spoke. "Yeah, but you don't have friends because you're a bitch. I'm just too pretty. Girls get intimidated."

For the first time since I could remember, Lily laughed. Really laughed—until she had to cover her mouth to keep the giggles in.

"God, I hate you sometimes."

"The feeling's mutual."

Lily nodded and wiped at the tears that had escaped with her laughter. "I'm sorry about Thanksgiving, Cora, really. I was upset, going through some things and I took it out on you. I shouldn't have said those things I did."

I sat there, my phone in my hand, and watched, holding my breath. Cora nodded.

"You're right you shouldn't have. But," she added when Lily's eyes widened and she opened her mouth to speak. "I think you had a point, and I'm sorry I yelled at you and said you were like our mothers. You're not," she said and smiled. She held out a hand and Lily grasped it.

"Really?" she asked on an expulsion of breath. "Because I am stuffy, and sometimes I feel like I'm turning into a shriveled up bitch, but I just can't seem to stop myself." I saw Lily's eyes fill with tears.

Cora shook her head and gripped Lily's hand while she struggled to reign in her own tears. "Lil, please, you're like ten times smarter than my mother. Even on your worst day you don't come close to her." Lily gurgled out a watery laugh and dabbed at her eyes.

I stepped away from the table to give them a moment. Throwing my cup in the garbage can, I flipped open my phone and sent a quick text to Max, hoping he understood.

"What are you doing?" Cora asked stepping up behind me.

"Making sure that Nina's not alone tonight."

"Oh, right, the secret operation. Please tell me it involves sexy Abercrombie Genius Boy."

"Mmhmm," I replied and turned. "Are you guys ready to go back?"

"Sure, and Lily," Cora said as we walked out of the café and onto the street. "You can pay me back for being so forgiving by letting me dress you tonight."

"Then I take back my apology and maintain that you're a slut."

Cora just laughed and hooked her arm through Lily's and then mine, connecting us all as we walked. "That trick won't work on me, besides, I need a project. This one here is wearing the dress your mother picked out for her."

"Mom picks your clothes out?" Lily asked with such shock in her voice that I felt heat flood my cheeks.

"Not all of them," I said defensively. "Just sometimes when she sees something that she likes or that she thinks I'll like."

"That's not the point, Mia," Cora said and shook her head. "You're going to be eighteen in May. Your mom can't continue picking out your clothes for you and telling you when they'll look good. And you can't keep letting her."

"It's a nice gesture," I said. "I don't have a lot of time to shop, so when she's out or in Phoenix and sees something, she picks it up for me. It's thoughtful."

"No, it's not, it's pushy," Cora said and we all stopped as we reached my car. "And you know it. You're too afraid to tell her no, Mia, and you're using the excuse of not having time to avoid confrontation. And I'm not just talking about clothing anymore. She's picked your date for tonight, too."

She was right, of course she was right. My mother had been picking out clothes for me for as long as I could remember—along with what people I should hang out with, where I should go to school, what I should major in. And I let her do it, not because I didn't care, I did, but because I was afraid that if I didn't live up to those expectations, I'd be forgotten, by her, by everyone. It seemed like the path she set out was the only one I was capable of following without seizing up from fear. I wanted to avoid confrontation—but more, I wanted to avoid failure.

I thought about the conversation I had with Ryan around Thanksgiving and about what I told him. I was a ruler follower and now I knew why. I didn't want to be forgotten. More, I didn't want to fail, and if I did as my mother asked, I never would. Not in her eyes, at least.

But what about in my eyes?

After watching her and my father interact with each other a few weeks ago, the last thing I wanted was what they had. Stanford, finally being accepted by my mother as worthy, it no longer mattered, not like it used to. What mattered was how I felt when I was with Ryan—alive and reckless and young.

There was a part of me that was still concerned about my mother and her acceptance of me, terrified that she wouldn't love me if she found out who I really was. Even still, for the first time in my life, the fear wasn't enough to stop me, it wasn't enough to rule me and make me bend to the responsibility of making everyone else happy. I just wanted to think about me, however selfish it sounded. And thinking about me meant thinking about Ryan.

"I actually have a different date for tonight," I blurted out.

Both of them stopped and looked at me. "Movie boy?" Cora asked and I smiled.

"And it won't be our first date since you were last here, either," I said and thought of the nights we'd spent together over the past few weeks—the moments of intense physical contact we'd shared, where I was left breathless and aching and unsure as to what was happening inside of me, only certain that whatever it was could only be ended by Ryan himself.

"Cousin, you do surprise me."

"Good, it's about time."

~

I wore the dress my mother picked out for me because I didn't have time to pick anything else out. The white on white ensemble with its sleeveless top and higher neckline that nipped in at the waist and flowed out into a full skirt wasn't really my style. It was simply too much, with its white polka dots that sat cheerily on the top of four layers of white skirt, which flowed out to swish around my thighs. It made me feel like I belonged at high tea with the queen. Which Cora told me more than once before I escaped downstairs, leaving her to torture Lily.

As expected, my mother praised my appearance to those around her even as she fussed with my hair, which I had put waves in and pulled over one shoulder. She fluffed and patted, bringing some of it to hang down my back before brushing at the front.

In a four minute inspection of me, she had changed half as many details in my appearance. So much for being my own person.

I thought wistfully of the chocolate stashed in my room underneath a pile of clean linens on the shelf in my closet. I'd only eaten one small morsel when I'd gotten home and I had a sick feeling it wouldn't be enough before the night was over.

"Where are your sister and cousin? I told them to be ready at eight o'clock sharp."

"Lily's just finishing up, and Cora's helping her," I answered. I didn't mention that Lily was also helping Cora into her dress, the one that could only be zipped when Cora lay flat on the bed on her stomach and Lily used pliers to yank the zipper into place. There were some things better seen in person.

"Well, I'll have to go get them because Jonathan Petersen is already here." She smoothed my hair once more before smiling at me. "Beautiful. I knew that dress was you the minute I saw it. So elegant."

I nodded, wondering how you told your mother that the dress she was sure was *you* was the exact opposite. That the fancy collar and full skirt were as far from "me" as it got. I didn't; rather, I smiled and walked in the direction she pointed me like a good little soldier, ready to serve her general. But I wouldn't be serving her all night, that was a vow I had made to myself. Ryan was coming, and after my conversation with Cora and Lily today, if there was one thing I was certain of, it was the fact that I wanted Ryan, and for the first time in a long time, I was going to go after what *I* wanted.

Chapter Eighteen
Ryan

I was already late for the party when I opened my front door and came face to face with Sarah and her cleavage. I'd be lying if I said I didn't stare for a moment, the sight of her in a tiny white sequined dress a trigger for a reel of memories to flash through my mind, many of which included her in significantly less clothing.

And then she spoke and her voice snapped me back enough to have me meeting her eyes.

"What?"

"I said, don't you look nice. You know how I love you in uniform."

"No, but you and I were never really big on what the other person wore. Or loved."

She smiled, and took a step closer, raising an eyebrow when I didn't move to let her in. "You're right—we were much better without clothes. Let me in and I'll remind you just how good."

Once, that would have been all it took. That throaty voice, low and sexy, the heavily mascara'd eyes looking at me, the invitation clear. Once, I would have grabbed her and had her undressed in under a minute, on the floor in less than two. But that was once, before I knew what it felt like to come back to reality and feel nothing for the person I was lying next to. That was before I knew what it felt like to touch Mia, to kiss Mia and hear her say my name, to feel her hands run over me in soft, hesitant touches that were enough to drive me crazy. Before I knew what it was to be with someone and care more about them and what they needed.

Now, looking at Sarah in her short dress that was so similar to the dress she'd been wearing the first night we slept together that I knew it was planned, I couldn't drum up one ounce of desire. And it reminded me exactly why we'd never been real in the first place.

She had been a convenience, a distraction that had filled a need inside of a sixteen-year-old boy, and with her, everything was easy from the very beginning.

We met when she threw a party at the end of our sophomore year that Max and I went to. I was in the kitchen, debating how much beer I could drink and still talk to my mom when I got home when Sarah walked in. She was in a white dress that was see-through to her skimpy bikini beneath and she walked straight up to me, pressing all 5'10" of herself against me and asking me if I wanted a tour of the house. That had been the first of many meetings for us. When she got tired of me, she saw someone else and I let her, just like I always let her come back a few days later. This continued for just over a year, but each night I was with Sarah, I had also been very aware of the girl next door.

And now I had her.

"I'm already running late, Sarah, and I still need to shower."

"I could use another shower," she said and I felt my stomach clench. It would be so easy…too easy. That was the problem.

"I don't think so," I said and watched her heavily lined eyes as they widened briefly in shock. Suddenly it struck me that I'd never seen her without makeup—without clothes, without shame, without her wits about her, but never without that shield of foundation and liner. Interesting. I stood in the doorway, blocking her entrance and watching as she dealt with the rejection I'd just handed her—only the second time I'd done that since we'd known each other. She stared at me, her thick, spidery lashes heavy over narrowed eyes, and then a smile played over her lips and she shrugged, seemingly unconcerned that I'd just shot her down. But I knew her just enough to know where to look, and her hands that gripped her purse were white at the knuckles.

Then she eased her grip and took another step forward, her body pressed securely to mine, her heavy perfume filling my nostrils. I waited for the memories to slam me again, for the desire that had always been so strong in the past to rush through me. Instead, all I could see was Mia's face after I'd kissed her the first time, hear her whisper my name the first time I'd touched her under the stars, when she'd finally trusted me enough to tell me who she was. Those images made everything I'd done and the person I'd been fade until all that was left was the person I wanted to be.

"How come you never come around anymore? You haven't been to a party in months."

"I've got a lot going on—not a lot of time for partying."

"You used to always make time." Her hand reached out and streaked up the front of my practice jersey, her voice going even lower. "The parties have been lonely without you."

"You've never been lonely, Sarah."

Her eyes snapped to mine and her hand stopped on its wayward journey back down south. "Don't be a dick, Ryan. Before you started dating Mia fucking Evans you weren't complaining. In fact, you were begging, and before long, she'll be off to college with all of those other Stanford geniuses and you'll be here, playing baseball and begging me to get you off, just like I always have."

I was left reeling as she stepped back, barely noticing as she turned to walk down the steps to her car. As usual, her darts were sharp and well-aimed—in a span of two minutes, she'd made me face the one thing that scared me more than not having Mia: not deserving her. She was going to Stanford, there would be a thousand other guys more suited to her, definitely more suited to her parents and what they wanted. Why the hell did I think I had a chance when all I wanted to do was play ball for as long as I could?

I looked across the street at the house that was all lit up and thought of her already there, already perfect in some dress that was sure to drive me crazy, already smiling, laughing, following her parents' instructions and living up to their image. And then I thought of her the other night, when she'd come to me because she'd needed me, when she'd wrapped herself around me and told me that not even her dream was her own.

Fuck it. Slamming the door, I bolted upstairs and headed for the shower. Late or not, I was going to see Mia tonight. I wasn't giving this relationship up without a fight, and certainly not because some crazy girl I used to sleep with had the uncanny ability to make me doubt myself. Tonight was about Mia, *just* Mia. After that, well, I'd wait and see.

Chapter Nineteen
Mia

Jonathan Petersen was no longer the small and socially awkward boy I remembered, with his dark clothes and darker moods. He'd grown since we had last seen each other, but that was expected. His arms and shoulders were still narrow and thin, though, a fact I think he tried to hide by wearing a cashmere argyle sweater over a striped blue and white button down. The combination of the two made it appear as if he was coming or going for a sail, but I didn't think it polite to ask if that was actually the case. The tail of his shirt peaked out from beneath the sweater just the right amount to rest against his perfectly pleated chinos. He was a direct replica of the Ralph Lauren models, with his perfectly coiffed hair that was just long enough for him to run his fingers through, while falling directly back into place after he did so, who wore too much cologne and showed all of his teeth when he laughed.

Which he did, constantly.

Everything was a great joke to Jonathan. Swiss boarding schools, college, Verrado, coming home, you name it. Nothing kept him from throwing back his head and barking out a laugh that had me cringing back a step and dodging spittle. Then he would lean down and repeat himself once or twice, as if what was said the first time was so funny it needed to be said again in order to really be enjoyed.

"I mean, hockey, crazy right? People are always throwing fists and slamming into boards, but the minute the coach saw me step on the ice, he said I was a natural."

This was another thing that accompanied all of his stories. It appeared Jonathan was a *natural* at everything. School, traveling, languages, hockey. And as the number of vodka sodas he consumed rose—drinking ages were so juvenile, didn't you know—so did the number of his many talents.

"It's so great being back in the states," Jonathan continued, while I contemplated the best exit strategy. My last few had failed, my pitiful attempt at making some excuse not even heard as Jonathan continued to talk over me. I was beginning to think my mother had given him a quick lesson before I arrived: *Margaret Evans's Abridged Guide on How to Steamroll Mia.*

Now, his hand was at my shoulder, holding me hostage and causing me to resort to plotting a diversion for escape. Then I could go find Cora and murder her for deserting me for a cute waiter while I was trapped in suburbia's definition of Hell.

"I mean, there are just some things that are better when they're done in America, right? Like the movies. God, I can't tell you how sick of subtitles I am. Not that I didn't understand what they were saying, as I said, I mastered the language no problem, but really, how boring is it when English is so much easier to understand?"

"Especially when we pilfer so many of our words from other languages," I muttered.

"What was that?"

"I couldn't agree more," I said and he nodded before continuing.

I tuned him out and searched the crowd for Cora. I spotted her in the corner by the double doors which were left open to invite guests to sit by the pool and enjoy the pretty desert air. She had a cocktail in her hand, so her flirtation must have been successful. I watched as she tipped her head back and let out a long laugh before touching her hand to the bartender's arm. Annoyed for reasons beyond me that she was having fun, I stared at her until I thought my eyes would bore holes into her back. It took over a minute for her to glance back at me, and when she did, I raised my eyebrows at her and gave a "get over here" look. She smiled and I glared, satisfied when she finally leaned up to whisper something in the bartender's ear before turning her back with a sashay of hip and wandering toward me.

"Cora, how lovely to see you." I vised my hand on her wrist in order to keep her from escaping, holding her much as Jonathan was holding me. She raised her eyebrows and sipped from her glass, her red lipstick leaving a small smudge on the rim.

"Eager to kiss me at midnight, Cousin? Sorry to disappoint, but even I haven't resorted to girls yet."

"I'd pay to see the likes of you two getting together," Jonathan interrupted with a loud guffaw and I winced. Cora raised her eyebrow at me and I widened mine, hoping she would understand the level of my desperation.

She sighed. "Fine, but you'll owe me."

"Name it."

"I'll think about it and get back to you."

Then she made me want to weep with gratitude as she slid her arm seductively through Jonathan's and began to talk to him in her low voice, laughing as he laughed, all the while steering him outside toward the pool and away from me.

The tug of guilt came fast and sharp as I watched them disappear around the corner, even as the relief washed over me. I'd go find them soon, I told myself. I just needed a minute to relax, to breathe, and to get the smell of Jonathan's Dolce cologne out of my nostrils.

Now that I wasn't searching for an escape route, I took a second to notice the people around me. Surveying the room, my gaze skimmed over Aunt Suzie who was now plastered to Uncle James's side as she nursed what was most likely her third cocktail of the hour while listening intently to a man I recognized but couldn't name. I watched her for a minute, noting her eyes—usually sad—had become hard and glowing after a drink, and the features that should have been strikingly similar to my own mother's were not because everything about her had been cut down to the bone after her last little tuck. Her cheekbones were too pronounced, her lips a little too large, her neck painfully taught. Her hair was platinum, like her daughter's, and worn a little shorter in a sassy bob that would have been cute if not for the spiked, hard look of it.

For a moment, I felt a stirring of pity as I watched her. She didn't want to age. Aunt Suzie wanted to be young and gorgeous forever, and because of that she'd peeled away all of the natural beauty she'd once possessed and covered it up with eye lifts and lip plumps and Botox injections that left her face looking like a sad doll. I sighed, wondering what it was about our family that made us so fierce to hold onto what was instead of being able to embrace the possibilities of what could be.

Without an answer for that particular question at the moment, I continued my scan, finding my own mother and father. They stood next to each, as close as two people could be physically without touching. Watching them, I noted the way they both spoke to the couples around them, the way they moved as a unit, making their way across the room, speaking with each person who crossed their path, and still, they never touched. My father said a few words, my mother followed with a smile and comment of her own, and then they moved on in their choreographed dance of duty.

Not once did their hands brush or their eyes meet—never did they stop and share a private word or a secret between just the two of them. They were strangers. Strangers who had shared almost twenty-seven years together, two homes, and five children, but who couldn't share a conversation, or a casual gesture of affection. Everything they were, everything they had been, had all been whittled down to who they were in name only. They weren't a couple, not in the sense that a couple should be. They were a merger, a successful business, and seeing them together made me realize that everything I had told Ryan was true.

Nothing was going to fix my family—not me, not Stanford, not anything.

And I was sick of trying.

That thought was as liberating as it was terrifying. Turning, I ignored the people around me as I walked through the kitchen and out the garage door, making what had now become the familiar trek across the street. I didn't question it this time, though, didn't question that I was making the same choice as Joe, that I was turning my back on my family and taking what I wanted. This time when I knocked on the door, I wasn't afraid, I wasn't nervous. I was sure.

Even when I had to knock again, nerves didn't threaten. Instead, pleasure bloomed warm and comforting inside of me when I heard a thud, a curse, and then the unlocking of the door from the inside before it was wrenched open. Ryan stood on the other side of the threshold, wearing nothing but a pair of black suit pants that hung on low on his hips, and a scowl. The scowl left his face immediately when he saw me, replaced by a slow smile that I barely registered as I stared at him shamelessly.

Sweet mother of God.

If I had conjured up a potion for a way to forget my night, it might not have been as effective as the sight of Ryan Murphy, shirtless and barefoot, with water droplets still glistening on his chest.

I'd never paid much attention to Cora as she ogled boys, had never given much credence to her rants about how a guy's body could make her melt. I just figured she was exaggerating. Now, though, staring at Ryan in black dress pants and nothing else, I realized that I may have been a little quick to dismiss the affect a well-toned body could have on a girl.

"Evans, I was just getting ready to come see you."

I nodded, unsure that I could find my voice as I continued to stare.

"Is something wrong?"

I blinked at the sound of his voice, ripping my gaze away from his stomach and raising my eyes to his. Blushing as he grinned, I shook my head. "I'm sorry, what?"

He laughed and reached out to take my hand, pulling me inside and closing the door behind me before leaning into me, giving me no choice but to wrap my arms around his warm, hard middle.

"Don't be sorry, I was enjoying the view myself. Nice dress."

I didn't have time to form the words thank you before his lips were on mine and his hands were in my hair. In the heels I wore I was closer to eye level with him, making it easier to stretch on my toes and close the rest of the distance. My arms snaked up his chest and linked behind his neck as I lost myself to the kiss.

Never had I dreamed that I would feel like this, not about anyone. Not *with* anyone. I had long ago decided that Joe had lost himself when he fell in love with Morgan, as Cora lost herself to anyone who was willing to love her for the evening, just as my mother had lost herself to my father. I was never going to lose myself, never going to let someone else be the reason I was unhappy. But kissing Ryan, feeling his hands roam over me as though I were a precious piece of artwork to be memorized and savored, I realized I wasn't losing myself. In fact, for the first time in too long, I felt as though I had been found.

When he released me, I stumbled back a step and had to lean against the door for support. He came with me, his hands caging me in as they landed on either side of my head. I tilted my chin up, courage I'd never felt before making me bold, but he avoided my lips, instead cruising his over my cheek, my jaw, down the line of my throat to my collarbone and back up again, where he the rested his forehead on mine.

"Hi."

I smiled. "Hi."

"Missed you."

Simple words, said simply, and still, they were just what I needed to erase the leftover cold from my parents' house. Everything inside of me went from tingling to melting and I opened my eyes to look at him. His were serious, dark with the passion he had just shown me, and completely steady on mine.

"It's only been a week."

"That's six days too long, Evans," he said and bent to kiss me again. My breath hitched a little and he pulled away to nip at my lips. "Didn't you miss me, too?"

Too much. He was all I'd thought about tonight and every night since Thanksgiving, but rather than tell him that, I shrugged. "Maybe a little."

He leaned back to raise his eyebrows at me. "A little?"

I bit the inside of my cheek. "I guess I thought of you, once or twice."

"Oh yeah?"

I nodded. "I wondered if you finished your paper for English, what grade you got."

He paused halfway to my lips and quirked his eyebrow. "Is that it? You thought of me and wondered how I was doing in school?" I nodded and his eyes got deeper. When he bent his head toward mine, I leaned forward to meet his lips, but he evaded, moving over to my neck. "You didn't think about this?"

I shook my head, and then sucked in a breath when he pulled away, instinctively going with him so that my body was pressed against his. I saw the gleam of triumph in his eyes before his mouth was on mine again. "Liar."

I nodded and this time I pulled his lips down to mine, greedy to taste him again, to feel that reckless, energized, drugged sensation. This is what I wanted, this passion, this need, this desire. Seeing my parents together had only made me realize just how much.

"I was on my way over to your house," he said as he pulled away. "Sorry I was late—practice was hellacious and then I was unexpectedly detained."

"I don't want to be around other people right now," I told him and saw his eyes widen briefly before going dark.

He didn't reach out to me and make my decision easier, he didn't do anything except look at me and wait. The choice was mine. For the first time in my life, I knew that, and even as it scared me to the bone, it invigorated me, freed me. He freed me.

Stepping forward, I stretched up to my toes and brought his mouth to mine, playing my lips over his even as he tried for control again.

"Mia," he began, but I wouldn't let him finish. Not tonight. He wasn't pulling back tonight because it was my choice, and I chose him.

"Are your parents home?" I asked, and his already rigid body stiffened until I was afraid it would snap.

"No," he said, and his voice was gruff and low. "They're at the Club for the night. Mia," he began again, but I stopped him by bringing my mouth to his and wrapping my arms around him in a move that brought our bodies together in one long line.

"Be with me, Ryan." I wasn't a brave person by nature, but instead of fear, I felt nothing but desire, nothing but need. For him, for this, for us.

His breathing became more labored and his eyes more intense as he stared at me. "I don't want to hurt you," he whispered and I smiled as I heard the fear in his voice. Strange that it was me who wasn't scared. "I want you so much, Mia, but I don't want to hurt you, not in any way. You have to be sure."

"I *am* sure, for the first time in my life. I'm making a choice just for me, Ryan, and I know that it's the right one."

He stared at me a second longer, his eyes intense as they stayed on mine. And then he exhaled loudly before pulling me against him a second before his mouth was on mine and his hands were in my hair. I met his demands, rising to my toes again as he brought me closer, wrapping my arms around his neck and sinking in to him.

His hands loosened enough to slide down to my hips and the back of my thighs, boosting me up until my legs were wrapped around his waist. He broke our kiss long enough to look at me, as if reassuring himself that what he was seeing was right, that we were real. I leaned in and kissed him again and he turned toward the stairs.

Chapter Twenty
Ryan

As I walked up the stairs to my room, my heart hammered and I stopped at the entrance to kick the door closed and kiss her one more time.

"You got your door back."

"Mmhmm. Last week. Thanks to the B- on my English paper."

I walked over to the bed and laid her down gently, settling my weight to the side. When she trembled lightly, I brought my hand to her cheek and swept her hair off of her face so it splayed out over my pillow as I'd imagined countless times. For the first time since I had opened the door tonight and seen her, I saw nerves dance in her eyes.

"Mia, we don't have to do this."

But she shook her head and tilted her face up for a kiss. "Be with me, Ryan. Be my first."

Christ. Everything inside of me tightened until I thought I would explode. I didn't know if this was right for her, but I did know I'd never felt like this, never needed like this and I couldn't stop myself from taking her lips with my own, from running my hand down her body and molding her figure as I brought it back up and under the hem of her dress, all along the smooth length of her thigh to her hip.

Her first. I'd been a lot of things in my life, but never that. Not with Sarah or any of the few other girls I'd hooked up with. It made me feel like a pussy that the thought of being Mia's first, her only, made me want to run as much as it made me want to stay. She deserved special, more than anyone else deserved anything, Mia deserved for this to be special, and since I was past the point of being able to walk away, of slowing this down, I was going to do my best to see that she got it.

I touched her gently, slowly, kissing her the entire time as my hands began to explore her in ways I'd dreamed of for so long. Her skin was soft and smooth and golden, and when I drew back long enough to unzip her dress, I saw the wonder and the fear in her eyes again. Forcing myself to go slowly, I didn't tear at the fabric, didn't remove anything else, I just kissed her, letting my hands roam over the newly exposed flesh.

When she relaxed in my arms again, I gently drew down the dress, sliding it past her hips and down the length of her legs until she was laying on my bed in nothing but her bra and panties. I took my time studying her, and wondered that my heart didn't burst from the sheer beauty that was Mia Evans. Her hair was fanned out over my pillow, its golden mass surrounding her so that she looked like some sort of goddess. Her eyes were wide and dark and a little unsure as she stared at me, her hands clenched together tightly over her flat abdomen, just above the low line of her white lace panties. Unable to resist any longer, I leaned forward and placed my lips on her neck, tasting her skin as I made my way down to her collarbone, lower until I could dip in between the fabric of her white lace bra.

Her breath hitched, her body tensed and I moved my lips back to hers, letting my hands roam until I felt her lose herself once again. When her own hands slipped over my back, gently pulling me closer, I shifted so that I covered her completely, the feeling of her skin sliding over mine almost enough to make me lose control.

My lips trailed down her body once more, following my hands as they stroked her skin, removing the barriers of her clothing and mine until we were pressed together with nothing between us. Her hands were less hesitant as they explored now, streaking over my back and lower, touching me until I was forced to roll her and pin her with my weight to keep from going insane. My lips played over hers as I found a condom and protected us, and her breathing shuddered out as my fingers and lips slid over her, preparing her, making sure that she was as lost in sensation as I.

And when we finally came together, when I heard her sob out my name, when I felt myself falling, I knew this was as much my first time as it was hers.

~

Later, as I walked her home, her hand clasped firmly in mine, the fireworks exploded around us. Stopping, I pulled her close and kissed her once more, unable to get enough. Her lips that had all but brought me to my knees earlier were hesitant and shy, as though she was remembering everything we'd just done.

Minutes, hours, I don't know how long we stood there in the middle of the street between my house and hers, wrapped in one another. I pressed my lips to her temple and brought her closer, still not able to believe that she was really here, and that she was mine.

"Happy new year," she whispered, placing a shy kiss on my jaw.

"Happy new year, Evans," I whispered back, and we stood, her snuggled against my chest with her head on my shoulder, and me with my arms around her, while the new year rained in around us.

Chapter Twenty-One
Mia

"I can't believe he just parked it on my couch and wouldn't leave." Nina rolled her eyes and sipped from her can of soda while she leaned on the reservations desk at the Inn where I was entering new guests into the system. It was New Year's Day, and I was working since Shane had called and begged me to cover his shift at the desk.

"Mia, I'm serious, I think I have the flu."

Since it was pre six a.m. when he called, I hadn't been happy with his excuse. "The flu, really, that's what you're going with? Did this flu keep you from going out last night?"

I heard a muffled groan and a higher pitched giggle. "If that's the flu, I recommend a visit to the doctor for a shot. You never know how bad it can be. You owe me," I said and clicked off without waiting for his response. Cora burrowed deeper into bed, mumbling something incoherent about payments and debts, so I left her a note telling her to meet me at the Inn around lunchtime before getting out of bed and going to do Shane's work.

Really, it wasn't that bad. Leaving early this morning gave me an excuse not to rehash the evening with my mother, or anyone else. I didn't know what I would say to Cora when she asked where I'd gone. I had to tell her the truth, but how much? What Ryan and I had done last night…I'd only been kissed by one other person in my life, and it didn't really count since it was in the seventh grade and it was more like being resuscitated than kissed. Nothing about being with Ryan made me feel like I was being saved—if anything, I felt as though I were drowning, one slow foot at a time, but every time I tried to climb my way back to the surface, he did something that pulled me under again. I was starting to wonder if I even wanted to get to the surface.

Being with him last night wasn't just about what we'd done physically, it was about everything—it was about feeling more than I wanted to feel and knowing I wasn't about to walk away. I knew I was on a road to disaster, and I still wasn't ready or willing to let it go. No matter what happened, I was determined that whatever time I had with him would be time I took, so that the next time I was somewhere doing something that was expected of me, living the life my parents had mapped out, I could look back on my memories of him and know that for a little while, I had been with someone who only thought of me. And I had been happy.

Now I realized why people kept picture frames with friends and frozen moments in them, not just monuments or paintings like in my family. Ryan was that moment, the one where I could move on from now and in five years look at the frame and remember the New Year's Eve when I had laid in his arms after sharing a part of myself with him that I'd never shared with anyone else, my head on his chest and his arms around me while our heartbeats made one rhythm. In that memory, I knew I would find joy, because no matter how our relationship ended, it was one of passion, one of need and love. It didn't even scare me to say it. I loved Ryan Murphy, and when I could no longer have him, I knew just the memory of what it felt like to love him, the overwhelming sensation of what he gave me, would be enough to sustain me through everything else.

"Mia, are you even listening to me?"

I snapped myself back to the present and looked up at Nina, guilt swamping me. "Sorry, I was thinking about these reservations. Give me just one minute and Cora will be here for lunch. Then we can talk about it when I'm totally focused."

She nodded, unconvinced as her eyes scrutinized my face. "I'll just go sit outside by the pool and bake away my misery with the rest of the skin cancer supporters."

"Get your tan on," I said as she marched away. Nina never left her house without putting SPF 50 on, and even then she had a long sleeve cardigan with her that I knew would be on before she stepped out on the pool deck.

Focused again, I looked at the computer screen in front of me, marking down the number of people and the dates, whether any of the groups had children under the age of twelve, looking for any special requests or comments before saving and shutting down.

"I'm done for the day, so I'm going to grab some lunch with Cora and Nina by the pool," I told Shane, who had finally arrived ten minutes ago.

He nodded. "Thanks for coming in this morning and taking care of things."

My eyebrows shot up as I stopped to give him a once over. "You seem to be feeling better. Get a shot for that flu?"

He grinned. "Nope, but I might just have a run in with it again tonight."

"Two nights in a row, that's a record for you."

"Yeah, what can I say? When you've caught it, there's no letting it go."

I shook my head as I walked to the pool, dumbfounded at the thought of Shane picking up yet another girl. This was normal for him, so I felt a tug of sympathy for whatever girl he was seeing. She was probably halfway in love, and he was showing her that he was, too. And he probably was, for now. Shane was a classic runaway, though. A week, two tops, and he would be pulling away, glad to have had his fun but ready for something different. Some girls were okay with it, but there were some who weren't ready to let go and those were the ones who came to work looking for him. It was never a pretty scene when one of them started crying—or worse, begging. Once, one of them had come in quiet as a mouse, thrown a vase at Shane, missing him by inches, then walked out again, never uttering a word. We told my mother that a rambunctious family had bumped into the end table and broken the vase, but I had to admit, I was impressed with the girl's flare for the dramatic.

Inexplicably, Ryan popped into my head again and I wondered if I would have enough gumption to throw a vase at him—or rage at him and tell him we weren't over. Never before had I thought I wanted to be that dramatic, that passionate, but thinking about last night, about how it had felt to be held by him, kissed by him, *touched* by him, I realized that there were a lot of things that I had never wanted before that I wanted now.

Pulling my phone out of my pocket, I stopped midway onto the deck as I stared at an empty inbox. No texts, no emails, no voicemails. It was just past noon and my mother hadn't tried to contact me once. Although relieved, a part of me wondered over her silence as I stepped the rest of the way onto the deck and found the table where Cora and Nina waited. Nina was sitting in the one spot that was completely shaded, her long sleeve cardigan on and buttoned, stuffing soup and bread into her mouth while sipping from a fresh soda. Cora sat next to her, gingerly sipping from a glass of water while she leaned back in the sunshine, sunning her bare arms and legs.

"Cousin," she said when I sat down and smiled at Robby the waiter as he set a bottle of water in front of me. "Why didn't you tell me Jonathan Petersen was a raving lunatic? We did shots of peach schnapps all night long. Who, under the age of sixty, drinks peach schnapps?"

"I thought the fact that I all but begged you to take him off my hands was the first hint that he wasn't completely sane. His laugh should have been the second."

She winced and rubbed her temple. "Please, don't remind me of the laugh. My head hurts enough already."

"Barbie, why didn't you just stop drinking?"

"Why didn't you just kick Max out?" Cora shot back. I saw her smirk when Nina scowled into her soup and said nothing. "That's right. Because it's not as easy to do the smart thing as it is to say *how* to do the smart thing."

"That doesn't even make sense," Nina grumbled.

"Sure it does," I answered and paused long enough to order the artichoke and tomato salad.

Cora cringed. "Christ, don't you eat anything that isn't grown in dirt? I'll have the cheeseburger, rare, with fries and more water. A pitcher would be ideal, actually." I saw Robby smile as he finished taking our orders.

"So tell me the story, Nina. What did Max do that was so horrible?"

"Parked himself on her doorstep and refused to leave until she let him in," Cora answered. "Some people would consider that romantic and may choose to enjoy it rather than complain about it."

Nina raised her eyebrows and flagged down the waiter. "Can I have another coke with a shot of peach syrup in it?" Then she motioned to me and Cora with a broad smile on her face. "Anyone else? A shot of peach to go in your drink?"

Cora shook her head and sipped from her water. "Well played," she said when it was just us again. "I won't make fun of you again if you promise to cancel that."

Nina smiled. "I won't cancel, but I'll keep it on my side of the table."

"Fair enough."

"Now that we've settled the argument, children, can we get back to the romantic story?"

"No, not romantic, Mia," Nina said. "*Annoying.* Use the right word. Romance is for stories, annoyance is for Max Canfield."

"What happened?"

She took a deep breath, like a diver going under for the second time before she pushed her bowl away and glugged the rest of her soda down. Switching to the doctored one that had just been set beside her, she drank again. I watched Cora lean back a little more and had to smile.

"I tried to ignore him," she finally said, "but he stayed out on the porch for almost an hour and I was afraid someone was going to call the cops on him. Which would have served him right. What's wrong with him?" she demanded and slammed down the spoon that she'd been using to stir her soda. "Didn't I already tell him I wasn't interested? Oh, he thinks he's clever, telling me he needed help with his physics homework. The idiot already had his packet completely filled out."

I bent over my salad to hide my smile.

"So, maybe he needed you to check his answers," Cora said, liberally salting her fries. After one bite, she groaned. "Thank Jesus, I might live after all."

Nina ignored her own food and sat with her eyes narrowed and her elbows on either side of her plate as she leaned forward. "That's what I thought, but like I'm about to check his answers when my packet's not done yet so he can think I cheated off of him. And you know what he does when I tell him that?"

I looked over at her. "What?"

"He said 'okay, you finish your packet and I'll wait.'" Her eyes were wide with disbelief and her wrists turned over so her palms were face up as she stared at us. "Then he just sat down on the couch, grabbed the chips and watched that annoying Ryan Seacrest and the rest of the New York City idiots bring in the New Year."

When Cora and I both laughed, her irritation only increased. "This is not funny. Do you know he didn't leave until after one o'clock and then when he did, he…he…" she trailed off, her face red, her brow furrowed. But it wasn't irritation that crossed her face. I set my fork down and looked at her more intently. There was embarrassment, a little shyness, and definitely pleasure.

"For Christ's sake, Nina, tell us what he did," Cora demanded.

"He kissed me," she blurted out and buried her face in her hands.

My eyes popped wide and Cora let out a hoot of pleasure. Nina hunched her shoulders and shook her head, her hand still covering her face.

"Kissed you how?" I asked when I could find my voice.

She jerked her shoulder once and finally looked up from her hands. "The normal way, I guess. How should I know?"

I put my hand on hers to settle her. "On the cheek?" She shook her head and her eyes filled with tears. I leaned back while she sniffled and rubbed her eyes. Tears for Nina were like snow in Hawaii—something you've heard could happen but you never expected to see.

"I believe this is my field of expertise, Cousin," Cora said and, apparently feeling better after her meal, smiled as she leaned forward. "Was there tongue involved?"

"Oh, God," Nina said and buried her face again.

"I'll take that as a yes, which means you had to have kissed him back, Nina Torres, because if you had been fighting him off, he wouldn't have had time to slip you the slippery one."

When we heard a sniffle, I looked at Cora and widened my eyes. She rolled hers but placed her hand gently on Nina's shoulder. "Nina, why are you crying? It was just a kiss."

"From Max Canfield," she sniffled again and sat up, scrubbing at her eyes until they were burning dry. "Why would he do this to me? Why would he kiss me and pretend to need my help and spend his entire night with me?"

"Because he likes you," I said gently and she laughed.

"Mia, this is Max we're talking about. He was just messing with me at the movies."

"No, he wasn't. He likes you, Nina. Why else would he enter into a Fun Run that you're at? Or go to the movies and only talk to you? Or purposely find eight ways a class period to annoy you so that you turn around and yell at him?"

The shock registered with my statement, leaving her face pale and her eyes dark. "But why?" she asked again. "Why now, all of a sudden? Nothing about me has changed."

I tried to find the right words to explain without scaring her off, but before I came up with an answer, Cora spoke.

"Maybe it's not about you, Nina. Maybe it's about him." When their eyes met, Cora smiled and gave her hand a reassuring squeeze in one of her rare and comforting moments. "Maybe it's his turn to look and see—not just notice, but really see what we all see. You're hot, girl, despite the fact that you dress like my grandmother."

The last part was meant to make Nina smile, but she didn't. Instead, she looked even more terrified. Cora sighed and shrugged. "There are worse things in the world than having an adorable and brilliant guy like you enough to kiss you."

She shook her head in denial at first, but I saw the understanding on her face, and the fear. "But what if he doesn't?" she finally asked. "What if he doesn't really like me and he's just doing this because he can? What then?"

"We ruin him," Cora said and raised her glass. Nina's lips finally curved into a smile as she raised her own glass and tapped it to Cora's.

"I'm smart enough to do it without ever getting caught."

"That's more like it. Kind of horrifying, but a nice change altogether. Now, Cousin, let's get out of this godforsaken heat and go back to your house and gorge on the chocolate your mother doesn't know you have. I'm almost through my hangover."

Chapter Twenty-Two
Ryan

Capture the flag was a tradition for the baseball team, and had been for the last several years when Coach decided we needed something a little less grown up to do with our time during the season. Translation: we needed something to occupy our time and keep us away from the parties.

So every year at the beginning of the season once teams were picked, we divided into outfield and infield, JV and Varsity combined, and we took over the town. Seniors were the only players allowed to bring a girlfriend, and when I opened the door to Mia on the last Saturday in February, I'll admit I thought about ditching the whole plan and yanking her inside to occupy her time with more pleasurable endeavors. Even in black workout gear, the girl was gorgeous.

Without giving her time to say anything, I tugged her inside and fused my lips to hers, grateful that my parents were out for the night and I didn't have to worry about holding back. It had been too long since I'd touched her, really touched her, and seeing her now made me want to do nothing more than kick the door closed and have my way with her.

If I thought what I felt for Mia was intense before we were together, it was a pale shadow in comparison to what I felt for her now. Everything I did, she was right there in the back of my mind, and uncontrollably, I'd be remembering what it felt like to be pressed against her, to watch and feel as she came apart against me. To know that I was the only one who'd ever made her feel like that.

Even now, almost two months after our New Year together, I could still recall every detail with vivid accuracy, and it was driving me insane. We hadn't had enough time together since that night, although I'd done my best to get her alone. With my increased time spent at the field getting it ready for the season that would begin next week, and her increased workload with track starting, we'd only been able to carve out a two nights together, and instead of easing this need inside of me, those brief meetings had only stoked it until it flamed brighter and stronger than before.

And it wasn't just a physical need, though I'd never known it could be like this with anyone, a craving that consumed me until I thought I would die if I didn't touch her. No, beyond that was the need to just be with her, to talk to her, hear her voice and laugh as she fought embarrassment for the things I would remind her of. Nothing was more enticing than Mia when she was blushing.

Like she was doing now as I pulled away. She buried her head in my shoulder and inhaled, her body curving into mine and making me rethink my commitment to the team. Really, one missed night of bonding wasn't going to kill me.

But then she was pulling back and raising her eyebrows at me, and the moment was light again.

"Are we robbing a bank on our way there?" she asked and I quirked my brow in question. She motioned to my outfit. "What's with the backpack? And the face paint? The ninja attire?"

"We're playing capture the flag—our goal is to be covert and unseen." I motioned to her clothing. "I thought I told you to wear black."

She raised her eyebrows and stretched out her arms. "I am," she said and indicated to her black workout capris and black and white half-zip jacket.

"All black, I mean. Evans, the point of capture the flag is to get the other team's flag without being noticed. You're white stripes are going to light up like a beacon out there."

"That's their purpose," she said with a frown. "I run at night—it's safer this way."

"Trust you to think of safety first," I mumbled. "Give me a second." I took the stairs to my room two at a time. Snagging a black sweatshirt from my closet, I jogged back down and found her standing in the same spot right inside the door.

"Take off your jacket," I told her and held out the sweatshirt. When she complied without hesitation, her fingers automatically lowering the half zipper before she peeled it over head and was left standing there in nothing but a black tank top that bared her midriff and arms, I tried not to groan. Everything inside of me was urging me to skip tonight and stay here, exploring her as I hadn't had the chance to do since our first night together.

And then I looked up and saw the shy smile on her lips, the uncertainty that was written across her face, and I reined myself in. She was different, and tonight, I would prove to her and everyone else exactly how different.

"Put this on," I said and handed her the sweatshirt. When she slipped it over her head, it fell to her knees and well past her hands, making me laugh when she held her arms out for inspection. Opening the can of face paint, I swiped some under her eyes despite her squeal and then snuck one last kiss in.

"Now you're ready, killer. Let's go."

Chapter Twenty-Three
Mia

I knew I was nuts when I pulled out my phone and texted my mother willingly on a Saturday night when I was out with my boyfriend. A boyfriend, I might add, that she knew nothing about. Yet, here I was, sitting in the passenger's seat of Ryan's truck, texting my mother because I hadn't seen or heard from her since this morning. The truth: I was worried about her because her overly enthusiastic, helicopter parenting was now lowering to an almost non-existent level. She hadn't hovered at the door to ask me where I was going and who I was going out with tonight, and I hadn't gotten a text about homework in weeks.

I didn't know what was crazier: that I cared or that I was texting her about it.

Of course, crazy appeared to be part of who I was these days, I thought as I looked over at Ryan in his black gear, and then down at myself.

The fact that I was wearing a sweatshirt three sizes too big, face paint that was sure to clog my pores, and going to spend the night playing a game that was usually reserved for elementary school kids should definitely make me want to rethink my mental stability, or in the very least, my relationship with Ryan. But it didn't.

Nothing had been the same since that day he'd begged me to tutor him. It had been better, and in the past two months I'd discovered something about myself that shocked me more than anything, even the physical relationship I had with Ryan: I was a fun person.

I wasn't as outgoing as Ryan, by any means, and it was true that I was still a rule follower for most things, saying no to him more than I said yes, ignoring my desire to be around him in order to complete homework, tutoring, and leadership duties. But on nights like tonight, when we could be together, it never failed to amaze me how comfortable I was with him.

And with myself. This was, perhaps, the biggest surprise of all. When I was with Ryan, I didn't feel the constant awareness of what I was lacking. Gone was the fear that what and who I was wasn't enough, and instead, I found myself understanding what they meant when they said *comfortable*. With Ryan, I was comfortable with who I was, and it was as strange a feeling as this physical desire he had awakened within me.

There were cars and people already in the parking lot at the high school when we pulled up. Getting out of my side, I ignored the urge to check my phone again and went around the front to meet Ryan, stopping mid stride when I saw Nina standing there glaring at Max as he held her hand securely in his and chattered on and on with Brian Mendiola about the team.

"Looks like he did it," Ryan said and I looked up at him.

"Did what?"

"Got Torres to go out with him. Apparently, her last answer was that she'd rather drink motor oil for breakfast, or something to that affect."

I grimaced. "That sounds like Nina."

"He won't let me go," she said the minute I walked over to stand next to her. She yanked her hand again, only to have Max tighten his grip and look over his shoulder and give her a wink before going back to his conversation. "He met me at the air force base today—God only knows how he found me there—and then he followed me back to my house like some kind of stalker and asked my parents if it was okay if we hung out tonight."

"Stalkers don't generally talk to their prey's family and ask for permission," I pointed out and earned a glare.

"What's with the face paint?"

I shrugged and watched as Ryan went over to another group of guys and started talking to them. "Ryan put it on me. Apparently, the outfit I was in earlier wasn't ninja enough."

"Oh, yeah, well, at least he just put paint on your face. Max came up to my room and picked out my clothes for me. He didn't even ask me if I wanted to come on this stupid extravaganza in the first place, and then he had the guts to go up to my room and pick out my clothes."

"Nina," Max said as he turned around. "I would ask if you would say yes, but since I know you won't, going around you is the only way."

"Maybe I don't want to hang out," she said through clenched teeth. And then Max did something I never thought I'd see in a million years. He bent down and pressed his lips firmly to hers, effectively shutting off her complaints.

"Maybe, I don't care because I want to hang out with you. Deal with it." With that he walked over where Ryan was, almost making it the whole way without tripping, and began talking while Nina and I stood there in our different states of shock.

She recovered first, enough to clear her throat and look up at me. "I can't get a handle on what he's doing. He's everywhere, all the time now. First, he spent all of January ignoring me, acting like he never kissed me. Then, he starts reminding me of it, like all of a sudden he feels like remembering. And now this—all of these 'dates.' This whole week he's been running into me in different places, irritating me into talking to him, maneuvering me until we're running a math study group together. We're meeting tomorrow at the coffee house at eleven." She took off her glasses and rubbed her eyes. "I don't know why he's doing this—he's proved his point, he can get to me. I think New Year's proved that. And you know what's worse? I don't know why I'm letting him. I could leave right now, or I could not show up tomorrow for the study group."

"But you won't do that," I said, understanding.

She shook her head. "No, because for some insane reason I like being with him, even when he irritates me so much I want to punch him in the face. Is that crazy?"

I looked over at Ryan and thought of how much he had come to mean to me in the past few months, of how much I wanted to be with him even when I knew I shouldn't. I shook my head. "Nothing seems crazy anymore."

An hour later, I was ready to retract that statement.

"This is crazy," I said as I sprinted down another darkened street close on Ryan's heels. Somehow, Ryan and I had been appointed the flag holder for our team. I thought this was a good idea until I realized exactly what that meant: we had to be in constant motion and everyone was coming for us. If they caught us, they could apply any means necessary to get the flag out of Ryan's backpack. Oh joy.

A high pitched laugh came from a few blocks over and Ryan veered to the right, snagging my hand to drag me with him. We came to an abrupt stop in front of a fence that was well over six feet. Breathing heavily after running for the past hour, I put my hands on my head and tilted my chin back. "This is ridiculous."

Ryan stopped next to me, leaning his hands on his knees while he caught his own breath. "What? This? No, it's fun."

Giving in, I mirrored his pose and tried not to think too much about what I looked like. We'd been running pretty much nonstop since the game started, and I was sweaty and out of breath. I was also still unclear exactly why we were running. What happened to the good old days when the people in charge of the flag made a perimeter around it and stayed in one place? The rules I had always used for capture the flag were not anywhere close to those that we were playing by now, and I was beginning to think that the boys' coach had conned them all into an extra workout.

"Fun? Ryan, we've been running down streets and hiding in corners for over an hour while everyone on your team chases us."

"Just the outfield—the infield is on our side."

"What side? I mean, what's the end goal here?" I stood up and eyed the fence. "Do you even know *where* we're running?"

"Of course I know where we're running—we've just had to take some detours on the way there in order to avoid getting caught. We get caught, it's over. They get our flag and the infield loses their three year winning streak."

"God forbid."

He grinned and stood, too, reaching out and snagging me around the waist. "Are you questioning my sense of direction, Evans?"

I couldn't help the smile, or the small shiver that ran through me when he lowered his head and pressed his lips just below my jaw.

"No, just your motives."

He grinned at that and then his lips were on mine and they were no longer teasing but firm and sure, playing over me and taking me to that place that made me forget. My arms snaked up his back and locked around his neck, and my back arched as his hands found the skin beneath my borrowed sweatshirt.

His lips trailed to my neck causing me to shiver as his hands continued to kneed the skin of my lower back. "Mia." He whispered my name quietly, almost reverently as he brought his lips back to mine.

It shouldn't be possible to feel as much as I felt at that moment—to want someone the way I wanted Ryan. I knew I was too far in, and despite what could only be a disastrous ending, I wasn't walking away. At some point I'd become completely his, the person he allowed me to be, and I didn't want to go back to being the Mia I was before Ryan, the one who took directions from everyone around her and never said anything about what she wanted or thought. I knew what I wanted now, and it wasn't to make my parents proud, it wasn't to live up to the Evans name and reputation: it was to be a person, one who lived for something other than status and appearance. One who knew, without a doubt, what it meant to be loved.

I wanted to be exactly who I was at this moment, and I didn't care what the consequences were anymore, though they were sure to be heavy. If I had learned anything in my life, it was that every action had a consequence.

All of the air left my body at this realization, so I was forced to pull back and drag in a deep breath. My chest heaved as I stared up at Ryan, his eyes so dark they were almost black, mine wide with fear and anticipation. As I opened my mouth to say something, anything, to explain what I was feeling, a flashlight and the sound of muffled shouts passed by us and had us both jumping back against the fence.

"Perfect timing," he mumbled under his breath and pressed one last kiss to my lips before pulling away. "We have to get out of here and circle back around toward the school and the baseball field. Max should've smoked out their flag holder already."

Since I had no idea what he was talking about and my mind was still racing as quickly as my heart, I just nodded. Then he crouched down and cupped his hands, holding them out to me in a makeshift basket. "Step in and I'll vault you to the top."

My head cleared enough at that and I took a step back. "Excuse me? Why? Why can't we walk out the way we came in?"

He rolled his eyes. "Because that's what they expect, Evans. They're taunting us, waiting for us to come that way instead of through the golf course and around."

I shook my head, my eyes widening as I backed up. "Golf course? Ryan, are you delusional? It's illegal to be on the golf course past the last tee time."

The only thing that changed in his demeanor was his grin. "Wow, you're cute. *Illegal's* a bit of a harsh word. *Frowned upon* is more accurate, and don't worry, we won't get caught. Come on Evans, up you go so we can win this and I can pick up where we just left off."

I don't know what prompted me to do it—whether it was the promise he made or the grin he wore. I certainly didn't care about winning the game in the first place, and whether or not we got caught by the other team was hardly a life or death situation worthy of jumping fences and trespassing. And yet, I found myself placing my foot in his cupped hands before levering myself onto the top of the fence.

Sitting there balanced, I looked to the other side. "How do I get down?"

"Give me a second to get over and then I'll catch you."

Before I could respond, Ryan stepped back a foot and then launched himself at the fence, vaulting over in one smooth bound. Impressed, I stared at him as he landed on the other side.

"Have you done this before?"

"Well, I wasn't always such an upstanding citizen, Evans. There were times in my past when vaulting a fence was a necessary part of my survival. Here," he said and reached up to put his hands at my waist. "Just fall back. I've got you," he said when I stared at him with a mixture of horror and disbelief on my face. "Trust me, Max has fallen back many times."

I laughed despite myself, and then I took a breath and created another first for my life. I leaned back into him and felt myself lifted and swung down, his arms neatly cradling me as I fell from the fence. Before I could catch my breath, he was dropping me gently to my feet and grabbing my hand, tugging me after him.

~

We won the game, but I have no idea how or why. Apparently, Max had analyzed and done a probability something-or-other that had told him exactly where the outfield's flag would be based on previous games before this, and low and behold, when Ryan and I arrived at the field twenty minutes after jumping the fence and escaping into the golf course, Max already had the other team's flag.

As we walked toward the parking lot, Ryan's arm was around my shoulder and he was whispering in my ear when someone shouted his name. With a groan that vibrated through him into me and sent shiver down my spine, he turned.

"Murph, wait."

"What's up, Sanchez?"

The gangly pitcher stopped in front of us and inclined his head to me. "Hey, Mia, how's it going?"

"I'm good, Manny."

"Sanchez, we were just leaving, so if you don't mind."

Manny shook his head and looked at Ryan. "We have some drunk JV kids, and one of them is trying to drive. He's already taken a swing at Max." Then Manny's eyes skittered to me and back to Ryan, communicating something that had my heart rate spiking.

Ryan's arm dropped from my shoulder as he cussed and raked his hands through his hair. "Where are they?"

"South parking lot by the field."

"I'll drive over and meet you there. Send Nina and Max this way so they can take Mia home."

I shook my head, but Manny had already nodded and started walking away. Ryan took my hand and began to tug me in the opposite direction.

"Ryan, who are the players?" I asked as we got to his truck and he unlocked the passenger side door to throw in his back pack.

"Just some idiot juniors who are pissed they can't make varsity and a couple of younger guys they've taken in."

"Let's go help drive them home, then. I don't need Max and Nina to take me home, Ryan. I can go with you."

He shook his head. "It's better you go. This could take some time and I don't know how many there are that need to be driven home."

He didn't meet my eyes as he closed the door and took out his phone to look at it. When he frowned and tapped a text into the screen, my heart continued its erratic beating and I turned and began walking back toward the field.

"Evans, what are you doing?"

"You're not telling me something, Ryan. I saw it when Manny was talking to you and I can see it now. I live in a family where faking things is like our religion, remember? So, if you want to keep lying to me and trying to ship me off like a little kid, I'll walk over myself."

"Evans," his voice was sharp this time, laced with panic, but I didn't stop. "Mia, goddammit, stop walking. I don't have time for this."

I whirled around when he yanked on my arm. "Then let's go, Ryan. Why wait for Max and Nina to come pick me up when they're already down there? Why not go down there and then pass me off?"

"Just wait by the truck, Mia. I need you to just trust me and wait by the truck for Max and Nina. Please."

"Why, Ryan? Why can't I help? What's going on and don't you dare lie to me." I stepped forward until I could look up into his eyes. And what I saw had my blood going cold. "Are my brothers down there?"

Chapter Twenty-Four
Ryan

I thought about lying. I thought about telling her no and pushing her away so I could deal with it. And then I remembered how much she didn't want to be like her parents and realized the only thing worse than telling her was *not* telling her.

"Yes."

I had to give her credit, she barely flinched even when I could see the words strike her like a blow. She stayed steady, with only the slight tremble of her lower lip to give her away. "Are they both drunk?"

I sighed and shook my head. "No, just Ethan."

"How long?"

"Mia," I said and reached for her. When she looked up at me, her eyes were hard and I stopped, dropping my hands and taking a step back.

"How long has this been going on, Ryan?"

"The first time I helped him was in December. I heard that was only his second time."

"Every weekend?"

I shook my head. "No. More often since January, though. In the past month he's escalated, but I think that's because he's with his teammates more often." Teammates I would deal with, I vowed silently. Standing there, watching her stare at me like I'd betrayed her was reason enough, but knowing what she would see when she went to get Ethan, and I knew she would go and get him, was an even bigger reason. A pleasant drunk the kid was not.

"And Joshua doesn't drink?"

I shook my head again. "From what I've gathered from Caitlin, Joshua goes along to make sure Ethan doesn't do something too idiotic and hurt himself. My guess would be that it was Josh who tipped off Max that they were all trying to drive."

"Caitlin?" she said lowly. "Caitlin knows?"

There wasn't a word to describe just how much of an asshole I felt like as I nodded. If she looked hurt before, she was devastated now.

"And you didn't think I should know? None of you, since I'm assuming Max and Nina had some idea this was going on as well. None of you thought you should tell me that my *fourteen-year-old* little brother was drinking regularly? How weak do you think I am?"

She stormed around me and I grabbed her arm, refusing to be intimidated when she glared at me.

"We don't think you're, weak, Evans, and yeah, we probably should have told you. But shit, Mia, you should see how you look right now, because this is exactly why we didn't, this is exactly why *Ethan* didn't. He knew you'd blame yourself."

"It wasn't your right to protect me."

Fuck that. "Then who's right was it, Mia?" I exploded. "Who else if not me, the person who knows you better than you fucking know yourself sometimes? Who better than the person who loves you more than anyone else? Who better than the person who's been *inside* you?"

Her face went blank, her body slack. Silently, she stared up at me, through me, and shook her head. "I had a right to know, and I have a right to blame myself if I want to, Ryan. He's my brother, which means he's my responsibility, not yours. Neither of us is yours."

I wanted to shake her, to tell her to look again because she was wrong, but I heard Max and Nina approaching, and with them I saw the twins.

"Mia." Josh said her name and she turned, her movements that had been defensive and emotional a moment before now brisk.

"In the car. Both of you. Nina, we need a ride."

Nina's eyes went to me and then back to Mia before she nodded. Taking Max's keys, she said something to him before turning. While they walked to the parking lot, Max came and stood next to me as I watched them go.

"So, I'm guessing that didn't go well."

It wasn't right to laugh, but I did anyway, because for a minute I was afraid I was going to cry as I watched the one girl that had the power to wreck me walk away.

"You could say that." When I saw the headlights to Max's car disappear, I scrubbed my hands over my face and started toward the parking lot. "When I get to Larsen and Katz, I'm going to fucking kill them."

"She'll come around, Murph, just give her time."

I nodded, but a part of me wondered if time was enough to fix us, or if I'd just fucked up the one thing that I cared about most by trying to protect her.

~

A week later, I had my answer.

I stood in the batter's box, staring at Sanchez as he shook off Max's pitch call, and tried not to think about the text Mia had sent me earlier this morning.

Can't make tonight. Busy all day with school and track, then work.

I might understand if she had made small talk, or if she had come to see me at lunch or before school like normal. I might even understand if she had called me and explained what was going on. *Might.* But a lame ass text, the second one this week, where she was blowing me off without a real explanation or a simple *see you later* was too much. Mia was pulling away, and even though I was standing right here, I couldn't do fuck all to stop it.

We hadn't seen each other since last weekend when she had

walked over to thank me for taking care of Ethan when she hadn't. Nothing had hurt as much as watching her stand there while she thanked me politely, her standard society smile in place, treating me like a fucking stranger, not the guy she'd given her virginity to.

When I'd reached for her, she had backed away and said she had to do some things with her family, that she'd call me later so we could talk. That was almost five days ago, and I hadn't received a call, but these goddamn text messages instead, blowing me off and telling me what I already knew without using words: we were over.

Sanchez threw the pitch, and because I wasn't thinking about the ball, I took a hard swing and cut right over it. Stepping out of the box, I let loose a string of cuss words and worked to relax my tensed shoulders.

I didn't know what hurt worse—the fact that she was pulling away, or the fact that she didn't expect me to question it. Or, from door number three, that I'd fucked up our relationship on the same exact night that I'd finally realized that what I felt for her was forever. What Mia was to me wasn't just a girl, she wasn't just a convenience or a good time. She was everything—so much that I had stopped looking at offers from schools on the east coast the minute she'd been accepted to Stanford. I might not be at Stanford, but I'd be somewhere close, because when I saw the next year, I no longer saw just me—I saw me and Mia. The where didn't matter, as long as we were together.

And now she was blowing me off in a text. *Again.*

I adjusted my helmet and took a few practice swings before stepping back into the box. I tried to focus on the feel of the bat in my hands, on my stance, my cleats in the dirt, even on Sanchez as he did his exaggerated wind up that somehow worked for him even when it made him look like a douche, but in the back of my mind was Mia, like she'd been for the past week, walking the other way at school with a lame excuse, running later and later every night into the darkened hills alone. Not calling me.

Yeah, I had worried after my run in with Sarah that Mia would soon see what I saw—that on paper, we didn't make sense. Even before Sarah had brought it to my attention, I had wondered what I was going to do to keep Mia. I had expected resistance when we started dating, and I had expected anger, a little hurt when she found out about Ethan, though I really hoped she never would. What I never expected was for her to fade quietly out of my life so that I could hardly remember what it was like to be with her, really with her, without any of the walls she'd built around herself in the last week. Because that hurt, my body tensed just as Sanchez threw his pitch.

The ball came fast and low, straight down the pipe, the pitch I'd prayed for every day since I first learned to play. And because all I could see was Mia, I took a hard cut at it again and heard the whiz of my bat just as the ball slapped into Max's glove.

Godfuckingdammit.

"Strike two, Murph. That's your pitch, man."

I worked on unclenching my teeth as I stepped out of the box and went through my routine again. Behind me, Max threw the ball back to Sanchez and started chattering, but I ignored him as I tightened my gloves, adjusted my helmet, scuffed the dirt with my cleats before stepping back into the box. Sanchez threw the same pitch and this time I at least got a piece, winging it foul down the third base line.

"One and two," Max said so cheerfully I wanted to bash the bat into his mask.

"I know what the fucking count is."

"Just being helpful," he said, and threw the ball back to Sanchez again. I hit two more foul and my frustration level rose.

"Shit."

"I'll say. Sanchez is throwing like my grandmother, son. You can't hit him, you better not think about hitting Rainoldi next month in the tournament."

When I whirled on him, Max grinned and popped his catcher's mask to the top of his helmet as he stood. "Go to hell, Max."

"Sure thing, right after you try getting to first, Murph. With

Sanchez, that is. I heard Mia locked you out from even that much."

I'd thrown my fist before it registered, was about to throw another when Max held his hand up and I heard shouting behind me.

"Knew that would do it," he said, and anger blurred my vision.

"What the hell is your problem, Max? You got something to say, just say it."

"Jesus, Murph. You're killing me, killing all of us with your shitty attitude and even shittier play. You and Mia are pumping the breaks, I get it. Let's deal with it so you can get back to helping us win a state championship. Or at the very least, deal with it so you stop being such an asshole."

"Truth," someone yelled from behind me and I held up my middle finger.

"Murph, you can't just sit around and do nothing. Figure out what you want and go for it, or get over it because it's ruining your game and pissing everyone else off."

Because he was right, I stepped out of the box and stripped off my helmet, swiping my arms against my forehead. "Shit. She won't talk to me, Max, and short of kidnapping her, I don't know what else to do. I've called, texted, emailed. I've said I'm sorry in a thousand different ways on every device I can think of. I even asked Nina if she could help." I smiled wryly. "To which she responded no, right before she threatened to kill me with various blunt objects if I ever hurt her friend again. Your girl's scary as hell, Max."

He grinned. "I know, it's what I like about her." Then he slapped me on the shoulder as Coach came our way. "Want some advice? Kidnap her. Don't let her walk away. Obviously, she's going through some shit right now, and obviously, she's mad at you, but you deserve a conversation at the very least. A chance to know where you stand."

I nodded and then Coach was yelling and we were all throwing our mitts to the side, lining up at home plate to run bases and serve our time.

~

Since Mia's car was still in the parking lot when I got done with practice, I figured now was as good a time as any and leaned against her driver's side door to wait for her. Twenty minutes later she came out of the school carrying her bags, her head down and her brow furrowed as she walked. She was halfway to her car before she noticed me.

When her eyes met mine, I saw the circles underneath hers, and I hated them, almost as much as I hated knowing I was part of the reason they were there. Shoving my hands into my pockets, I stayed where I was and waited for her to finish her approach before speaking.

"Evans."

"Hi. I thought you had practice."

I nodded. "We finished a little early today and when I saw your car, I figured it was a sign."

She stopped, leaving enough distance between us that I couldn't reach out and touch her. Though I wanted to stand and yank her against me, to demand that she forgive me, that she trust me enough to listen and understand, I didn't. She'd had too many people tell her what to do and how to do it in her life, and I refused to become another one who did, so instead, I just stood and waited.

"I'm sorry I can't stay and talk, Ryan, but I have to go to work. That's why I left my own practice early."

"I know. I got your text. I miss you, Mia." When I stood up completely and reached for her, she took a step back. I froze, and though every cell inside of me was raging, my voice was calm when I spoke. "I'm sorry I didn't tell you about Ethan. I realize you think I was lying to you, and maybe I was, but not in the way you think."

"Ryan, I already told you I overreacted that night. You were trying to help him and I'm grateful, really, and I'm sorry that I yelled at you. It was just a shock."

But there was more to what she was saying, more that she wasn't saying. "Why are you avoiding me then, Evans? What else happened?"

Her eyes shifted down to the ground as she fumbled around

for her keys. "Nothing happened, and I haven't been avoiding you. I've been busy, like I told you."

"Fine. When aren't you busy? Let's hang out then."

Her hand shook for a moment, her fingers tightening and then relaxing on her keys before she finally looked up at me. Her voice was calm and detached, just like her expression. "I don't know, Ryan. I've got a lot to do to get ready for graduation, with school and track and making sure Ethan doesn't slip up."

"Evans, he won't slip up. He's fourteen, he made some bad choices, people do that."

But she was already shaking her head, making me want grab her shoulders and yank her against me, rage at her to stop thinking and just see me. "It's not just about the mistake, Ryan, and it's not just about Ethan. There's just so much on my plate right now with the end of the year and track and finishing school. Plus, Mrs. Rogge is making me write an article for the newspaper that I've been putting off, and Prom's right around the corner."

"Let's go."

"Excuse me?"

"To prom. If that's the next time you're free, I can wait until then." I took her hand, panic making my grip more forceful than I intended. "Go to prom with me, Mia."

I saw the rejection before it left her lips, had seen it, really, the moment she'd walked out of school and seen me waiting for her. This was the end, and try as I might, I couldn't stop the crash that was coming.

"I don't usually go to dances with anyone, Ryan. It's easier not to have to worry about a date when you're running around making sure the DJ and photographer and caterer all have the things they need."

She might as well have punched me, the way the air clogged my lungs and fear seized my body. Working to keep it cool, I took a breath, in and out, and then another, my eyes never leaving her face.

"Evans, are you telling me you don't want to go to prom with me because it's easier for you if you don't have to watch out for someone while you make sure everyone gets a piece of chicken for dinner?"

I saw her hand tremble slightly as she reached for her door handle, but her voice stayed calm and even. She was using her tutor voice, the one she spoke in when she was trying to convince someone to see what she already knew. "It's not like that, Ryan. It's not about wanting to go to prom with you or with anyone, it's about what's best."

"And what's best?" My voice was low, a direct contrast to the panic I felt bubbling up inside of me. "What do you think is best for us, Mia?"

For the first time since we'd started this conversation, I saw her eyes flash with something—anger, fear, pain—before she looked up at me. "I don't know."

But she did. *I don't know* was her way of telling me she wasn't ready. The girl who had come to me the day she'd been accepted to Stanford, the same one who had come to me the night of New Years, was long gone and buried, replaced with the scared girl who had been there the first month we'd hung out, the one who was too afraid to say what she felt. Or didn't feel.

Standing there, I stared at her face for a full minute, searching for the girl who'd been with me the past few months. But she wasn't there. Instead, there was a wall between us, as impenetrable as anything made out of brick and stone and twice as dense. Something had happened to make her withdraw from me, whether it was the fact that I'd lied, or that Ethan had been in trouble, or something else I didn't know, but whatever it was, she was holding onto it and using it as a shield, as a weapon, against her feelings and against me.

"Are you done, Evans? Are we done?"

She shook her head and looked down at the ground before whispering, "I don't know."

"Liar." My voice was no longer soft, my words no longer guarded as they whipped out of me. My chest was heaving with a pressure so great I wanted to scream, and an ache formed in the back of my throat as I tried to draw in air that didn't want to come. "You do know, but you don't want to tell me, just like usual. You're waiting for me to make the call, to tell you what to do or what you want, just like you do with everything else." She winced and I felt a small zing of satisfaction snake through me, glad for even an instant that she felt a tiny shred of the pain I was feeling.

"Fuck that. If you're done, Mia, you have to say it. I won't just walk away, and I won't just let you go along with whatever I want so you can blame me when it fails."

Her eyes filled with tears and the sight of them was as effective as a fist to the face. My anger fled, and with it, my shield. All that was left when I stepped back was the ache, the pain burning a hole in my chest and obstructing my throat.

And then she said it.

"I'm done."

Chapter Twenty-Five
Mia

I'd known the minute I saw him waiting for me that this moment was coming. As much as I wanted to avoid it, as much as there was a part of me that wanted to take it back, the other part of me understood that this was my consequence.

In the very beginning, I had told him that the results of us being together could only be bad. He hadn't listened to me, and in the end, I hadn't listened to myself. Now, I was paying for that, leaving him like this when all I wanted was for him to reach out and tug me against him, for him to wrap me up and take me to that place only he could take me, where I was light and free and happy. Instead, I was stepping back, stepping away, and picking up the responsibilities that I had let go the past five months while I could only think of him.

Ryan continued to stare at me but I avoided his eyes, focusing instead on the few people who were walking to their cars, some ignoring us, some waving to us like it was normal that we were there together. But it wasn't normal, and it was wrong that I kept pretending it was, or ever could be.

A month ago I might have thought it was possible to be with him, for however long he wanted me, for however long we could make it work. I was able to ignore what I knew and just see him and what he made me feel. But now, the image of my brother Ethan when we had gotten home the other night, stumbling and belligerent, and then sobbing and sick, left me unable to believe that anymore.

"You're drinking now, Ethan? How grown up, I missed the day you turned twenty-one."

I was on his heels as he walked into his bedroom and stumbled, tripping over his feet and falling face first into the wall. When I reached for him, he shoved me away and righted himself, leaving his hand on the wall to stay steady.

"Go away, Mia."

"Not a chance, Ethan. I want to know what you were thinking, not only getting drunk, but being drunk at a team function and then driving with someone who was drunk. Have you no sense, you idiot? Don't you know what could've happened to you?"

"Go away." He leaned against the wall, his head tipped back, his face pale. But I wasn't done.

"What's Mom going to think, Ethan? Jesus, what do you think is going to happen to her when I tell her you were drunk, and that it's something you do all of the time now, apparently."

"Nothing," he said and finally looked at me. "She's going to do nothing, except what she does all of the time now, which is go out to her social functions, and pretend her children are perfect, even when she knows that's not the truth. The truth, big sister, is that she lost one son, and now she's forgotten the rest of us."

My heart broke at that moment, the crack slicing right down the center until all I wanted to do was slide down the wall and weep. How had I missed this? How had I not seen that he felt this way? "That's not true, Ethan," I started, hoping somehow to make it right, but he laughed and shook his head.

"I got a D in biology, Mia. Not just on a test, but on my 3rd quarter progress report. A D. You know she said, Margaret Evans, control freak extraordinaire? Nothing. Because she didn't see my report card, because she doesn't know I'm here anymore. Just like she doesn't know I see Dad when he slips into the guestroom at night, or when he walks away from her without saying goodbye and she has to bite her lip to keep from crying."

He'd been sick after that, and locked himself in his bathroom where Joshua assured me he was all right. One look at Josh's face and I knew what Ethan had said was true. No one noticed them anymore.

Not even me.

That was the breaking point, the point at which I realized that it didn't matter what I wanted, I had responsibilities to my family, ones that I'd been ignoring because all I could think of was Ryan and how he made me feel, of myself and what I wanted. I hadn't cared about the consequences, but that was when I thought I would be the one suffering them. Ethan and Joshua would never suffer for me, or because of me. Not again.

The image that Ethan had painted of my father walking into the guestroom instead of the room he shared with my mother was stuck in my head, reminding me every day that living for the way someone else made me feel wasn't responsible, and it wasn't smart, because in the end it was everyone else around me who suffered.

Joe had done that when he'd left all of us for a girl and how she made him feel. He'd shattered our family for a dream, a feeling, and because of him we were broken, and we were suffering. Ethan was right about that, and he was right about our mother. She was still reeling from his loss, still accepting what little my father could give her and acting like it was enough, still allowing his moods and wants and needs to dictate her happiness, as Cora had let every boy she'd ever been with. As I had let Ryan.

Hadn't I learned my lesson? Hadn't I seen what a relationship did to a person every time I looked at my own parents, my own family? This relationship wasn't fair to either of us, and it wasn't right, no matter how much I wanted it to be.

"This isn't right, Ryan." The words were out before I could think about them. The shock hit me, but I ignored the sinking in my belly and continued on. "We're graduating soon. It's silly pretend that this is going anywhere real when we'll both be going to different places next year."

I waited for him to say something, a part of me silently hoping that he wouldn't back down, that he wouldn't accept less than everything, that he would make this choice for me and *show* me that no matter what, he wanted me. Instead, he just stood there, his arms folded across his chest as he stared at me. Nerves made me want to crumble, but I held my ground, meeting his eyes until it became too much to bear.

"I have to go," I said and motioned toward my car.

He nodded, one quick slice of his chin, and without a word he turned on his heal and walked toward his truck, never looking back. I stood alone and watched him, staying where I was even when he disappeared.

~

Over the next month, I went from never being at home to spending the majority of my time there, and it took only a week for me to see that Ethan was right. Mom wasn't there. The way she fluttered around and went from function to function, planned meetings and social events, followed my dad around, running errands for him even when he was in another state, made it impossible for her to focus on the family around her.

She'd become this other person, transitioned from the overbearing, over protective, and over involved mother, to the surface mom, the one who put her name all of our papers and then never took the time to talk to us or attend any of our events.

It took a week longer for me to realize that no matter how hard I worked at being there for the twins, it wasn't going to make a difference, not the one they needed anyway. Ethan had become sullen, and between Joshua and I, we had no idea how to pull him out of it.

"Goddammit, Ethan, what do you want? You know your homework matters, you know I care, you know I want to be here for you. Do you want me to sign it in blood so you believe me? Will that inspire you to do your work, to effing try?"

We were standing in the kitchen on a Friday after a particularly long week, and I was staring at his grades online, which hadn't improved, not one percentage point, because he hadn't done an iota more of work. I wasn't normally a person to use bad language, but *Jesus*.

"Do you think that failing is going to get their attention? That Mom and Dad are going to come running just because you can't pass freshman English?" I slapped the phone on the table under his nose so he was forced to look at his grades that were on the screen. After a minute, his eyes shifted and he just sat there with his arms crossed and his eyes fixed on the countertop in front of him. "Well?"

When he finally looked at me, his eyes were glossed over with tears and I was struck with just how young he looked. It didn't matter if he had five inches and twenty pounds on me, Ethan was my baby brother, and everything inside of me wanted to protect him, from himself and everyone else.

"I don't want their attention, Mia, and I don't care what they think anymore, because it doesn't matter. I don't want to be like them, only caring about but what everyone else thinks."

If only you knew, little brother, if only you knew. My thoughts had been exactly the same since the day they'd taken me to dinner and barely spoken to one another. Every day since I'd tried to be a person who lived her life, not just ran through it like a checklist. But somehow there had to be a balance, because like Ethan, I'd gotten so far off track that I'd become oblivious to the important things, too. "Is that why you started drinking? To show you didn't care?"

He jerked his shoulder once. "Maybe, I don't really know. It was just easier, you know? Easier than working hard to make them happy and then realizing they had no idea who I was. Easier than worrying over every little missed point or unmade free throw. Dad hasn't been to one of my games all year. I play three different sports," he murmured, his voice tight with the emotion clogging his throat. "I just started wondering why I should care so much when they don't."

"You can't always play for them, Ethan." Suddenly, everything I'd done since Joe left made me feel silly. Everything I'd done in the past three years had been to prove a point to my mom and dad, to myself and everyone around me, and really, what had it changed? Now, looking at the same results in my little brother, I knew the truth. "You can't worry that what you're doing isn't good enough for them, Ethan, because it will drive you crazy. Or to drink," I said and saw his lips twitch a little. "You just have to know that what you're doing is good enough for you."

"How do you do that?"

My laugh was humorless and a little shaky as I gave in and ran my hands through my hair, wondering what the hell had happened that I'd gone from screaming at my brother to think of my parents to explaining why it was important that he thought only of himself. "Honestly? I have no idea, I'm kind of struggling with it myself. But I do know," I continued when he frowned, "that drinking your way through high school is not one of the signs that you're doing something right."

I kept my voice light and was rewarded when his lips curved into what looked like a genuine smile before he said, "I think you might have a point." Then he scrubbed his hands over his face and I had to stop myself from reaching out and resting my hand on his shoulder. He wasn't a kid, and he'd made a choice that he had to deal with. Hopefully this time he would trust me to help, but I couldn't smother him, no matter how badly I wanted to.

"Hey Mia?"

His hands were still covering his eyes, rubbing them, and I smiled at the echo of his voice. "Hmm?"

"What's going to happen next year when you're gone, like Lily and Joe? What are Joshua and I going to do?"

I sat on the stool next to him and stared straight ahead, wondering just how oblivious I'd been the past few months. It was almost amazing how blind I'd been to believe that I was the only one who felt the loss of everyone around me. The twins might have been young when Joseph left and Lily went to school, but they weren't immune. They needed security, just like me. "I'm leaving for school next year, Ethan, but I won't stay gone, not like you think. I promise to come home during breaks and see you, and to call you and Skype you and Facetime you. You'll hardly even know I left."

His lips trembled, but after a moment, he nodded his head, a brisk acknowledgement of trust that meant more to me than any words. He was scared, but he believed I'd do as I said. We sat there a while longer, making a plan for how to get his grades back up, sketching an outline of what he was going to say to his teachers in order to get them to let him make up missed work, because despite how much he said he didn't care, Ethan did. And despite how much I hated it when my mother hounded me about my grades, it also meant she noticed me. I wasn't about to let Ethan feel like he was going unnoticed again.

"Go get Joshua and we'll go to The Authentic for dinner. Louise is cooking Paella and Mom went to Phoenix for a fundraising dinner."

Ethan scrunched his face. "He's with Caitlin at her house, why don't we walk over and get him on our way?"

I met Ethan's eyes, and this time, they were direct and clear. Pushing away from the counter, I grabbed my phone and tapped out a text to Josh, asking him to come home so we could go.

"Done, now we don't need to walk since it's hot outside. I'm going to change. When Josh gets here we can leave."

"He didn't tell you because I asked him not to." I stopped at the entryway to the kitchen and turned. Ethan was watching me from his same spot at the counter, and for a minute I was reminded of the day Joe left and I had sat and waited for him.

"He only knew because one of the guys from the team told him they'd seen me at a party, and when he asked Caitlin about it, she couldn't lie to him. He confronted me about it, told me to pull my head out of my ass and think about what it would do to me if I got caught. Then he told me how you would feel if you knew how I was acting. I didn't care enough to stop," Ethan whispered and I blinked my eyes. "But he cared enough to try and stop me, every time. He had people call him every time they saw me, and he always came to get me when they did."

Of course he did, because that's who Ryan was. Despite how I tried to insist that he was frivolous and spoiled at the beginning of our time together, Ryan was one of the most selfless, giving people I'd ever met. If there was a chance I could be with him and somehow keep everything else...but there wasn't, because I'd already proved that I wasn't capable of focusing on anything but him when we were together. Because of that, he'd known my little brother was hurting and I hadn't.

"He's a good person, Ethan, no one is denying that."

"He is a good person, Mia, and I think he cares about you a lot." Ethan swallowed. "I'm sorry I messed it up."

This time I knew what to say when I walked over and sat down next to him, when I waited for his eyes to meet mine. "It's not you, Ethan. We were headed here from the first time we went out, we just didn't want to believe it."

"But why?"

I sighed as I tried to explain to him what I barely understood myself. "When I was with Ryan, everything else was just less. I didn't care where I was or who I was, as long as he was there. That's dangerous, to me and to him, because no one person should be the reason you do something." I paused and thought again, amazed at how easily the next answer came. "I need to be the reason I do things, the reason I'm happy. I depended on him too much, used him as an excuse to ignore things and be a different person, and it wasn't right."

I stared ahead as the truth of my words echoed in my ears. No, I hadn't walked away because of Ethan. I had walked away because Ryan had become to me what Morgan had to Joe, what my father had to my mother; the controlling factor that told me who to be. No matter how happy it had made me at the time, I understood now that I couldn't live for him or the way he made me feel. I had to live for me, be comfortable with who I was alone.

Ethan nodded, and as I stood to leave, he stopped me one last time. "It just seems that if you liked who you were with him, maybe you already know how to be that person. He just makes it easier."

~

Ethan's words haunted me the rest of the month leading up to spring break, and because of it, I avoided Ryan like the plague. I was afraid that if I gave in and saw him, I would beg for him to take me back, and however much Ethan might have a point, I knew that I had been right to walk away. I felt it, even as I felt the hurt from it.

It wasn't easy to avoid Ryan when I lived across the street from him, but I gave it my best effort. I left for school earlier each day, rationalizing to myself that I was helping Ethan get back on track with his schoolwork, and I used my track workouts as an excuse for why I stopped running at night. I worked hard to convince myself it had nothing to do with the fact that Ryan still sat on his porch every night but the success of this was mediocre at best, especially since I checked religiously to see if he was there. He was, but he never strayed from that swing, never took a step in my direction or made any other move that showed he felt the same gravitational pull toward me as I did him. If a part of me was disappointed at how easy it was to avoid him, I ignored it and convinced myself I was glad that we hadn't seen each other in over a month.

Thirty-four days to be exact. Not that I was counting.

Avoiding him at school was even easier as we had none of the same classes and he was gone more and more with the baseball team. Spring break came and went—he went to Vegas with the team, which I only knew because Nina told me that's where Max had been, and I stayed home and worked at the Inn, making sure to go to every baseball game the twins had.

In my dedication to avoiding Ryan, I had been spending more and more time at home, the only place I was sure I wouldn't accidentally run into him. If there was one benefit to this, it was that my constant presence appeared to reinvigorate Ethan, and the happy, carefree brother I'd once known had returned full force, teasing, talking smack as we played Wii, being a general nuisance. He hadn't gone anywhere without Joshua since the night of capture the flag, and Joshua hadn't even gone to Caitlin's without him.

While my relationship with my brothers got better, my anxiety about my mother's lack of communication or general neglect of her motherly duties only got worse. The only thing scarier than my mother obsessing about my achievements and planning my future for me was the mother who said nothing at all. Which was why I was sitting across from her at dinner, a dinner I'd invited her to under the guise of a girl's night, wondering how to broach the subject.

"Mia, are you listening to me, honey?"

I looked up from the lettuce I had been pushing around my plate and met my mother's quizzical look. "I'm sorry, what did you say?"

"You haven't said anything all night and you've barely touched your food. Are you all right?"

"Why does Dad sleep in the guestroom?"

There had never been a more effective way of silencing my mother. Her mouth dropped and her eyes widened, but she made no sound. It took her a stunned moment to form any words, and when she did, all that came out was a harshly whispered, "Excuse me?"

Setting my plate aside, I ignored the shocked expression on her face and leaned forward on the table so I could keep my voice low. "Ethan saw Dad going into the guest room last month. The other day I walked in and all of his stuff was in the closet."

"You shouldn't encourage your brothers, Mia, and you shouldn't be poking around things that aren't yours." Her voice was stiff like her shoulders and laced with disapproval, but when she reached for her water glass, her hands were shaking, trembles so strong that the water lapped dangerously close to the edge and she set the cup aside without drinking from it. Pushing back the guilt and grasping the courage I had so badly wanted those months ago when faced with my father, I forged on.

"It's hardly poking around when we live in the same house. Answer the question, Mom, please."

She stared at me for a full minute, so long that I began to think she would do it. I leaned in a bit further, trying to reach my hand over and settle it on hers to offer a bit of comfort, but that bit of contact snapped her. Throwing her napkin on the table, she grabbed her handbag from the floor. "No."

Stunned, it took me a minute to get up and follow her, and she was already halfway down Main when I caught up to her. For the first time, I wished that we lived in a town where you needed to drive places so we had some privacy.

"Mom, wait."

"Mia, I won't have this conversation with you. My relationship with your father is no one's business, and where he does or does not sleep is certainly not for you and your brothers to speculate about."

I almost stopped. I could hear the tears in her voice, see the strain in the way she carried herself, so I almost stopped, let it go, walked away. This was hurting her, and despite how much she might drive me crazy, she was my mother and I loved her more than anything. Hurting her was the last thing I wanted to do. But then I remembered her at dinner, and at the party, shrinking smaller and smaller with every minute he was near her, every comment he made designed to show her she wasn't as important as he was.

And I remembered Joseph walking away because no one cared what he wanted, and Ethan walking into the house drunk because he was done trying to live up to expectations when no one showed him he mattered without them. She wasn't the only person who was hurting, and it was time she saw that.

"Mom, I'm your daughter, he's my father. How you feel about each other affects me; it affects all of us."

"Don't be dramatic. Where he sleeps has nothing to do with you."

"Jesus, Mom, why won't you tell me?" For the first time, my frustration leaked out and guided my actions. I grabbed her arm, forcing her to stop or make a scene by yanking out of my grip. She turned, her eyes heated and wide, her face as pale as it was back in the Club. "Why can't you open your eyes for one second and see that your lies are fooling no one? Why can't you trust me enough to tell me the truth?"

"Because I don't know the truth!" she shouted, two splashes of color appearing on her pale cheeks as her breath heaved in and out of her lungs. "Damn it, Mia, I don't know the truth. I don't know why he doesn't stay in our room when he comes home, or why he so rarely *comes* home anymore. Is that what you wanted to hear? That I don't know why I'm not enough for him, that I can hardly function when I think about him, so I don't? Is that what you want?" I barely heard the last words as they dribbled out of her mouth, her chin dropping and her shoulders sagging.

It was instinctual to reach out and bring her close, to rest my arm over her shoulders and my head against hers, running my hands up and down her back as we both clung. And though we were both in pain, though I hated knowing that I had caused her to feel everything she'd been trying to block out, I finally felt like I had my mom back. For the first time in three years, I had her with me, and even when I wanted to erase the pain for her, I never wanted her to go back to being the perfect shell that she had been; unnatural and unapproachable, just there.

Gripping her tighter, I leaned into her and reveled in the feeling of holding my mother.

"I'm sorry, I'm so sorry. I didn't mean to hurt you, Mom. I just need to know, to try and understand. To try and cope," I said gently. Holding her like this, I could feel exactly how small and frail she'd become, and it worried me to know I was the one protecting her now. "Somehow we all have to learn to cope, Mom, because this is tearing us apart."

She shook her head as she pulled away far enough that she could see me clearly. Cupping my face in her hands as she used to do when I was little, her eyes were sad, her voice low but sincere when she spoke. "I barely understand, Mia. And *I* don't want to hurt *you*. I'm not worried about me, but I can't stand the thought of hurting another one of my children and having you leave." Her eyes filled and she closed them. When she opened them again, they were clear of tears and although shadowed, I thought I saw a hint of strength in them, too. "I won't have one of you walking away, not again."

"Then trust me. And stop pretending, because we all know, and we all hurt, and when you act like nothing's wrong, it hurts more."

It took her a moment and a long breath, but she finally nodded and we turned to keep walking, our arms linked as we wound our way through town and into our cul de sac. We didn't say anything, just walked together, the silence oddly comforting after years of unspoken words. When we reached the edge of our driveway she stopped and stared at the house, her arms hanging limply at her side.

"I remember the day we came here, how quiet everyone was when we stepped inside." Her voice dropped, got smaller as she did, her shoulders hunching, her head drooping until it seemed she was barely there, a woman who was nothing but the shell her family had left her with, hollowed and broken, trying to weather the storm. "It's still in there, the quiet. It echoes when I'm alone, and it scares me."

I nodded but I wasn't looking at the house, I was looking at her, seeing her for the first time in a long time. "Even when we were shouting, it was quiet, like we were incapable of filling it with the love it needed, incapable of *filling* it so that it felt like a home. The day your brother left, I don't think anything's ever been so quiet." Her voice broke, thick with tears and heartache and I reached down to grab her hand, my own eyes filling. "I never said what I wanted, never told him the things I should have to make him stay, or at least want to stay, even if he had to go. He went without knowing how I felt, and our house stays quiet." Finally, she turned to me and I studied her colorless face, her thin, barely there body caving under the weight of her admission. But her voice was full of conviction when she spoke again, and for the first time in a long time, I saw a hint of the strength that used to be my mother.

"I was silent because I thought it would save you and your brothers, that admitting there was something wrong would only make it harder." I shook my head, but before I could speak, she spoke again, her voice quiet again. "I don't want to be silent anymore, because I don't ever want you to feel like this."

"Like what?" I asked and she gave a wry smile, wiping a stray tear as it escaped down my cheek.

"Unnecessary. Achingly unnecessary."

Chapter Twenty-Six
Ryan

I sat at the table in front of the trophy case in the athletic hallway of the school, the championship banners from the years before hanging in the cases behind me, my mom and dad and Caitlin to the right, Coach and Max to the left. There was a small crowd of people behind the cameras that faced me, and in them I could see Nina, already scribbling furiously in a notebook.

I couldn't resist the urge to search the crowd for the familiar golden hair, even though I knew she wouldn't be here. She had a meet against Bradshaw and Willow Canyon at home. She'd been at the track since two o'clock and would be there well past six since she ran the first and last events.

"Ready?"

I looked over at my parents and nodded, resisting the urge to yank on my tie. I sat down and smiled at the cameras as the athletic director greeted everyone and went into his spiel about student-athletes. When he finally introduced the coach from ASU, I stood as well, reaching over and shaking his hand as he handed me a Sun Devils hat.

"Glad to have you, son."

I nodded and took the pen he offered me, leaning down so I could sign my name. As I signed, flashes went off and questions were shouted out.

"Why ASU?"

"They're one of the top ten baseball universities, and it's home."

"Are you going to red shirt?"

"No. I want to play, and I don't want to wait."

"There was a rumor earlier in the year that you were looking long and hard at Cal State Fullerton. What made you change your mind?"

More like who. Until a month ago, Fullerton had been my top choice, over Arizona, over South Carolina, over the Oregon schools. Fullerton was exactly six hours from San Francisco and Mia. Now, six hours, six hundred miles, it didn't matter. She didn't want me.

"California isn't home, and I want to play at home."

I answered a few more before turning away to shake hands with my coaches and set up a time to meet and go over my summer workout. When I turned to leave, I caught a glimpse of long golden hair and sun kissed skin as Mia slipped out the side door, almost completely gone before I could take a step in her direction.

"Hey, Murph, you okay?"

I looked down at the hand on my arm, and then up into Ethan's face. I saw it right away, the recognition, the pity, and then the understanding. "She had to go and she didn't want to interrupt you." He cleared his throat and looked around before settling his gaze back on me. "Um, I'm going to walk down to her meet in a minute if you want to come. I need to say some things to you anyway."

At his tone, I finally focused on Ethan and noticed his dejected pose; the hands in the pockets, his head down, shoulders hunched. We hadn't really spoken since the night of capture the flag. The same night Mia had decided that we weren't worth it after all. Looking at him, I couldn't help but see her, and I wondered if he felt as alone as she did sometimes.

I nodded and looked out at the thinning crowd. Waving to my parents, I motioned for Ethan to follow me as I excused myself and headed toward the track.

~

I hadn't been to a track meet since I was a freshman and heard that Mia ran track. That was the first and the last meet I'd been to, as even the true love of a semi-stalker couldn't combat the absolute boredom I had felt that day. Until now, when seeing her up close, or closer than I had in longer than I could remember, had sent my neglected system into overdrive and it now craved just one more look.

I only had an hour, an order from my mother who had stopped me on my way out the door of my own college signing.

"You have one hour to go do what you need to do, Ryan Phillip Murphy, and then you better have your head out of your ass or I'll put my boot up there and make it doubly crowded. Understood?"

Ethan's eyes were wide and filled with admiration as he watched her.

"Did your mom just tell you to pull your head out of your ass?" he asked as we walked away. I looked over and laughed at his shocked expression. Truly smiling for the first time in weeks, I nodded and walked out into the heat.

Now, I stood in my white t-shirt and suit pants, having ditched my tie and letterman's jacket before trekking down to the track next to Ethan, who had pointed me toward the fence near the starting line. I was positioned perfectly to see her, according to him, and I wondered if this was the best idea for me. It felt odd to be looking for Mia again, twice in one day, since I'd been doing my level best to avoid her for the past month, hoping that with time and distance my feelings would ease off and fade away.

One glance at the back of her head today and I realized I was about as over her now as I had been a month ago when she'd ripped out my still beating heart and stomped on it before handing it back to me, along with my invitation to prom. And because, despite all of that, I couldn't shake her from my mind, here I was, embracing my equivalent of self-mutilation on a day that should be one of the happiest in my life, as the sun beat down on me and I watched gawky boys who weren't coordinated enough to play a real sport run in a circle while I waited.

"Jesus this is a stupid sport."

I didn't realize I'd spoken aloud until I heard Ethan laugh. "I know, I'm always telling Mia that. I mean, how much athleticism does it take to run in a circle?"

"So, you and your sister are talking again?"

I couldn't help but feel a little satisfied when a red hue of embarrassment crept over his face and neck as he nodded. I had known from day one that Mia would be hurt when she found out that Ethan had been lying to her and that I had known about it. It was twice as bad because of the way she found out, and I placed the blame for that squarely on his head. Just like I placed the idiot move to get into a car with a drunk kid on him.

"Yeah, she's been hounding me about my grades, about caring about my future and my goals for my life. Said she would tell Coach herself that I have a D if I didn't get my shit together."

"She can be demanding that way."

"Tell me about it. I think I liked it better when she was too busy thinking about your failing grade to notice mine."

Although I laughed, the tightness in my chest peaked at an almost brutal level, and when I saw her walk out onto the infield and begin doing some sort of hinky warm-up that included leg swinging and skipping, I had to remind myself to keep taking deep breaths of air.

I hated that she could make me feel this way, especially when I knew she wanted me to do nothing more than forget her. Watching her as she peeled out of her warm up shorts and t-shirt to the black running spandex and tank she wore as a uniform, a part of me wished for the same thing, wished for that easy dismissal to come so maybe it wouldn't feel like there was a hole being drilled into my chest, deeper and deeper each day, until there was nothing but a gaping wound that let the life slowly leak out of me.

"She's been the steady one in our family for as long as I can remember."

Ethan's words pulled me out of my trance and I broke my gaze from Mia long enough to shoot him a glance. He was staring at her, too, but his expression was thoughtful, careful, and I waited for him to continue.

"I don't remember a ton about my older brother. He was cool, but we're pretty far apart and he was busy. I remember more about from the time we moved here because there was less to remember, if that makes sense." I nodded and thought back to the day that Mia had sat on the porch, crying for him. A part of me wanted to punch him in the face for making her do that, and another, larger part of me wanted to call him and ask why? What did he think leaving would accomplish when his family was right here?

"Mia's told me about Joe, Ethan. She even told me a little about your parents."

That had his eyes moving to me and studying me. Then he nodded.

"Then you know she's been the steady one. My sister Lily doesn't come home from school if it's not a holiday, and I don't really blame her. My dad—" he stopped to take a deep breath, and for a minute I was left wondering what it would be like if I didn't think my parents loved me.

I couldn't even imagine in it.

Even with all of the ass kickings my mother has doled out, both verbal and physical, with the intense "you've really done it this time" stares and head shakes my dad's given me over the years, I never once had to wonder if they loved me. Not even when I was wondering if they were going to kill me.

"My dad's never been a big part of our family," he said on a small expulsion of air, and I stopped moving as I watched him fight for control. "Mia doesn't really remember that because until we moved here, she had Joe. She didn't really think about the fact that Dad wasn't ever around, and that when he was, he wasn't really here. It just never affected her because Joe did everything, so when he left, she blamed him, but the truth is, our parents have always been this way."

Ethan's words hung in the air and I switched my gaze back to Mia and watched as she joined the crowd of runners at the start line, as she surged forward with the shot of the gun and steadily worked her way through the pack.

I wanted to view her objectively, to find her controlled demeanor and set facial expression cold, the rigid set of her shoulders unbending. I wanted to be able to step back after being apart from her and realize that my feelings were no stronger for her than they'd been for anyone else, that it had been all heat of the moment and chemistry, nothing more.

But I couldn't.

Instead, I could remember the way her face would brighten when she laughed, as if she hadn't been expecting it and the feeling was foreign, or the way her body melted into mine when I touched her, the way her entire being went pliant as she trusted me to take her where she'd never been before. The way she buried her face in my neck and cried for the family she was watching break apart and helpless to stop, no matter how hard she tried.

I watched the entire race with Ethan next to me, neither of us saying anything. My eyes never left Mia in the eleven minutes that it took her to run the two miles. At the home stretch, she pushed, digging down to keep her lead, her face contorting ever-so-slightly with the effort, and when she crossed the finish line, continuing through the curve of the track before she slowed to a walk and evened her breathing, I watched her even more closely, looking for those signs of struggle, of pain, but her face never showed it again.

As she cooled down, her expression was barely discernible, only I had seen the pain for that brief second, and it made me wonder how many other times she'd been able to control the pain without anyone noticing.

"Don't quit on her, Ryan. I was an asshole—I didn't want the one person in my family that notices me to leave, so I did the one thing I knew that would bring all of her attention to me."

I raised an eyebrow. "That's pretty enlightened, Ethan."

He smiled, and for the first time today I saw the happy kid that he was in it. "Her highness not only demanded that I get my grades together, she demanded that I talk to my counselor at school, especially since I didn't 'trust her enough to talk to her.'"

"Wow, she really has you on lockdown."

"You have no idea."

"Well, drunk Ethan was kind of an asshole, so I'm not sorry to see him go."

I said it lightly and was rewarded when he grinned. "Yeah, Josh's been all too happy to tell me that this past month."

"I'll bet. But you're lucky to have him, Ethan, and your sister. You might not think your parents love you, and maybe they can't, not the way you need, but you have someone who does, and that should count for a hell of a lot."

He nodded, and his face was serious again. "Mia needs you, Murph. I know I messed it up, but she needs you."

My eyes traveled to the track again where she repeated her warm up process in a slightly different order. Her face was blank, her breathing deep as she focused wholly on what she was doing. She never stopped to talk to the girl next to her, or laugh or take a break. Mia, being Mia, had a job to do, and she was doing it without detours. I was a detour, and she was back on her path to success.

"I'm starting to wonder if we would have ended up here anyway, Ethan." I glanced at him and shrugged. "I'm not part of her plan. Deep down I wondered if we were crazy because she's always going to want to be perfect and I'm never going to fit that image."

"What do you want?"

I stared out at Mia, watching as she continued her cool down with a stretch, her face serious, her eyes dark. "Her," I said quietly and realized how deep that truth went. "It seems like I've always just wanted her."

Shortly after that, Ethan left to go to his own practice and though I should have left with him, I found myself waiting by the fence. It took another ten minutes for Mia to collect her things from the infield and say goodbye to her coach, and I was cutting it perilously close to the end of my hour when she finally made her way over to where I was standing. Whether she had seen me before this moment or not I couldn't tell as I stood where I was—my hands shoved into my pockets so they didn't do something stupid, like grab her and never let go—watching her walk toward me.

"I figured you'd be out celebrating with your family."

Her voice was normal, controlled, and I worked to match my tone to hers. "I'm headed that way. Ethan was at the signing and since he wanted to talk, I walked down with him."

We stood a foot apart, staring at each other, our eyes drinking in every detail. When the air around us changed, when the familiar charge of electricity began to snap, I took a step back, breaking the eye contact. She did, too, and without a word, we began walking toward the parking lot.

"I'm glad Ethan spoke to you. I know he's been wanting to make up for putting you in such a bad position, helping him when he was breaking the team rules by drinking."

Her voice was formal and stiff, and for a second I imagined gripping her shoulders and shaking her until she spoke to me like we had slept together instead of like I was one of her mother's society friends. "I've broken a few rules myself from time to time so I understand," was all I said.

She nodded and we continued to walk, the silence around us deafening as both of us wondered where to begin.

"Congratulations, Ryan. Your family must be so proud of you."

Safe topic change. Point to her.

I nodded. "They know it's what I want, so they're pretty happy. Of course, my mom's just glad I didn't get rejected because of an F in English."

A small smile formed at her lips as she stared at the ground. "I don't know if you would've failed. Gotten a D maybe, for terrible grammar and even worse spelling, but you would've passed. And really, I think Mrs. Friedman is just as happy to never see you again as you are to be leaving her class."

I felt a real laugh bubble up and out and for a minute, I almost forgot the past month and the fact that I'd been avoiding her. It felt like it had since that first night, the one where she'd finally snapped and shown me who she was, deep down, without the perfect pretense.

"The signing today—I didn't think you'd be there."

She kept walking, her head down, but I could tell her mind was moving, picking its way through the awkwardness and trying to find the right words that wouldn't give away too much.

Point for me.

"I felt like an idiot when Nina told me."

She looked up then and answered the question she must have seen on my face. "I didn't even know where you wanted to go to school—after all that time we spent together, after everything I shared with you, I never bothered to ask where you wanted to go to school. And then they mentioned Fullerton…"

I stopped and she stopped with me, both of us turning to look at the other. "You can ask me now," I said softly, and she stared at me for a minute, her eyes dark and full of secrets I didn't know. Suddenly desperate, I stepped closer. "Ask me, Evans."

"Have you always wanted to go to Arizona State, Ryan?" Her voice was barely there, closer to a whisper, but her eyes never left mine and I found that I could see much more than ever before in them. And what I saw had me wondering why she'd ever walked away, why I thought I'd ever be able to let her.

I shook my head slowly side-to-side as I watched her. "As a kid, I wanted to go to South Carolina, get away from home and be a part of the legend. Then, a few months ago, I thought I might play at Cal State Fullerton because for a second, I thought California had everything I ever wanted."

Her already dark eyes filled and I stood still, staring at her, hoping that she saw what I was saying loud and clear: I would have gone anywhere for her. For us. The minute she had become mine, my dream had altered and she had become a very real part of it.

"And now?" she asked, her voice so soft I barely heard her.

I held her eyes a moment longer before stepping back and breaking the contact. Whether or not she'd wanted to walk away or she'd felt she had no other choice, she'd left me and I had to remember that. When I started walking again, she fell into step next to me, leaving the space I had put between us. "Now, I'm going to Arizona State and my family can come and see me play."

She said nothing as we stopped at her car, but stared down at her keys as her brow furrowed. "Are you happy, Ryan?"

I nodded, my heartbeat picking up its rhythm and beating wildly against my ribs as I watched her watching her keys. "I've dreamed of playing ball in college my whole life. The dream just came true."

She inclined her head, finally looking up and meeting my eyes. Wondering if it was my last chance, I took a step forward so that there was only a whisper between us. "But I had another dream, too, Evans."

"Ryan—"

"I know why you walked away," I said in a rush and watched her hand tremble. Risking it, I took my own out of my pockets and gripped her fingers until she looked at me. "I know you were mad and scared, and I guess I don't blame you. But you were my dream, too, Mia, for a long time. I thought that if I had you, I could do anything. And then when I had you, I knew I had everything. It took you walking away to make me realize that a dream doesn't change even if you can't have it. It just waits."

Taking her face in my hands, I cupped the back of her neck and leaned down until our mouths were as close as our bodies, until her eyes fluttered and I could feel her heart beating into me. "I'll wait, Mia, because you're worth it, because we're worth it, even if you don't know it."

Chapter Twenty-Seven
Mia

Tears were as useless as regret, and still, I felt both welling up inside of me as I stood in the parking lot and watched Ryan walk away from me again.

Because we're worth it, even if you don't know it.

I replayed Ryan's words over and over as I drove home. I wanted to ask what he meant, but he had already turned, already walked away, and deep down, I already knew. I was scared of Ryan, scared of him leaving as easily as everyone else did, scared of myself and who I would be if I stayed with him.

It wasn't a matter of worth, though, not really. It was a matter of strength. Could I be strong enough to be with someone, especially someone as powerful and open and consuming as Ryan, and still be myself? Still be a person, even if I was coming to see I had no idea who that person was? There it was, the fear that Ryan had talked about the day I'd backed off, the hypocritical desires within me, one asking for guidance from everyone to save me from decisions, the other refusing anything from anyone in fear that it would make me less.

As I pulled into the driveway, I turned off the ignition and sat there. I thought of the other night when my mother had finally confided in me, when she'd sat down across from me and explained exactly what had changed her.

Unnecessary.

She'd pushed so hard for so long, not because she didn't believe in me, but because she didn't believe in herself. Her oldest son had left and she'd done nothing to stop it because she wanted to please a man who never gave her the same consideration. Now, like me, she waited for the next disappointed person to make their move. Thinking back, I realized that my analysis of her actions hadn't been that far off base, I only wished that I had said something sooner.

I wondered what would happen now. I didn't believe my mother would leave my father, not only because it wasn't in her DNA to forfeit or quit on what she considered her responsibilities and promises, but because despite all he'd made her feel, or not feel in the past few years, she really loved him.

"Why?" I had asked as we sat at the kitchen table that same night, both of us with a cup of coffee in front of us while she told me she didn't want to give up on my father, even if he'd given up on her. "He barely sees you when he's here, and when he does see you he ignores you or makes you feel like disappearing. I've seen it," I said as she shook her head. "You shrink when he's here, Mom, literally."

Her eyes got a little cloudy as she nodded and sipped from her cup, but that didn't stop her from answering. It seemed like no matter how much it hurt her, she was going to make good on her promise to never stay silent again. "Because no one person changes a relationship. I changed, too, Mia. I became the mom more concerned with the things than the people. After Joseph left—"

She stopped to take another sip of coffee, and I watched her throat move, her hands tense on the cup. Just as I had earlier, I reached out and placed my hand over hers, only this time, she didn't run. She stared at it for a moment, and then she turned it over until our fingers were linked.

She looked at me, her eyes wide and unsure, and my own reflection from so many times was thrown back at me. Somehow, when I hadn't been watching, my mother had been broken, and now it was up to me to make sure she stood up again.

"He was my son, and I never talked to him, really talked to

him. In all of those months of fighting and moving and forcing him to go to school, I never asked your brother what he wanted. I never asked my *son* what he needed, Mia, when it was so obvious that what he needed was for me to do just that. Now I've done the same to you and your brothers."

"Why?"

Her smile had been sad then, and more than a little self-deprecating. "Because I only cared about making everyone else happy—and I thought that if I did that, nothing could go wrong. I thought if I made things seem perfect, they would be."

But perfect didn't exist, not the way our family thought it should. Life was messy and complicated and heartbreaking. I don't know if it made me feel better or worse to know that my mother actually knew that.

~

The last week in April, the countdown to prom was on and everyone was in a frenzy—sans Nina, who simply played Scrooge and vetoed half of the ideas we came up with.

"Seriously, if that idiot Marci makes one more ridiculous suggestion, I'm going to stab her."

I laughed as Nina and I walked to newspaper together. "She's supposed to make suggestions, she's the chairman of the decorating committee. *Cirque de Soleil* might not be original, but it will be beautiful."

"Please, Mia, you can't tell me that you didn't think her idea to have actual people hanging from the rafters and doing tricks on their ribbons wasn't asinine. We're a school, for shit's sake, not a casino. Even if we could afford it—which we can't—it's a huge liability."

She had me there. "At least try to be a little gentler when you shoot her down. She's on edge since her chandeliers aren't going to make it on time."

"Chandeliers we already paid for."

"Five days, Nina, and then you never have to hear the word prom again."

"Thank Christ," she said and slammed through the doorway into the newspaper room.

We were both brought up short at the sight of Ryan sitting on the desk of a sophomore girl who was twirling her hair around her finger as she looked up at him from under her lashes and giggled. The air left my lungs, my whole chest constricting when a laugh rumbled out of him. I heard Nina mutter "son of a bitch," but I was too concentrated on trying to draw a breath to say anything.

It had been almost two weeks since we'd spoken, when he'd told me that we were worth the wait. I had wondered if he would push after that, show me everything we could be together, but instead of becoming a larger presence in my life, he'd taken avoidance to a whole new level, never once coming within twenty feet of me. Until now, when he was shamelessly flirting with another girl in a place he had to have known I would be. Anger rushed through me, and suddenly I had to resist the urge to scream at him.

Worth it, my ass.

The sophomore reporter, oblivious to the daggers Nina was shooting her way, giggled once more and ran her hand through her hair again, her voice buzzing in the background of my consciousness as I stared at Ryan who was still smiling down at her. Nina, having had enough, marched straight over to the desk and planted her hands on her hips, all five feet of her looming over the girl. Ryan looked at her and barely got out a hello before she shoved him hard enough that he didn't have time to catch himself before he fell off of the desk and hit the ground with a thud.

"Moron," she said and turned toward the sophomore whose mouth was now agape as she stared in terror.

"Shawna, what are you doing?"

It took more than a few seconds for her to stutter out an answer, halfway through which Nina cut her off. "I need the article on the baseball team, and I needed it yesterday. Ryan Murphy is not the only person on the team that's to be interviewed, clear?"

Shawna's head bobbed, but I didn't hear her reply as I watched

Ryan shift from his side to his feet, dusting his pants off as he stood. When he raised his head, our eyes met and I saw something flash in his before they went carefully blank. A small smile played over his lips and he nodded before turning to Nina.

"Whoa, what'd I miss?"

Battling the overwhelming desire to march over and shove Ryan down again, I looked over at Max who was standing beside me, hands in the pockets of his jeans, his eyebrows raised at Nina and Ryan as Nina yelled "idiot" and stomped off.

"A reporter was flirting—Nina didn't like it."

My voice was controlled, level, not betraying any of the anxiety I felt at knowing Ryan was ten feet away. Closer than he'd been since the day he told me I was his dream…and then run away.

Max tilted his head and looked down at me, raising his brows. "Just Nina?"

I stared for a full minute before nodding my head. "Just Nina. I'll be at my desk when you're ready," I said as I saw Ryan make his way over. Stepping to the side, I turned and walked away, not looking back, trying not to listen as Ryan greeted Max and I heard them both laugh.

As I set my things down at my desk and prepared to interview Max and Nina—the Valedictorian and Salutatorian, both National Merit Scholars and now a real life couple—I thought of Ryan's small smile of acknowledgement. His casual greeting and calm demeanor that had my chest squeezing and my throat aching with unshed tears.

Turns out, I didn't need to avoid him. He was over it.

Since my breath was starting to come in pants again, I concentrated on my computer and the questions that were already written there, grateful when Max and Nina sat down. He reached for her hand, linking their fingers and she scowled, tugging hers back. Max simply placed his arm across the back of her chair and started fiddling with her hair.

"Stop touching me. We talked about this."

"No, you talked about this. I disagreed with you."

"Canfield, I swear to God I will punch you."

He looked straight at her and pressed a kiss to her lips, stilling her and stopping her protests as she melted into him. "Do your worst."

The envy that snaked through me came so suddenly, so forcefully that I could do nothing to stop it. Max wasn't about to give up, no matter how much Nina pushed him. He wouldn't back down just because she asked him to, just because she'd been scared and overwhelmed. No, he wasn't leaving, because he loved her. People who loved one another didn't just walk away…which should logically mean that I had never loved Ryan and he had never loved me; therefore, seeing him had only hurt because I'd been unprepared.

"Mia, can we get this over with so Princess can take his sparkles and get out of here and I can get back to work?"

"She adores me. It's almost embarrassing the way she fawns over me."

"Keep dreaming, Canfield."

"Only of you, darling."

Before Nina could snap back, or before I snapped and punched one or both of them in the face—apparently I was through the depression stage of mourning and headed fast into anger—I interrupted. "Okay. You're the top two students at school, but also in the state. Your GPAs are only one thousandth of a point different. What do you have to say about that?"

"I wish I'd taken Spanish honors instead of Latin I my freshman year so my GPA was better than his."

"You'd still have your PE grade," Max said and Nina sucked in a breath.

"College decisions yet?" I asked to save him.

"Embry Riddle. I committed in January." Nina crossed her arms over her chest.

"Why Embry Riddle when you got offers from all of the best schools in the nation?"

"I want to be an aeronautical engineer. They're the best at that.

Logically, that will make me the best at what I do later on."

I nodded and wrote down the answer, though I'd already known it. "What about you, Max? You both attended a week long seminar in Tucson this summer for engineering. Do you have the urge to build?"

He shook his head. "No, not roads and bridges at least."

I raised my eyebrow. "Airplanes and Space crafts?"

He grinned. "No, I'll leave space to Torres. Medicine," he said before I could ask again. "I want to study biochemistry and go to med school."

"What about baseball? Was that a factor in your school of choice?"

He shook his head. "No, I'm a catcher, and I'm not the best there is. If I want to do baseball and school, I'll try to walk on. It's Ryan who can play baseball anywhere he wants. I'm just the one behind the plate who gets lucky enough to throw out a steal runner every now and then. But with medicine," he lifted his hands in a *wow* gesture. "With medicine, I can learn to save people and give them something more. I can learn to give them a life they may have never had otherwise."

"So you have a God complex?" Nina asked. "You have an ego that demands you be able to give people the one thing that no one else can?"

Max stared at her for a minute, and then just shook his head. "No, Torres, my ego isn't nearly as needy as yours. I want to help people while working toward advancements in the medical field that can be taken to other countries and help make their populations healthier, their hopes bigger. That's not ego," he said and tapped Nina's nose when her eyes widened. "It's called a heart, Tinman."

"Have you chosen a school yet? The deadline is fast approaching and you're still listed as undecided."

Nina smiled and said *no* at the same time that Max answered *yes*. "Southern California. University of."

Nina gaped at him while Max smiled at me. "When did you

decide this?" Nina asked before I could.

"A month ago."

"Why?"

He turned to look at her. "Why what?"

"Shut it, Canfield, and stop playing games. You got accepted to Harvard. I know you've wanted to go to Harvard Medical School since you were little. You told me."

"And I still can. USC is only the first step, Torres, and I really like the sunshine. It rains in Massachusetts. I hear it even snows."

"Max—"

"Why USC?" I repeated Nina's words, cutting her off. She scowled at me, but I ignored her. Max looked down at his hands and shrugged.

"It's like you said, Torres and I can both go to school anywhere; I got a lot of offers and one of them was from USC. I took it because it's a great school. Plus, it's close to where I want to be. And who I want to be *with*."

"Oh, God," Nina whispered and I smiled.

This time, it was Max who turned toward her. "Prescott and L.A. aren't that far away, I Googled it."

"You're an idiot."

"So you've said." Reaching over, he linked his fingers with hers and this time, she didn't try and shake them loose. "Got your prom dress yet?"

"Oh, God."

~

For the first time in a month, I ran at the end of the day, chasing the dying sun as it bled pink and orange over the horizon while the muted grays snuck in and sucked away the color, leaving only a glowing gray in its place.

The gravel crunched under my feet as I forged ahead, switching to the dirt as I pushed up the mountain and away from the town and the lights, away from the responsibilities that were all precariously balanced. Here in the darkness, away from the everyday, I could admit what I couldn't back there to anyone: I didn't know what I wanted, and more, I didn't know who I was.

Watching Nina and Max together today, I recognized a large part of what I wanted, and it was simple to say. I wanted love. Not the kind my mother had, or that Joe had for Morgan, I wanted the kind of love that let me be whoever I was, the kind that helped me grow, that someone gave me not because of what I could do, but because of who I was.

The kind I had felt with Ryan and walked away from. Only now, he was the one walking away.

Like it had the night that Joe left and I began running here, the hills and the darkness offered me peace, a kind of salvation that I had needed since that day that my family had crumbled. We were still a little broken, even though pieces of our foundation had been carefully reset in the past weeks; still, we were so fragile that I felt if I moved wrong, it might shatter all over again and this time the damage could be irreparable.

I ran, my legs pushing me up the dirt road that was surrounded by cacti and other succulents and towering rock formations, but the peace that once surrounded me when I hit this point was getting harder and harder to find as the world below seemed to follow me.

Ryan hadn't been wrong when he'd said it was easier for me to follow a decision that someone else made; that's exactly what I did, followed the plan someone else set out for me in the hopes that if I succeeded, I'd be worthy of them. In the past two weeks, talking with Ethan had forced me to see what I'd previously refused: sometimes, it just didn't matter. All we could ever do was be ourselves and recognize that sometimes, people hurt us. We couldn't change that, any more than we could change their feelings. As I had been trying to do my entire life—make my parents love me, love each other, love our family as much as I needed them to.

Now, my mother was trying, working with Ethan, not rushing to check his grades but to check on him. She'd even come to my track meet this week, then taken us all to dinner afterward. And still, I wanted more and I was afraid I was always going to.

More from her, from my dad, from myself. From Ryan.

Tears leaked out of my eyes and my lungs burned, but I pushed on, further and further into the darkened hills, trying to find the peace that had once saved me.

Chapter Twenty-Eight
Ryan

I didn't go to prom, despite the fact that Sarah asked me several times. Each time she asked, her method got more and more creative until the Friday before, I found her on the hood of my car wearing a t-shirt with my name on it...and nothing else.

That was one of her more persistent moments, and since I had been slightly tempted despite myself, I decided it was safer to stay completely away from her and any other temptations she had up her sleeve. As the clock ticked away to eight, I thought about getting drunk and having a party of my own while I waited for all of the after prom ones to start, and then I decided I just didn't have enough energy, which was probably good. I hadn't had a drink since November, and though it was my desire to be with Mia that had brought about the change, I was finding that I liked the person I was now better than I liked the person I'd been.

And being hung over sucked. I never realized how much until I'd spent this much time *not* hung over.

Deciding that if I wasn't going to get drunk I needed to find something else to do with all of my energy, I slapped on my running shoes and headed downstairs. There was no way I could stay in this house all night without going insane. On my way down the stairs, my mom called out to me and I detoured to the kitchen.

"No dancing shoes for you tonight?"

I shook my head and grabbed a bottle of water from the fridge before sitting down with her and my dad at the table. "Nope. Just gonna go run."

Quirking her brow, she reached for my forehead and laid her hand on it. "Run? Are you feeling all right? Are you ill?"

I smiled and knocked her hand off. "I'm fine. I need to be in better shape for July workouts with ASU anyway, so I figured I might as well start early. And it's not like I'm doing anything right now."

"I'll say," my dad mumbled and continued thumbing through the magazine in front of him.

My mom choked on a laugh and I narrowed my eyes at him. "What was that, old man?"

His eyes met mine over the edge of his magazine and I waited. Even when my mom shifted in her seat, I kept my eyes on his, waiting for him to speak.

Lowering his magazine, he looked straight at me, his gaze strong and steady. My lips wanted to twitch as we stared at one another, but I kept still and waited. This was his tactic—a pitcher, he'd always been good at psyching his batters out. I'd learned long ago not to anticipate what he was going to throw at me, but to wait and take the pitch as it came.

"Well, son, I think it's about time you stopped being such a pussy and went after what you wanted."

I don't know who was more shocked, my mother or me, but as my father raised his magazine again, both of us simply stared at him.

"Phillip!" my mother said after a minute and he shrugged without looking up.

"I call it like I see it, Jojo, and for the first time in his life, our boy's giving up."

"Giving up on what, Dad? Didn't I just say I was going for a run so I could be in better shape for next season? Next season with the *Sun Devils*."

"I never said you weren't motivated, Ryan, but baseball isn't what's hurting you, and we all know it. That girl walked out and you let her. Now you're doing anything and everything to get over her, when maybe what you should be doing is talking to her, telling her how you feel. At least then you can walk away knowing you did everything you could."

"Phillip," my mother said again, and again he shrugged.

"I know you don't agree, Jojo, but that's because she hurt your boy. If you step away from that for a second you'll see I'm right. Whatever happens to them, he needs to tell her how he feels right now, because if he doesn't, he's going to think about it for a long time, and it's going to hurt. Regret always hurts."

"So does rejection," I snapped back. "I didn't give up on her, Dad, she gave up on us. If there really was an *us*."

"Of course there was. This is what I'm talking about. Why would you say that? Why would you even think that?"

"Because she doesn't trust me!" I exploded and water spewed like a geyser out of the bottle in my hand as I clenched my fists. "Something happens and she shuts down. Someone hurts her and she shuts them out, shuts me out. She comes to me and says she needs me, tells me she wants to feel, to be with me, and then I make one mistake, don't tell her one thing because I don't want to make her life any harder, and she shuts me out." Deflated, I scrubbed my hands over my face and pressed them to my eyes, mortally afraid I would cry. "I've wanted her since the first day I saw her, and once I had her, she was all I could think about. Even now, after she's rejected me and girls are lying naked on my car, she's still all I can think about."

"Excuse me?" my mother said and I had to laugh at her expression.

"Don't worry, I didn't do anything, which is why I'm going for a run instead of going to prom."

She nodded, leaning back again, and I looked at my dad. "I'm not a quitter, but eventually, isn't there a time when you can't fight anymore?"

"No," he said and this time, he leaned across the table. "Even when it's the bottom of the ninth and you're down by five with a full count, and you can't possibly make up those runs, you fight until the game's all the way done. Then you go to practice the next day and fight some more."

Heading out of the house, I wondered if my dad was right. Was I giving up? Or was I moving on? Was I ready to move on?

I was eighteen. Logically, a lot of eighteen-year-olds had intense moments with someone and then broke up, because really, who stayed with their high school boyfriend or girlfriend after high school?

Even as I thought it I knew I was making an excuse. Whether or not Mia and I would have been forever, how I felt about her was stronger than some moment, some connection that was just to avoid boredom during my senior year. How I had felt about her, how I still felt about her, was consuming, and when I'd told her I'd wait, that we were worth it, I hadn't been lying.

Mia was everything, and though I knew my life would go on without her, I wondered if my dad was right and I had just given up because rejection was hard to take. Isn't that what she expected, anyway? People to give up on her and find their own lives, their more important lives while she stayed behind and did the right thing?

Winding my way through town, I didn't recognize where I was going until I was there, until I looked up and saw the horizon, almost completely dark now, only one small sliver of silver light outlining the hills where the sky rested. My future was like that, the steady hill that stood no matter what. I wasn't going to stop living because the person I loved didn't love me back. Or wouldn't let herself love me back.

As I pushed forward, I remembered the nights we'd come here, first after she was accepted to Stanford, and after that as a place to be together, to feel together. Touching Mia was unlike anything I'd ever known, and being with her, feeling her need me as much as I needed her had been everything. So thinking, I pushed further, feeling the familiar and hated burn in my legs and lungs, stripping off my shirt and tucking it into the waistband of my shorts as I continued. Maybe my dad had been right, and I was just being a pussy—a word I never thought I'd hear from him in my life. My mother, yes, but Phillip

Murphy, the master of the quiet game and silent looks? Never. So maybe he had a point and I was just giving in too easily.

I wanted Mia, had wanted Mia for what felt like forever. I wasn't going to break without her, not again, but I also didn't want to wonder my whole life if I had given up too easily, if I had quit when all she had needed was for me to ask. Or to show her.

I wondered about the timing and if I should talk to her now or give her more time as I jogged back down the hill and into our cul de sac. Then I glanced over at Mia's house and saw her stepping out of her car in a dress that was so light it reminded me of the light against the hills as it glowed against her skin and fell in one long line to her ankles. Her hair was swept over one bare shoulder and left to rain down to her elbow.

The sight of her struck me as it always did, and even though I was prepared for it, I took a minute, steadying my heart rate and my breathing, controlling the overwhelming desire I had to run—whether it was toward her or away I wasn't sure. I knew that this was my chance, my opportunity to say what I wanted, to tell her how I felt, and still, the part of me that wanted to run also knew that I was opening myself up to be rejected again and fear of that was holding me back.

"Jesus, I *am* a pussy."

Purposely turning away from my house, I jogged over to where she stood staring at her phone.

"Must have been some date if you're home before ten o'clock and staring at your phone."

It might have been immature of me, but seeing her jump and stumble a little smoothed out most of my nerves. Nothing was more intimidating than masked Mia. And nothing was more entertaining than the real Mia. If I irritated her enough, she always got real, and it turned out I was in the mood for real.

Score one for Dad on the motivation.

I kept moving until I was only a step away from her and when I stopped, I was too close for her to be comfortable, which meant that she would have to be rude and take a step back if she wanted more space. I was betting she did, just as I was betting on her manners winning out.

"Nice dress." Because I wanted to, and because I knew how much she would hate it, I reached out and traced a finger along the dress, watching her eyes as I traced the sheer material, brushing her ribs as I did. To her credit, she never broke eye contact, never cringed or stepped back. If I didn't know where to look, I wouldn't have any idea she was remotely affected by me. But I did know where to look, and one quick glance at her fingers clenched tightly on her phone told me what I needed to know: she wasn't as immune to me as she wanted to be.

Thank God.

"Not having fun at the dance?" I asked. When she didn't answer, I grinned and motioned to her phone. "Or was your date just that bad? Just so you know, if you'd said yes to me, we'd still be there, I can guarantee it."

That snapped her out of it enough that she did step back a tiny fraction, squaring her shoulders as she went. I had to admire the way she carried herself, even as I was about to make it my mission to crack her.

"I was done setting things up so I decided to come home."

"So you would have had time to dance with me. Which means you're a liar."

Her eyes narrowed and her fingers clenched even tighter on her phone. Almost there.

"Excuse me? It's almost ten o'clock, the dance ends in an hour. I don't think having one hour to spare for your date constitutes as time."

"Depends on where you're coming from. Me, I would have considered an hour spent with you worth it, but that's just me. I'm not a liar and I say what I mean."

"I am *not* a liar," she ground out, through clenched teeth.

"Oh yeah? Prove it." I took a step and eliminated all space between us, lining up our bodies as they had so many times before, pressing all of me to all of her and leaving our mouths a scant breath apart. "Prove that you're not a liar, that you really don't want to be with me like this. Prove that you can just walk away, Evans, because from where I'm standing, you're in just as deep as I am, only I'm honest about my feelings. Can you be honest, Mia?"

"Of course I can," she said, but instead of the conviction of her words earlier, her voice came out a little strained, a little breathy, and I could feel her heart racing.

"Then tell me you're done again. Say it when we're here like this, and you can see everything I feel." I leaned a little closer, my lips brushing hers. "Say it, Mia."

Chapter Twenty-Nine
Mia

The words trembled on my lips, anger pushing me to say what I had already told him once, to throw the words in his face and walk away just to prove that I could. And then I wondered what that proved, really. That I was a great liar? That I was firm in my idiocy?

Before I could think I leaned closer, my body drawn to his so that my lips brushed his jaw, over and down his throat as my hands snaked up and over his shoulders to lock around his neck.

I heard him mutter something, an oath, a prayer, I barely understood let alone comprehended his words as his lips found mine and took, bringing back everything that I had worked so hard to forget in the past two months. And because he was right, because I was being a liar, I took this one time, this one moment, to have what I wanted.

Feelings overwhelmed me as I met Ryan's frantic pace, my lips seeking as his did. Rising to my toes, I pressed myself more truly to him and changed the angle of the kiss, allowing his tongue to tangle with mine, for his fingers to lose themselves in my hair. As his hands wandered down my back and over my dress, as he broke the kiss long enough to press his lips to my throat and murmur incomprehensible words, sensations swamped me and left me short of breath. And then he said my name, just my name, and everything I'd felt in the past month came rushing back to me.

"Wait, Ryan." I unlocked my arms from around his neck and

stepped back, lifting my hands so that he could see I needed a minute. He didn't step back, but he did release me, his hands going up and palm out in a mirrored movement of mine.

"I'm sorry, that was too fast. I know it was too fast. I can't seem to help it, though, Evans. I miss you." When I went to speak, his eyes narrowed and stopped the words on my tongue. "Are you about to tell me you don't feel what I feel? That what just happened was instinct, that it could have happened with anyone, not just me? Because I call bullshit, Mia."

"That's not what I'm about to say."

"Then what are you about to say, Mia? Jesus, I can see it on your face and you haven't even spoken." Raking his hands through his hair, he took a step back, and then another, before turning and pacing the length of the driveway and back. "If you want me as much as I want you, then why are you walking away, Evans? And don't tell me you don't want me," he said in a barely there voice. "I deserve the truth, not some excuse."

I knew he was right, but try as I may, I couldn't find the truth. All I knew was that he was too much right now, what I felt for him was too much when what I needed was to focus on me for a while. Not just my family, though they were a part of it, but me. I had told Ethan the truth when I told him he had to start living for himself. Now I needed to do that, and that included not allowing myself to be swept up in Ryan Murphy.

"I do want you, Ryan," I said and he stepped toward me. I held out my hands to stop him. "But I'm not ready for you. I wasn't lying that day when I said I wasn't ready. I'm not. What I feel for you is too much and it's too fast. I barely know who I am and when I'm with you, I don't care. All I care about is you, and I can't be like that. I *won't* be like that."

"I'm not your dad, Mia."

I shook my head. "I don't think you are, but I think *I* might be. I'm too wrapped up in who I am and what I need right now, to think clearly. I'm always going to run away when things get hard, and that's not fair to you."

"So stop running."

"I'm working on it." I took a deep breath and stepped closer, wrapping my arms around his stiff middle, waiting, waiting until he finally relented and put his arms around me. Resting my head against his heart, I stood there and breathed him in before stepping back and letting go.

He stood there, staring at me, his eyes dark and steady as they stared at me. "I meant what I said, Evans. I can wait."

I shook my head, though my chest constricted at the knowledge that he was telling me the truth. "I'd never ask you to do that, Ryan. It's not fair to you."

"Fuck fair," he snapped out and stalked over to me. "You do your thing, Evans, take your time and find yourself or whatever else you need to do. But you hear me: some feelings never go away, no matter how hard someone tries to ignore them." He pressed his lips to mine, fiercely, before stepping back. "I won't ever ask you to change, Evans, and I won't stop fighting just because you don't know how to. I love you, Mia. Eventually, you're going to believe it."

I watched him go, keeping my eyes on him until he disappeared inside of his house. "I think I love you, too." Wasn't that the problem?

Giving in, I sat on the front steps and put my head on my knees. I had done the right thing, but that didn't make it any easier. He deserved someone who could give as much as he did, and right now, I wasn't that someone. I was wrapped up in me, in my family, in everything we were going through, and to accept what he was offering would have only lead to heartbreak for him. I wasn't done running yet.

I don't know how long I sat there brooding into the darkness, but when I finally stood to go inside, I heard the sound of an engine. It was faint, almost a flutter, but as I listened it got louder, and for the second time that night I watched a car pull into the driveway. I didn't recognize the dark sedan, but as the driver's side door opened a flood of memories came over me, paralyzing me.

His hair was still a little long, a little darker than my own, but his face had lost that hollowed out haunted look. He stepped out of the driver's side and moved around to the passenger door, and I stood watching as he opened it and the one behind it, a smile on his face as he held out his hands. Curious, I stepped closer as he helped two people out, and my heart rate increased when I saw the pale blonde hair glow in the twilight, a stark contrast to the platinum blonde next to it.

When Joe shut the door and turned, I sucked in a breath as I stared at Lily and Cora. They both looked at me then, but it was Joe who spoke first.

"Hey, Mimi."

~

"Cousin, your dress is fabulous. Did your mom pick that one out? I'm shocked at her taste."

Cora and I were in my room twenty minutes later, having left Joe downstairs with our mother who had begun to cry the minute we all walked in the door. I'd had tears in my own eyes as I watched her get up from the couch where she'd been reading, knowing that the reason she was there was because she had been waiting up for me, something she hadn't done since before Christmas. Then, as Joe went straight to her and embraced her, my tears fell for a different reason entirely. She wouldn't be alone anymore, not like she has been.

I stripped off my dress and threw it out of the closet, replacing it with a pair of sweats and a tank top before walking out to sit on the bed next to Cora. "No, I picked it out. I've been getting better at that. *We've* been getting better at that," I corrected.

"So, you and your mom have really spoken, huh? And it worked?"

I nodded. "I think so, I mean, we talk almost every day, she doesn't keep secrets, she doesn't shut down as much, and when she does, she works to pull out of it for the boys." I thought of her face when we had walked inside a few minutes ago, the shock and then the excitement, quickly followed by what could only be regret. "She doesn't know how to be a person anymore, and for a while, the only way she could function was by making sure *we* functioned at an optimum level."

"That's good, I'm glad we came when we did then."

Staring at her, I quirked my brow. "Why did you come?" I finally asked. "And when did Joe come back home? And how are you with Joe and Lily?"

"If by back home you mean into the states, then right after Christmas, which you would know if you ever read your email and responded to people. Then, he showed up in California around late February. He's been there since, working, thinking about going back to school."

"And you? How did you end up in California and then driving to Arizona?"

She smiled. "Lil needed some expert advice and since I took online classes and graduated last week, much to my mother's undying regret, I decided now was as good a time as any to make a road trip."

"What expert advice did Lily need?"

"I can't tell you everything because it's not my story, but I can tell you she had an interview for an internship, and I helped her pluck her eyebrows and saved her from wearing the world's ugliest matching pant suit. Not to mention the date I helped her get ready for."

"Cora. Shut up. Lily had a date? She called you to help her? What was her interview for? Oh my god, where have I been?"

"Martyring yourself, from what Josh's email said."

My head snapped up and I gaped at her. "Excuse me?"

"I just thought we should cut to the point."

"And what is the point?" I asked with my teeth clenched.

"The point, Cousin, is that Joshua emailed your brother and sister a few weeks ago and said things at home were bad, though he didn't tell them specifics. Basically, he asked them to come home, to help you and the rest of your family. He was scared," she said and I felt my eyes prick with tears. "Mia, what's going on?"

I shook my head and wondered where to start. "A couple of

months ago, Ethan saw our dad walk into the guestroom when he got home from his business trip. Apparently, he's noticed how distant Dad is, how cruel and cold, and when he saw that he kind of snapped. He started partying with older kids, acting out in public, failing some classes. I found out about that and we fought initially until he explained why he was doing those things. Now we've turned a corner, worked out how to get him back on track and back to being who he wants to be."

I pressed my hands to my eyes and took a deep breath. I was too tired to cry, too numb to feel anything more than weighing sadness. "The worst part was that my mom didn't even notice. Ethan's failure was like some kind of experiment to see if she even knew he existed. Two years ago? He'd have been ex-communicated or sent to boarding school for those grades. Two months ago? She never even knew."

"Did you tell her?"

I shook my head and stared at a spot on my comforter. "No. I promised Ethan, and he's been trying, hasn't been drunk again, hasn't gone anywhere without Josh. But I did ask her about my dad sleeping in the guestroom. She cried," I said and finally looked at Cora. "She cried and said she doesn't know why he doesn't love her, why he doesn't want her anymore. I wanted to see them work it out after Joe left, Cora, to see that they still loved each other. Now? All I can see is that they may never have loved each other in the first place, and it bothers me because I don't know what that says about our family."

"Oh stop, it says nothing other than they're human and have issues. About damn time someone in this family admitted it."

Surprised by her harsh tone, I sat up to stare at her. "Did you miss the part where I said Ethan was out getting wasted every weekend since God knows when? Isn't that messed up enough for you?" Irate that she could be so insensitive, I continued. "Or how about the fact that my mother didn't notice, because newsflash, she barely notices anything unless it's what someone else thinks about our family. My father barely knows who we are. Is any of this messed up enough for you?"

"Oh, stop, you know I care and you know I don't want your family hurting. What I want is for you to realize that you shouldn't have to accept that this is your responsibility. Why didn't you email or call Lily? Why didn't you ask Joe for help? Or me, for godssake, why didn't you at least text me and vent? Why did Joshua have to do it, Mia?"

"You were in Oregon, Lily was at school dealing with her own life, and I haven't seen Joe in three years, what would I say to him?"

"Anything!" she shouted. "Jesus, say anything, Mia. Whatever you said would be better than sitting here, being mad at everyone, sacrificing your life for theirs."

Angry because she was angry, pissed that rather than sympathy she was blaming me, I stood. "You don't know what you're talking about."

She rolled her eyes. "Oh please, Cousin. I don't know what I'm talking about? I live with a selfish, self-absorbed mother who's hated me my entire life because I'm younger than she is, and a father who walks around smiling because he doesn't know what the hell else to do." Her voice was tight with tears and though I wanted to, I didn't go to her, didn't reach out and hold her because what she was saying shamed me.

"Life sucks, Mia, don't delude yourself into thinking you're the only person who suffers. People leave each other, people fall out of love. Or, if you're lucky like me, people never really loved you to begin with. No matter how hard you try, no matter how much you give up, how much you just plain *give*, shit happens. But you have to keep living, and you have to learn to ask for help, Mia, otherwise, you'll never make it."

Lily walked in and her eyes were wide as she stared at Cora and me standing ten feet apart, both of us with our arms crossed and tears in our eyes.

"What's going on?"

When I made no move to answer, Cora gave a wry smile. "Mia

was just explaining to me why her life is harder than everyone else's. Your family's not perfect, so she has to give up everything in the hope of being perfect for them."

"Oh, yeah, I heard that somewhere. I also heard she's the only one who can do it, like the Chosen One of the Evans' household. Impressive."

"Oh go to hell, both of you."

"If I were religious, I'm sure that would be my path. It's definitely Lily's, since she's a judgmental bitch. Regardless," Cora continued as I narrowed my eyes at her and Lily barked out a laugh, "the point isn't us, it's you. What are you doing?"

I went to answer, to tell her exactly what I'd been doing the past few months, but looking at both of them, my sister and my cousin, smiling at each other as they acknowledged their flaws, the words disappeared.

"I don't know." And this time, it was true. Sitting down on my bed, I raked my hands through my hair and curled my legs to my chest. "I thought I was doing the right thing, following the rules and being the person Mom and Dad wanted. I thought I was doing what was best for Ethan and Joshua, setting a good example and all of that, acting as though there was nothing wrong with our family."

"They're not idiots, Mia."

I laughed despite myself and nodded at Lily. "I've noticed. Seeing Ethan drunk like that..." I trailed off and shook my head. "He looked so little all of a sudden, so *not* Ethan. He was like a kid playing dress up and I couldn't believe I hadn't known about it. Everyone else knew except for me."

"And me," Lily said, raising her eyebrows at me. "You finally found out and instead of telling me, you tried to take care of it all on your own."

"And it worked," I snapped. "I'm sorry if I wanted to avoid having you come home and judge our little brother for being sad, like you judged our older one for wanting something different, but I won't apologize for not calling you when you barely call home as it is."

"Mia," she started but I shook my head.

"No, Lily. You left—both of you left," I said when I saw Joe standing in the doorway. "Maybe I should have called or emailed or texted, but I didn't because I honestly didn't think of it. Neither of you has been here, really been here since the day you walked out, when you made it clear you didn't want to be here."

"I didn't walk out, Mia, I went to school. Just like you're going to next year."

"And I've already promised Ethan that I would come home, and stay in touch, and still remember him. He disappeared," I said pointing to Joe, "but you left, Lily, and even when you come home, all you're doing is thinking about leaving again. So, sorry if you're mad that I didn't call, but I'm mad at you, too. At both of you, dammit."

"Well look who's all grown up with a temper," Lily mumbled and I raised my eyebrows at her. With a sigh, she shoved her hands in her pockets and rocked back on her heels. "Fine, you're partly right. I did leave, and I did stay away because it was easier than being here, but that doesn't mean I didn't want to know if something was wrong, that I wouldn't have tried to help. Despite what you think, Mia, I do care." I let out a slow breath and nodded as she sat down next to me. "And I understand how you're feeling right now. Part of the reason I was so eager to leave was so I could just get it over with, just go and do and see if I was really good enough to be a part of the Evans' legacy, or if I was going to have to ride the coattails of our name for the rest of my life."

Remembering the way she had apologized to Cora this winter, the way she had admitted that she wasn't as positive about her life track as she had once been, I began to understand that Lily, too, had her moments of insecurity. "What did you decide?"

"Oh, I'm smart enough. By the time I graduate, Dad will be begging me to be a part of the company, and I'll have to decide if I want to or not." She grinned, but I could hear the relief in her voice, the life that had been missing five months ago when she'd been home.

"I'm glad for you, Lil. I was a little worried about you over

Thanksgiving, wondering if something had happened."

She nodded and her smile turned pensive. "Nothing major, just some insecurity that took me a bit to push through, to conquer and realize that I'm good enough, better than most actually, even if neither of our parents remembers to tell me."

I reached out and gripped her hand, relieved to hear those words from her, as if my own feelings were validated. She looked down at our hands and then turned hers over so our palms were touching. "Seriously though, Mia, you have to tell people these things. Maybe you don't think you need to, but you do. Maybe we're messed up, but we're a family and I want to be a part of it."

"I know you do, Lil, and to be honest, there were other reasons I didn't call." Looking at Joe, I gave a half smile. "I guess a part of me thought this was payment—my consequence, if you know what I mean."

He stared at me and I stared back, wondering why it was as if he had never left, as if he hadn't walked out and never turned back, even to wave to me one last time. "Consequence for what?" he asked and Cora and Lily turned to look at him.

"For thinking about myself more than my family. I stopped caring about anyone but me and how the boy I fell for made me feel, and in the end, my family paid for it. Just like you."

Chapter Thirty
Ryan

The flash went off one last time and I saw spots. Blinking furiously, I prayed there was no permanent damage.

"Look at the camera, Ryan."

"I can't see the camera, Mom. Jesus, is the flash satellite capable? White lightening?"

Smiling, she lowered the lens a fraction so I could see her whole face, only slightly out of focus now that my vision was returning. "I bought the camera last year when I didn't know if I'd be taking graduation photos, or long distance pictures of you in the yard in your orange jumpsuit while you served your time."

"I can't believe you doubted me."

"I can't believe you graduated."

I grinned and walked over to her, grateful to be shedding the ridiculous cap and gown. "I had some help."

She motioned to someone over my shoulder. "There's your help now."

I knew it was her before I looked, and still, I couldn't prepare myself for the onslaught of feelings that raced through me. Watching her there in her yellow sundress and matching shoes, surrounded by people that looked too similar to be anyone but family, though I didn't know any of them except for Ethan and Josh, I finally understood that sometimes shit didn't go your way, no matter how much you wanted it to.

I had my life, my future. And for a brief while I'd had Mia. Maybe that's the way it was supposed to be.

"I was talking about you, you know," I said turning back to her. "You didn't let me fail, and you didn't shut me out. Even when I was wearing an orange jumpsuit on the side of the road and picking up garbage, paying the city for my sins, you never disowned me."

"Don't think I didn't consider it," she said, and I laughed as I swung my arm around her shoulders. "Look, I'm going to drag your father away from the cookies and head over to the Club with the Canfields to get our table. Why don't you say your goodbyes and get Max? You can meet us there."

I leaned down and kissed her cheek, suddenly grateful that she'd always been there to kick my ass. "Thanks."

She hugged me fiercely and then stepped back. "Don't lollygag, I'm hungry." And then she was walking away and I was left standing there, wondering if I should just skip all of the goodbyes, go find Max and be done with it. Besides, hadn't I said everything there was to say a few weeks ago when I'd told her I'd love her no matter what? After which she'd rejected me, *again.* How many times could a guy really take that kind of beating and get up from it?

Thinking that it was cowardly but wise, I turned and started to look for Max, my eyes sweeping over the crowd. I made a small circle without spotting him, and just as I brought out my phone to text him I heard my name. Glancing up, there was Mia three feet from me, waiting patiently, all of her glorious hair long and loose, spreading over her shoulders to tempt me.

Apparently, this guy needed one more good punch before it was all said and done.

"Looking for someone?" she asked and a myriad of answers filtered through my brain.

My pride, I seem to have left it with you. Along with my heart...and my balls. Pretty sure those are in your back pocket, too, otherwise looking at you wouldn't make me want to curl up on the ground and weep like a schoolgirl.

Clearing my throat, I nodded my head. "Max."

"He, um, walked Nina to the parking lot with her family. They left about two minutes ago."

I nodded. "Thanks, I'll catch him out there."

I started to head past her, my eyes skimming over and around her, landing anywhere but on her face. It was better this way, simpler. She would go north, and I would go south and our lives would continue as they had before we had ever become a *we*. End of story.

"Ryan, can we talk for a minute?"

I stopped and closed my eyes, wishing for a brief second that I could just ignore her and keep going, walk as far away from here and her as possible so I could begin to get over what had never really been there in the first place. Not the way I thought, at least.

"I don't think that's such a good idea, Evans."

I heard her step lightly around me and when I opened my eyes, she was there, directly in my vision. "At least let me walk to the parking lot with you. Please, Ryan," she said when she saw me hesitate. "I have some things I'd like to say to you."

Jamming my hands into my pockets, I gave a small nod and we turned to begin our walk, so similar to the day when I'd told her she was my dream, the day I'd told her I would wait for us because we were worth it. I wondered now if it was better or worse that I knew there wasn't a chance for us, if this moment should be liberating in some way because I was free to begin a new chapter in my life.

Because I didn't have an answer, I stopped thinking about it. "You better start talking or you're going to miss your chance."

She flinched slightly, as if my sharp tone physically hurt her. Irritated because it made me feel like an asshole when all I'd wanted was to love this girl, I kept walking.

"I, um, I guess I wanted to say goodbye." When I stopped to stare at her, she blushed and looked down.

"You could have sent a text if that was really all you wanted to say."

She nodded and brushed her hair off her face, forcing me to

clench my hands into fists inside my pockets. "I'm sorry I wasn't who you wanted me to be, Ryan, more sorry because I wanted to be that person, too."

This was unexpected. I kept my eyes on her as I inclined my chin slightly. "Who do you think I wanted you to be, Evans?"

Her eyes found mine and in them I saw everything she refused to say, refused to give to me, and it was like a blow to the head. Everything I wanted, and still, no matter how hard I worked, how patient I was, it may never be mine. "Someone who could love like you do, someone confident and open and free and happy. Someone who made you happy," she whispered.

"I guess I'm sorry, too," I said and watched her face fall. Stepping closer even though my brain screamed *warning* at me over and over, I risked myself once more and cupped her face in my hands, brushing them through her hair at the temples, all the way back and through to the tips. "I'm sorry that you thought I wanted you to be anything but who you are. I loved you, Mia, from that first day that you sobbed into your knees, to the last one we had together when you were laughing and jumping fences because you trusted me. I loved every part of who you were, and I'm sorry you can't see that you *are* all of those things."

Her eyes brimmed with tears as she looked up at me, and her voice shook when she whispered my name.

Because I knew what she needed, because everything she felt, I felt, I leaned down and rested my forehead against hers one last time, breathing in her scent, memorizing every detail I could. Squeezing my eyes shut, I raised my head enough to press my lips to her brow.

"Miss you."

This time I didn't look back as I walked away, and she didn't call my name.

Chapter Thirty-One
Mia

Walking up the stairs at the end of my own graduation day, I recognized just how different the sounds around me were from the previous two. I could hear doors slamming and the twins shouting. Cora's laugh echoed throughout the great room below, followed by a quick insult from Lily. I could even hear my mother talking. Stopping at the top landing, I surveyed the wide hallway in front of me, noticing the doors that were open or cracked, a light left on to cast a small glow on the carpet.

It was as if people had moved in and begun living in the house overnight. Where there had been closed doors and muffled conversations three weeks ago, suddenly there were messes and shouting. With a small smile I wondered if my mom knew her wish had come true; the house wasn't quiet anymore.

"It's a nice sound, isn't it?"

Joe stood in the doorway to his room, his hands in his pockets, and even though he'd been home for the better part of a month now, I jolted at seeing him there. We hadn't really spoken just the two of us since he'd come home, and I'd wondered if we would. I couldn't explain it, but there was a tension between us that had never existed when he'd lived here before. It was odd because nothing of the sort lived between Lily and I, and before, she was the one I hadn't been able to talk to, to understand, to really get along with. Now, whether it was Cora's influence or her own acceptance of the fact that she was good enough, something had changed in her and we had found a place in our relationship that made us both happy.

Joe and I, however, were walking on eggshells, neither one of us sure of how to approach the other, how to begin a conversation that was more than surface talk.

"Want to take a walk with me, Mimi? There are some things I want to tell you."

It was so like him not to demand, not to just say, 'let's go,' and still, I found myself resisting. "I was about to put on my gear and go for a run."

He winced slightly, and I was tempted to laugh, remembering that Joe was a basketball and baseball guy, just like the twins. Exercise just for the sake of exercise wasn't something he enjoyed.

"It's almost a hundred degrees out," he started and I lifted my shoulders and let them fall.

"It's June in Arizona; almost a hundred is relatively mild."

"How far?" he asked and again, I shrugged. "Jesus, okay, but if I die, at least try to resuscitate me. Don't make this a mafia-type moment and leave me there to get my broken and bleeding self home."

"I'm not the one who leaves people to fend for themselves."

He stared at me as the barb hit him, and then nodded. "Point taken."

Feeling guilty because I couldn't seem to stop myself from making snide comments when all I really wanted to do was throw myself at him and weep, I started toward my room. "I'll meet you downstairs in five minutes."

He was already waiting for me when I finally walked out of the side door near the garage, and without a word we started through the neighborhood and onto the walking path that traveled the golf course and through the town. We kept our pace steady, neither of us ever moving ahead or falling behind the other as we made our way to the hills. Lost Creek came into view, and for a minute I saw Joe glance at me in my peripheral, but I said nothing and neither did he as we continued on and up.

I pushed harder than necessary, a small sense of satisfaction coating me when I understood that he wasn't being silent out of respect for me, but because he was breathing too hard to talk. I took the hill at a pace that had my own heart racing and lungs burning, but I didn't back down, not until we made it to the top of the crest that allowed us to see out to the hills beyond where we stood.

When we finally stopped, the sun was shifting into its downward descent and the hills that I never quite conquered were lit, their stark brown taking on a pinkish, mystical hue, one that would change colors a dozen times in subtle ways as the sun bled its way onto the horizon and down, making room for the moon to rise and have its turn. I'd never thought of it that way, never considered that the sun disappeared each day so the moon could shine, too, even on days when the moon was covered by clouds, or when the Earth's orbit was just so that all that could be seen of the moon was a small sliver. Yet, sliver or not, the sun always set, it always disappeared and made room.

"After you left, I wondered if I could run far enough, fast enough to make it over those hills and see what was on the other side. Like getting away from the city, from our house like you did would somehow make me understand better, understand more, and be able to accept it."

We stood next to one another with the city below us, but we didn't look down. As if it was our nature, we looked up and out, we looked ahead into that horizon and wondered what lay beyond.

"And then, after almost three years of not being able to understand, of not wanting to understand, I met someone who showed me exactly how it felt to let go, to leave the person I've become for the person I wanted to be. And like that, I understood how you felt when you left, and I think I understood why." I finally turned away from the hills and looked at him, looked at my brother for the first time in three years. "What I want to know is if it was worth it?" Clearing my throat of the tears that wanted to lodge themselves there, I tried to bring my voice above a whisper. "Did you find what you needed, or do you regret it?"

He sighed and bent down to rest his hands on his knees, his breathing still a little ragged. "I don't know how to answer that, Mimi. Leaving was what I thought I had to do, what I thought I needed to do. Looking back? It's always easier to wonder, to ask yourself what if, to think you could have done it differently, should have done it differently. I missed you, every day, and it hurt when you didn't respond to my emails and I thought you had forgotten me."

"You walked out, I didn't know what to say other than 'congratulations for escaping—life's even more miserable without you,' and that didn't feel very appropriate."

"I thought it was my price to pay, like you," he said and stood up. "I left, so you forgot me. That was the consequence for me. I had my freedom, but it came at a price. You were the price—you and Joshua and Ethan and Mom." He wiped his brow with the corner of his t-shirt. "If you're asking if that was worth it, then no, it wasn't. But I didn't know how to change it once it was done."

"I thought I would be like you," I said and he paused to stare at me. "When I was little, when I was growing up and you were always there, I thought 'one day I'm going to be just like Joe, strong and smart. Then Mom and Dad will love me like they love him.'"

"And then I left."

I nodded. "And then you left, and I was ashamed because a small part of me still wanted to be like you. Even when I hated you for what you did, something inside of me always envied you, always wished that I could be half that courageous."

He let out a bitter laugh, one that had me narrowing my eyes at him. "Leaving wasn't courageous, Mimi. The exact opposite, actually."

I shook my head. "How can you say that? I hated you for leaving but even I think what you did took guts."

"Staying takes guts. Being here with Mom and Dad and still being the person you want to be? That's courageous. I left because I was angry, Mia, and I stayed gone because I was scared. Scared that no one would want me to come home, scared that if I did come home I would fall into line because it was easier than saying what I wanted and making decisions on my own."

"Morgan?"

He laughed, a true laugh for the first time since he'd been home and I was whooshed back into the past when Joe had laughed every day. "Morgan was an excuse; I loved her as much as you can love someone who wants to change everything about you. I was eighteen and wanted to love her, wanted her to matter so that I could say what I was doing was for love. In reality, I was running away. It took a week after I left here for me to realize that I wasn't the picketing, service, do-gooder type. I just don't care enough to chain myself to a tree or ride my thumb all the way to Alaska so I can save some whales that I know nothing about." I smiled at that. "It took me slightly longer to admit to myself, and Morgan, that I wasn't any happier riding around the United States saving endangered animals and poverty stricken humans than I had been when I was forced to apply to college. After I finally told her, I found a job as a bellhop at a hotel in Southern California, and kissed Morgan goodbye for the last time."

"So what you had was fake?"

He shook his head and stared out at the city lights this time. "I don't think of it like that."

"Then how? How do you think of it?"

He sighed and stayed silent for a minute, gathering his thoughts as if what he was about to say was the golden ticket to understanding. "Life's messy, Mia, emotions are messy, and when you come from a family like ours, where everything is very controlled, very civilized and businesslike, messy emotions overwhelm you."

I thought about Ryan and everything I'd felt since he had walked into my life, the anger and the happiness, the frustration and confusion, the need, both physical and not. I had been overwhelmed by him, still was, because now what I felt scared me. I wore love like a scratchy, ill-fitting sweater that I wanted but didn't have a clue how to manage.

"The first time I ever really felt what it was like to be the center of someone's world was with Morgan," Joe said and I looked up at him. "From that moment on, she was the center of mine, and right or wrong, she made me want to be a different person. The problem was, she wanted me to be a different person, too, her kind of person, and I didn't see it until it was too late. I just liked that someone could make me feel like that. I never thought about who I was as a person, only who I was when I was with her. In the end, neither of us could be who the other needed."

Joe's words so closely echoed my own spoken to Ethan in the kitchen that I had to shake my head to process all of it. I thought of Ryan and saying goodbye to him, of what he'd said to me. He hadn't tried to change me, but I *had* changed since I'd been with him. Was that the same thing?

"Do you regret choosing her?"

"It's stupid to regret what you can't change, and I don't."

"But if you could," I insisted, finding that I was desperate to know, to understand. "If you could change your decision, if you could decide to go back and never meet Morgan, or never fall in love with her, or never leave us, would you?"

He barely thought about it before shaking his head. "No. I regret that I lost so much time with you and the twins, that I hurt Mom and made life harder here, and still, I know enough now to know that avoiding mistakes, looking for a way to make life perfect isn't reality. Reality is mistakes, failures, and heartache. I've had all three, and I'm finally in a place where I can say what I want."

I wondered if he was right, if there was never going to be a perfect moment in life for everything I felt or wanted. Considering, I looked up at him. "What do you want, Joe?"

He looked at me and there was a question in his eyes, a pleading that made me want to weep it was so powerful. "I want to come home. I want to come home and be with the people who matter."

I nodded, and he let out a small breath. "I want that, too. God, I was so mad at you," I said with a laugh and threw my arms around him. "And I'm so glad you're back. We need you, Joe."

He squeezed me tightly and nodded into my hair. "I need you guys, too. It gets lonely out there, traveling alone, seeing new things and knowing you have no one to share them with. Knowing that the people who matter don't know how you feel about them, that you miss them."

I closed my eyes and hugged him harder. "I'm sorry I didn't write back, sorry that I was so mad at you that I couldn't see that leaving was hard on you." I stepped back and wiped at my cheeks, clearing the tears from them and my eyes so I could look at him. "But I'm not sorry that you came home, and I'm not sorry to ask you to stay. We need you, Joe; Mom needs you, Ethan and Joshua need you." I offered him a weak smile. "I need you."

"Have things really been as bad as Joshua's email said?"

I nodded and wondered what it must have taken Josh to write that email, what it must have cost him to admit that he was scared. "Mom's trying since she and I talked, but it's a slow process. Dad's never home, and when he is he's so wrapped up in work or other people that he never gives anyone attention. I thought it was just me," I said, almost to myself. "But then I saw Ethan so wasted he could barely walk, and Mom so hurt she could barely focus, and I realized, we all depend on him, and we all feel let down when he chooses something else. And he always does," I murmured. "He always chooses something over his family. And we always let him."

He nodded and wrapped an arm around my shoulders. "My coming home won't necessarily make him change."

"No, it won't, but you'll be there, and sometimes that's enough."

He nodded as he reached out to throw his arm around my shoulders. "I've missed you, Mia."

"I've missed you, too." I leaned into him for a second, reveling in how comfortable I felt. Joe was home, and though we weren't perfect, or anywhere near it, I was beginning to think our family would be okay. Energized, I pushed away from him and grinned. "Come on,

I'll race you back." He groaned as I sped off, and I laughed the entire way home.

Chapter Thirty-Two
Ryan

"Dude, I'm telling you, she was totally checking me out. I bet she still is. I can feel her eyes on me. I have a sixth sense where the ladies are concerned." Jace Fuller wiggled his barely there eyebrows and inclined his chin in a "c'mon" motion. "She is, isn't she?"

I glanced over my shoulder to see the girl in question flipping her hair and shamelessly flirting with a guy who had on a bro tank and was sporting twin tats on the back of his spaghetti noodle arms. Classic fraternity douche. When she pulled out her phone to take down what could only be his number, I turned away.

"Well?" Jace prompted. I looked at his freckled complexion that only seemed to get redder in the relentless October sun. His hair was the same white blonde as his eyebrows, his eyes an eerie color of light blue. If it weren't for the freckles, he'd be sort of ghostlike.

"Totally checking you out," I said and he fist pumped. Reason number one Jace wasn't the chick magnet he claimed: the fist pump. For tacos, for a passing grade, a base hit, the rare time he actually got a girl's number. He fist pumped for everything. Reason number two: he thought he was a chick magnet, which gave him an immense amount of confidence when it came to talking to girls. Unfortunately, that confidence didn't come with common sense, and phrases like "So, how about we try each other on for size?" popped out of his mouth with terrifying regularity. He hadn't been on a second date since we'd been here, and the way he was going, the first dates were starting to dwindle off, too.

"So, Murph, you've got a hot glove, an even hotter bat, you're kind of ugly but since I live with you I can attest to the fact that you might have what the ladies term a 'hot body.'" He waggled his eyebrows and I snorted out a laugh as we pushed through the midday campus foot traffic together on our way back to our dorm from the field house where we'd just put in two hours of running, hitting, and fielding. Fuller had a hot bat, hotter than any other freshman and most of the upperclassmen. No matter what you threw him, he hit it, and he mostly hit it home. Which was a good thing, since he didn't have a hot foot, or a hot body. He was barely six feet and thick with it, his chest, his waist, and his hips all one width from shoulders to knees.

"You asking me out, Fuller? Cause I have to say, you're not really my type."

He barked out a laugh that was a cross between a polar bear and a braying donkey and shook his head. "I could change your mind, big boy, but that's for another time. What I'm asking is how come you don't got a hot girl to go with that hot glove? And don't say you're saving yourself for marriage or some such shit because I'll know you're a liar."

I laughed and shook my head. "No, I am most definitely not saving myself for marriage."

"Then what the fuck is it? Because if you wanted some, you could have it, trust me."

"Just staying focused, man. I'm in the groove, and I don't want to risk a slump."

"Humping means no slumping, son, just remember that."

"Jesus," I said as my body shook with laughter. Fuller was from Iowa, or Idaho, or some other potato or corn bred and fed state, and his thoughts revolved around two things all of the time: baseball and sex. One he was great at, the other he just dreamed of being great at.

"Seriously, though, there's a girl in my Comm class that knows who you are. She has a cute friend, too, and she mentioned we should all go out sometime. This chick's so hot you'll be batting .500 when you're done with her."

Though I laughed, I shook my head. It wasn't the time, and I wasn't the guy for that, not yet. Right now, I was satisfied playing baseball and figuring my shit out from there. I had enrolled as a Sports Communication major, like most other athletes, and I actually liked some of the classes. Of course, I was also taking an entry level English class that was making me want to gouge my eyes out, but it wasn't really the professor's fault. We were reading Shakespeare, and even though I told myself not to, I thought of *her* when I was in class, and thinking of her made me wonder about her, where she was, what she was doing, how she was doing. If she thought of me.

We hadn't spoken since we said goodbye at graduation, and though I'd seen her around during the summer, we'd never breached the barrier and crossed the road. I learned from Max that her brother was home, and that her family was working some things out. I didn't know if that meant she and her parents, or she and her mom, but I did know that whatever was happening, on those last days of summer when she'd gone for an early morning run and I'd been coming home from my own workout, she'd looked lighter, freer, not so weighed down.

It had been enough to see that and let her go, to know that maybe she was going to find a way to make herself happy for real.

It didn't stop me from wanting her, but it made the wanting easier for some reason.

"Jesus, would you look at her."

The sound of Fuller's voice brought me back to reality and I glanced up as we walked toward the front entrance of our dorm and did a double take. When the familiar sight of golden hair entered my vision again, I stopped completely.

"Now she's definitely worth a second look. What do you think, Murph? Should I go over and see if she wants to help my batting average? I feel like she could make me a starter."

Before Jace could walk toward her, I reached my arm out and stopped him, my eyes never leaving Mia. "She's taken." I was already three steps away when I heard him yell "lucky bastard" and I ignored him. She was really there, I thought as I got closer, drinking in everything from her bare legs to her light blue dress, the pink polish on her toes and the pink bracelet on her wrist. My bracelet, I realized, and felt a small glow of satisfaction.

I'd given it to her as a silly gift, something I'd won in one of those quarter machines you find at pizza parlors and grocery stores. I'd put it on her as a kind of joke, a token of my affection, I had called it, and though I had expected her to laugh and take it off, she'd worn it almost every day we were together. When I had looked at graduation, she hadn't been wearing it, but now, she was sitting on one of the benches outside of my dorm as she looked around at the trickling of people going in and out, and she was wearing the bracelet I'd given her when she'd been mine.

My heart was beating painfully, its loud thumping like a drum beat in my ears as I got close enough to say her name. When our eyes met, I saw everything I'd ever wanted in hers, and it brought me back to that first day in the library when I hadn't been able to breathe from wanting her so badly.

Now, I'd had her and lost her, and because of that, I was paralyzed at the sight of her.

"Evans," I said again as I stopped a few feet in front of her. I didn't say anything else, just stared at her, my eyes on hers as she did the same. The air between us was palpable, and immediately I wished that I was in street clothes instead of practice gear so I had somewhere to put my hands. I clenched and unclenched them a few times, the urge to reach out and touch her so strong that I was dizzy with it.

"Hi," she said after a moment and stood, bringing us one step closer together. "I, um, called up to your room but no one answered. Then I figured you might be in class so I waited. I didn't even think that you might be at practice," she finished and her eyes darted around, looking beside me and behind me, never focusing *on* me. Her hands fluttered nervously before she locked them together in front of her, her knuckles going white with the effort.

Before I could figure out what to say, or how to say it, Jace was at my side, introducing himself and making some asinine comment that made Mia laugh. Grateful, I inclined my head at him.

"Mia, this is Jace, my roommate. Jace, this is Mia. We went to high school together," I said lamely.

She reached out to take the hand he offered and I saw hers tremble slightly. Jace was babbling, keeping his mouth running a mile a minute while he still held her hand, and for a second I was amused watching her as she glanced between her hand caught in his, to his face, to me, back to her hand. True to form, she never asked him to let it go, and because it amused me, I didn't say anything either.

At one point, Jace looked over at me and inclined his head. "You gonna go change and take this lady out, or are you gonna stay sweaty and dirty? Go," he said before I could respond. "I'll keep Mia company down here while she waits for your girly ass to finish primping. It's all his hair," he said and I took a second to flip him off before I turned to sprint upstairs.

Ten minutes later in a clean pair of shorts and t-shirt, I came out to find Mia laughing, really laughing, and Jace making some idiot face while he gestured with his hands. Since I'd seen this bit before, I rolled my eyes and kept walking toward them.

"Fuller, you mind? Not everyone needs to hear that story."

"You ran into a pole showing off your speed, Murph. That story cannot be told enough."

Grinning at me like he knew what he was doing, he turned back to Mia. "Mia, if you decide Murphy here isn't your style, a little too puny and all that, you know where I live." Then he kissed her hand like the moron that he was and turned to leave. "Hey, Murph? Forget everything I said earlier. Your batting average is going to be just fine."

I laughed and shook my head and he began whistling some country tune as he passed me. Mia stood up and waited, the ease she'd displayed with Jace two minutes ago gone, replaced by the nerves she'd worn since she saw me. Her hands were clasped firmly again, and every muscle in her body was rigid as she watched me.

Grateful for the pockets in my shorts, I shoved my hands into them and tried a smile. "Let's take a walk, Evans. I'll show you around."

~

"You seem happy."

Sitting at an umbrella table at a café on the outskirts of campus, she sipped from an iced coffee while I devoured a sandwich and a bag of chips. We'd walked around saying nothing important for over an hour while I showed her where all of my classes were, the baseball and practice fields. She'd asked questions about my major and my team, how I was liking it. I'd waited for her to bring up why she was here, what she needed or wanted, but since she didn't, I didn't ask. Whatever I had learned in my brief time with her, it was that she may not know what she was doing here yet, either.

Now, while I ate and she sipped, she finally spoke.

"Does that surprise you?"

She shook her head. "No, not really. You're a happy person. It's one of the things I admired most about you, the way you can be happy just doing what you want, what you like." She gave a shy smile and I was hit with an urge to reach out and touch her, just her hair, her cheek, anything to make that connection and feel her.

I picked up my water and sipped instead.

"What about you, Evans, are you happy?"

Her eyes stayed on mine while she thought about it, and then she smiled, that slow, blooming smile that always took a second to form, as if her lips had to remember what to do. She nodded her head slightly. "I am, I think. At least, I'm getting there. I'm transferring to USD at semester."

I raised my eyebrows. "What happened to Stanford?"

She shrugged and sipped from her coffee again. "Nothing really. I guess I just needed to know if I could do it, if I could go there and succeed, be a part of the Evans tradition and all of that."

"And?"

"And," she said with a small smile, "I can, I did, but I don't want to anymore. Smart people are weird," she finished with a laugh and I couldn't help my own. "Everyone there seems to have a cause they're fighting for, a thing or an idea or a place that drives their ambitions. I just want to go to school, to get away from home, and figure out what I'm doing. And I want to enjoy it."

I choked on my water at her last sentence, and she leaned forward to pound on my back. "I'm sorry," I said waving her away. "Did you just say you wanted to enjoy something? The same drill sergeant that tutored me in English actually just said she wanted to go to a school where she could enjoy herself?" Using the back of my hand, I felt her forehead. "Are you all right, Evans? Is there something in the water at that smart kid school of yours?"

She batted my hand away, but I saw her laughing. "Seriously, though, congrats. Looks like you finally figured it out."

She nodded and we stood to throw our trash away before walking back through campus. The sun was finally setting, and though it was quieter than it had been that afternoon, people still milled around us. As we walked, she got quieter and quieter, her eyes watching her feet as we headed up the street to my dorm. "Evans, why did you come here?"

Her eyes flashed to mine and I stopped, putting my hand on her arm so she would stop, too. Pulling her to the side, out of the way of traffic, I asked again. "If it was just to tell me about USD, you could have texted, though that would have been weird, too, since we haven't talked since June. When we said goodbye."

She nodded and looked down at her fingers, twisting them together and unlocking them, over and over again until I laid my hand on hers and she stopped. "Talk to me, Mia."

"I *did* come to tell you about USD," she said, looking up. "I came to tell you that I went to Stanford, not because I thought I was going to save my family," she murmured, "but because I thought I needed to try, that I should see if it was what I really wanted."

"And it wasn't," I finished for her.

"No, it wasn't."

Her voice was barely there, and her eyes never left mine. Praying that I was reading her right, that I saw what she was giving me and not just what I wanted, I stepped closer and cupped both of her shoulders in my hands. "What do you want, Mia?"

Taking a breath, she stepped forward an inch, her tiny toes brushing mine. "I want to go to USD and be the person I discover there, whoever she is. I want to study physical therapy and nutrition, I think, not hotels and business like my father. And I want you," she said, her eyes filling and her voice cracking. My heart stopped, my lungs froze, and everything in me went on high alert.

If this was a dream, I was going to kick my own ass when I woke up. If it was real, I needed to be sure that I understood her, or I was going to have to kick my own ass for being an idiot.

"What about not being ready, not being able to be with me and be there for your family, for yourself?"

Blinking furiously, she cleared her throat and gave me the words. "I want to be with you, Ryan, not because I don't know how to think on my own or make my own decisions, but because when I'm with you, I feel right. I don't know how else to say it. I left because I was scared, and I was scared because you meant too much too fast and even though I cared about you, I didn't care about who I was, or what I was, when we were together. I forgot about my family because all I could see was what I wanted, and it terrified me that I could become as careless as my parents with everyone around me."

"You've never been careless, Mia, no matter what happened to your family. Ethan needed someone and you were there for him. That's not careless, it's selfless."

She nodded, her eyes still shining with tears that she refused to let fall. "In the end, maybe, but for a time I was so wrapped up in what you could give me that I never thought of what I needed to give anyone else. Even you," she said softly. "I never really asked about you, I only talked about me, my plans, my fears. My mother is like that, talking and talking but never listening, and my father, too, with all of his demands. Both of them are so obsessed with other things that they don't see the people around them all of the time, not until they've hurt them and even then, they can't always fix what they've broken."

She took a deep breath and I continued to stare at her as my heart pounded, but this time it wasn't fear that drove its beat, it was something else, something lighter, something freer. Happier.

"What do you see now?" I asked her.

"I see you," she murmured. "Every time I think about my future, my life, I see you."

"Are you still scared?"

She nodded but stepped forward, a contradiction of action and words as she aligned our bodies and stared up at me. "Yes, but not of this."

I remembered those words from the first time we laid in my truck and she had trusted me with her secrets. "Of what then?"

"That your dream changed just as I realized mine," she whispered.

My hands were in her hair and my mouth was on hers before I could think. Everything in me that had frozen when she told me she wanted me sprang free at that moment, urging my entire body closer to her to touch, to hear, to breathe in. Bringing her to her toes, I wrapped my arms securely around her, banding her to me as I assaulted her lips, tasting every part of her before pulling away, only to bring her back and do it all over again.

Here she was, the girl I'd been waiting for forever. I kissed the tip of her nose, her eyelids, her cheeks, back to her mouth again, taking her deeper and deeper until somewhere in the background someone whistled and she pulled away to bury her face in my neck. My fingers stroked her back as our hearts kicked into one timed beat together, over and over again, just as they had countless times before.

And then she gave me the words I'd only ever given her.

"Missed you."

Smiling, I rested my forehead against hers and closed my eyes. "Missed you more."

Epilogue
Mia

Sometimes it was hard to breathe when I remembered that he was mine. We spent weeks, sometimes months, apart, but then we get to be together and I understood he's all I need. How does this happen to people?

I used to think that this type of connection, something that's the result of need and desire, was unhealthy. There was a fear instilled in me from a young age, and it made me think that anyone who had power over me was wrong. I watched my mother be the smaller person in her relationship for my entire life--and even now when she's learning to stand on her own two feet, learning to stand up for herself, she'll still always feel like her place is second. I have never wanted that.

With Ryan, I was first. I knew this, because he was first for me, too. First, last, everything. Who he is to me, who he is *for* me, it all makes me a better person.

I watched him come down the steps from the house and onto the sand. His hair was longer, shaggy because he has gone all season without cutting it--not until they lose, he said. I loved it like this, long and curling at the ends, flipping out of his baseball cap when he was on the field. I could watch him walk all day, that gait of his that's lazy at the same time its purposeful, the deception of who he is.

I once thought he was lazy and unmotivated--the gorgeous athlete who only cared about lifting weights and being wanted by girls. Now, after almost three years with him, I knew he was so much more. He was happy, but his happiness didn't come from getting everything he's ever wanted, it came from believing that with hard work, he would achieve something great. He trained harder than I ever imagined, lifting, running, doing plyometrics and working on his swing, his agility, all of those things that made him not only a better individual athlete, but a teammate who could be trusted to do his job.

He once told me that was what he wanted--to be the consistent one on the team, the one his teammates understood wouldn't let them down.

I couldn't help but think of that moment now when I realized he was the consistent source of love and desire in my life, too.

I thought back to the day I introduced him to my parents all those months ago, the day I brought him home and showed him that I wasn't afraid anymore, that I wouldn't let him down like I once had. Despite the cold reception of my father and the overly bright praise of my mother, he stood as he always did—relaxed, comfortable, confident. When my father attempted to break him down over his choice to play baseball for as long as he could, Ryan just grinned.

"I like to play. It's not a game, it's not life and death, it's my job, and I'm lucky to have it."

My father hadn't known what to say to that--how do you argue with someone who can love what they do, understand the absolute commitment it takes, and still realize that it's just a job they are lucky to have? Not even my mother had made an attempt to respond.

Now, we were ending our junior year in college, done with year three of long distance, and I knew the time apart was only going to get longer the closer to his dream that Ryan got. He deferred the draft with his teammate, Jake, both committing to their senior year and the shot at that title, but I knew he would enter next year, and when he did, I knew his road trips would be even longer than they were now.

And still, as I watched him walk toward me, I knew I would spend the majority of every year alone as long as I could have him at the end of every season. He brought me back to life, brought my vision back to Earth, and showed me that living meant finding something to live for, and it had to be myself first and foremost.

His walk didn't slow once he reached me; not until his arms were around me and he was lifting me off my feet, bringing me up to meet his lips. I wrapped myself around him, losing my hands in his hair and angling my head so he could take the kiss deeper. In the back of my mind, I was aware that this moment with the setting sun and water and sand was about as romantic as it could get, but that's not what I cared about.

This was *real*. No sun, no sand, no surf... it would still be romantic, important, *special*, because it was real. That's ultimately what got me over my fear of loving Ryan Murphy. However scary, however overwhelming my feelings were, I knew he was real.

I pulled back when he did, just enough so that I could look into his eyes. "Missed you."

He grinned and captured my mouth again, swinging me up until one hand was around my back and the other underneath my legs, before turning and walking toward the house. "Me too, Evans. Me too."

~

Ryan

I was laying on my side next to my girl, her hair spilling over her naked shoulders and down her back. Her eyes were closed and she was laying on her stomach. Her hands were tucked underneath her chest, her cheek resting on the pillow with her face turned toward mine. Her breaths were slow and easy.

The sun has finished setting and the room was shrouded in darkness, except for the harsh spill of the bedside lamp I had just turned on. There was rain coming, so the stars were covered and there was no moon to speak of. I could hear the ocean, the choppy lap of it while the wind brought in the change in weather.

It has been just over two months since I saw Mia, and this time would only be for twenty-nine hours when it was all said and done. Jake and Jace razzed the crap out of me for it when I was racing around our apartment and gathering my shit to leave, but like I pointed out to both of them, they don't know what I can do in twenty-nine hours. That elicited an entirely different conversation that I ended up walking out on.

Now, I was spending some of my minimal time left staring at the girl who stole my heart almost six years ago before she even knew my name. That same heart was beating as if I had just run a marathon, and I knew it was because I was about to take the largest gamble of my life.

A little over three years ago she walked out on me—on us. She thought that being in a relationship meant giving up every part of herself that was worth anything, until she was only what I needed her to be. When she left, I didn't think she would ever come back. She is strong and independent, two qualities I admire as much as I fear them. I needed her like I needed to breathe. When I was with her, I felt like my world was right on its axis.

But, Jesus, did it hurt to watch her walk away and know that I had to let her go.

Now, she was back; she was mine and I was hers, and as much as I loved her, I was still scared shitless of her, too, because in my life she was the only thing that has ever brought me to my knees, the only thing I've never been able to battle my way to keeping. She had to decide to keep us—all I could do was love her. And I did, ridiculously.

Even as I thought it, she opened those gorgeous eyes and looked at me, her gaze soft, her eyes still filled with clouds of sleep. I stayed where I was, looking at her, memorizing everything about those eyes, that face, the perfect little nose and slashing cheekbones. She was tiny, small enough that I sometimes worried I was too rough with her, that she was easily bruised, and then she would do something to remind me just how strong she was.

"I love you."

Chills popped out on my skin at the sound of those words. She didn't use them often, not because she didn't mean them—which was once what I feared—but because she was private, quiet, easily startled by emotions. Where Mia came from, no one voiced their feelings, no one shouted when they were mad, no one cried when they were hurt, no one cheered when they were happy. Everything was *rational*, and love wasn't always so easy to comprehend and compartmentalize. But when she did say them… for her to say them was for her to mean them, to need them, to be reassuring me that I meant to her what she meant to me.

"So you say," I told her and she smiled. It was our game, the one we played now that we could look back and laugh at the time between, when we weren't an *us*. Now, we were RyanandMia, one word, one unit, the people you expected to see together. And still, looking at her while she looked at me, I couldn't shake the fear. I knew the moment she came back to me that our love was forever. Now, I just had to figure out how to make it official.

Christ, my hands wanted to tremble and sweat, but I kept my voice steady when I spoke.

"I'm going to enter the draft."

Needing to touch, I reached out and brushed a hand over the

silky skin of her shoulder, slipping my fingers through her golden hair to comb it off her face and reveal more of her to me.

"It's going to be busy—if I get drafted, there isn't going to be a lot of time between my senior season ending and my Short A season beginning."

She nodded, her head still on the pillow, but I could see her eyes getting a little wary. "I know. We talked about this last year when you deferred. I'll wait, Ryan. I'll be here, no matter what."

My nerves eased just a little. I reached over and slid my hand under her pillow until it found hers, our fingers twining together, our noses nearly brushing we were so close. "That's the thing, Evans. I don't want you to wait."

Her whole body froze—her eyes widened, her breath hitched, her fingers clenched in mine. I sat up, bringing her with me, my hand still holding one of hers. "I'm done living this far apart, getting twenty-nine hours and no understanding of when we will see each other next."

"Ryan..." She swallowed. "What are you saying?"

My heart slammed once, twice, and then settled. Bringing her hand to my lips, I brushed them over it and then looked straight into her beautiful blue eyes. "I'm saying I don't want to live without you—ever. It might be selfish, it might be asking too much, but I want you to be with me forever, Mia." Dropping her hand, I cupped her face and tilted her eyes up so I could look straight into them. "I want you to marry me, Evans. More than anything in the world I want you to wear my ring on your finger, I want you to write my name next to yours, and I want to know that no matter where you are or where I am, we'll be going home to the same place."

I was talking too fast—I could hardly breathe, reverting back to the guy I was when I loved this girl and she hardly knew who I was. Mia Evans, kryptonite for Ryan Murphy. Every time.

Taking a deep breath, I swallowed, brushing my thumbs across those cheekbones. And then I leaned down and rested my forehead on hers, closing my eyes and breathing her in. "Will you marry me, Mia? Because I want to marry you—more than I want anything, I want to marry you."

"Me, too."

Barely able to hear over the pounding of my heart, I leaned back. "What?" My hands tightened on her face when I saw her eyes fill. "Evans, what did you say?"

"I said, 'me, too.' I want to marry you more than anything, too, Ryan."

"That's a *yes*."

I scooped her against me, ignoring her laughter when my mouth took hers, hands diving into her hair. "That's a *yes*," I repeated against her lips.

She leaned back enough to look into my eyes. "That's most definitely a *yes*."

ABOUT THE AUTHOR

I'm a hopeless romantic with an addiction to caffeine and large dogs. I've recently found my way back to the Pacific Northwest, and I am so grateful for the rain after eight years in the desert. I hate sad endings and I believe in happily-ever-after, even if it can only be found on the page. I write about young adults because we all remember what it's like to be at the awkward, I'm-an-adult-but-not-a-grown-up stage in our life, and how messy it can be figuring it all out. Relationships drive my writing, and my husband, my daughter, and my great dane drive my life… with a lot of help from my Verismo. Connect with me at any of the following places to chat:

Twitter: @KKehoeAuthor
Facebook: facebook.com/authorkristenkehoe
Website: www.kristenkehoe.com
Instragram: Instagram.com/authorkristenkehoe

Keep Reading for a look at Cora's story, released October 2014!

The Light of Day (a beyond the horizon novel)

Chapter One
Jake

When you're twenty-two and watch every dream you've ever had drain down the toilet in just under two minutes, there's not much to do except bend over and take it. People try and cheer you up, try to see the glass half full and all of that bullshit that some optimistic prick has made millions writing about, but you know it isn't, and it won't be because one look at the doctor's face when he took out the x-rays confirmed what he hadn't yet: you're done. Find a different dream.

I was twenty-two and six days old when this occurred. Twenty-two and six days old and eight weeks away from entering the Major League Draft, the one that I had been working toward my entire life. I'd chosen to finish my career at ASU, to go my senior year because all I wanted was a title. What I got was a busted elbow and a crushed career. Yeah, I shattered that fucking glass.

Now, at twenty-two and forty days old, I've got a hangover on the horizon and my eye on a brunette who walked in an hour ago. She's tall, long and curved, not bony like most girls I've met in the past few years, but healthy looking. No nose candy or other recreational drugs for this one. Nope, her skin's too clear, her curves too toned. Healthy is what I'd describe her as. And fucking stacked. I can't see her eyes clearly from here, but I'm sure they're clear, too. I haven't seen her drink anything but water since she came through the door, and I haven't looked away from her in the hour she's been here.

That's also something new. In the past month, there has been little to keep my attention for more than a few brief moments. Which is why I took medical reprieve from classes with the intent of going somewhere else in the fall and starting over. Just the phrase makes me swig from my bottle. Starting over. Finding something else. Looking beyond what I was to what I can be, which isn't what I wanted to be. Fuck. Not even Jack can cure that thought, no matter how deeply I gulp him down. But another look at the brunette has my eyes finally meeting hers. I recognize the golden haired angel she's standing next to, but I can't place her at the moment. I haven't slept with her, that's for sure; too innocent. The brunette looks clean, but there's something darker about her, something mysterious, like a secret that she's wearing on the outside, showing the world without saying a word. The angel next to her looks just that: angelic, sweet, pure. I'm not pure, and I'm not looking for it. I'm looking for hard, rough, mind numbing…something. Anything to finish what the alcohol can't and make me forget for a while.

I keep my eyes on the brunette as I set my drink down. It lost its appeal an hour ago when I saw her, and as a result the drunk I was headed toward has now softened to a buzz. I can't explain the pull that I feel, but I can say I don't want to let it go. It's been too long since I've felt this need, this force to do something besides wallow and I'll be goddamned if I skip over it.

Standing, I wait for the ground to settle beneath my feet and take my first step toward her.

Chapter Two
Cora

When your cousin asks you to be her maid of honor, you accept, even if the thought of it makes you want to vomit, not because you don't love your cousin, but because the idea of happily-ever-fucking-after is a joke you've been sold one too many times. Worse than that, looking at your cousin makes you want to believe in it and that just pisses you off all over again.

Despite how nauseous the whole idea makes me, I watch Mia as she readies for her big day and I can't help but be just a little envious of her. She has it; if ever someone has a chance at happily ever after, it's her. And she deserves it. Maybe this is one of those times that justice actually comes to those who deserve it and Mia, the nicest, most giving person I've ever known is getting hers in the form of finding someone who loves her beyond all bounds. And maybe that's why mine has never worked out; I don't have a nice bone in my body, and rehabilitated or not, I'm no better a person sober and celibate than I was drunk and promiscuous. Drunk just gave me an excuse.

"You okay?" Mia asks me and I nod. No way I'm going to tell her that being at a party two days before her wedding is making me want to find a razor and end it. Or just end those people around me;

I'm not really big on self-harm, but I have been known to fuck up a few of those people around me. Hence the rehab.

"The question is not if I'm okay, Cousin, the question is if you're okay. We're closing in on your last days of freedom, any wild wishes you need to live out before the big day?"

She laughs and shakes her head before sipping from her drink, her first and I'm betting only for the night. Yep, where she's a poster child of self-control, I'm the opposite. Eleven months clean and I still think about taking a quick drink, finding an easy mark who's looking for the same thing and checking out for a few hours because it's nicer in the dark than it is in the world.

But the world always comes back, I remind myself, and when it comes back after a night of overindulgence, it's a lot uglier than it was when you checked out in the first place, and so's the person you wake up with. So, instead of giving in to my urges to drown myself in a bottle and/or a body, I grab some water and sip from it, keeping an eye on Mia as she watches the door for her betrothed while scanning the room and observing those people around me.

As expected, there are more girls than guys, but that's because we travel in packs. Well, most of us. I never have. Mia has been my one and only true friend since we were little and as I was growing up I thought that was okay. Other girls were the enemy, my competition, the person who stood in between me and whoever I wanted and so I rejected them, making sure to stay alone. Now, at almost a year sober and celibate, I'm realizing that connections and relationships are necessary in order to live. I can't explain why except that without people, I want to find that dark hole and sink. It's Mia's who's pulled me out time and again since our freshman year of college, when I decided I was going to be the person my mom always thought I was, but Mia wouldn't let me sink all of the way. At the end of our sophomore year, she'd had enough and sent me to rehab, a thirty day detox where she visited me every chance she was allowed. Not because she wanted to check on me, but because she wanted me to know that I wasn't alone.

Then I transferred cities, moved to San Diego to work and move in with her. For the past year she's been my backbone, my base, and now it's time that I stood for her. In two days, she's marrying her first and only love, and I'm going to stand there in the champagne dress she's picked for me and smile even if it kills me. For Mia, I can do it, even if I'm still learning how to be strong for myself.

When my eyes meet the dark brown ones across the room, I'm surprised to feel the small jolt of electricity. Interesting, is my first thought. And dangerous. I was in the game long enough to know a train wreck when I see one, and this gorgeous package has CRASH written all over him.

From his seated position I can't tell his entire height, but I've assessed enough men in my life to know it's more than most of the guys here, an easy six-four or six-five. I take in his shaggy brown hair that screams baseball player with its curling ends and sun lightened spots that my trained eye knows are less calculated than those from a stylist. His skin is olive, darkened to a bronze from what I can see on his arms, arms that carry one distinct swirl of black ink on the inside, but its shape I can't tell.

When Brown Eyes sets his drink aside and stands, I wonder if it's smart to be looking at him. When he starts over to where I'm standing, I go from wondering to knowing it's a mistake to keep my eyes on his, and yet, I don't look away. For the first time since I got out of rehab, I'm tempted by the opposite sex. I'm not thinking of safe and healthy, I'm not even thinking of alcohol, which is usually where my temptation comes from. I'm thinking of his skin, warmed and golden from the sun, and how it would feel against my much paler skin, which suddenly feels cold as I look at him. I want explosions, mind numbing explosions and warmth, touch and feeling, cravings that remind me I'm still alive.

And that line of thinking is what sent me to rehab in the first place. Straightening my shoulders, I bring myself up to my impressive five-nine and meet Brown Eyes head on as he stops in front of me.

"Name," he says in a voice that's low and scratchy, like he

hasn't used it in a significant amount of time and he isn't happy about using it now. Shivers break out on my arms and I think *well done*. And then I remember that the girl I used to be is the one who would have responded to that in under twenty seconds, had his shirt off in double that. I'm different now, because Mia believed I could be and because I want to be, deep down underneath all of this stuff and these feelings, I want to be different, too. *Uh-uh, Cora*, I tell myself. Explosions are only so fun, especially when someone else is lighting the fuse.

Thinking that I need control so this doesn't get out of hand, I raise my brow. "You first."

Acknowledgements

Thank you, first and foremost, to my husband, Jan, for believing in me and helping me realize just what words were living inside of me. Thank you to my family, for loving me and always reading my work. Thank you to Sara Huggins, for being that friend who supports me unendingly, by way of funny cat pictures and sexy stories, and just hilarious text messages. Pashugs, you're the best.

Thank you to Tessa Marie for the beautiful book cover, and Ashley Blevins at Mark My Words Book Publicity—you keep me on my toes... one day, your invaluable outlining help may actually demand I know the ending of a book before I write it. (Maybe.)

Lastly, thank you to the people in my life, students, friends, strangers, who have shared their stories with me and trusted me with them. As it says in the beginning, this book is for anyone who's ever struggled to find tomorrow, for anyone who's ever forgotten what love feels like. Here's to you and your strength. Remember to keep living, taking it one day at a time.

xoxo

Kristen

58106589R00175

Made in the USA
Charleston, SC
01 July 2016